BRAVE HEART!

Angeline waited just long enough, then brought the knife down swiftly. She felt the blade sinking into the brave's left shoulder and saw the sudden grimace on the Indian's face. He whirled angrily to punish her. The knife went flying.

The other Comanche riders shouted taunts at the brave Angeline had stabbed. It was clear that they felt she had bested him, having drawn first blood. As they howled derisively, emphasizing his disgrace, the brave's face darkened in fury.

Angeline tried to duck away, but he caught her by the arm and yanked her close enough to catch her on the side of the head with a hard, bludgeoning fist that sent her spinning to the ground . . .

SPECIAL PREVIEW!
**Turn to the back of this book for a sneak-peek
excerpt from the exciting Western series . . .**

FURY

. . . the blazing story of a gunfighting legend.

— TOM EARLY —

SONS OF TEXAS

Book Five

THE BOLD

B
BERKLEY BOOKS, NEW YORK

SONS OF TEXAS: THE BOLD

A Berkley Book / published by arrangement with
the author

PRINTING HISTORY
Berkley edition / July 1992

ISBN: 0-425-13334-6

A BERKLEY BOOK ® TM 757,375
Berkley Books are published by The Berkley Publishing Group,
200 Madison Avenue, New York, New York 10016.
The name "BERKLEY" and the "B" logo
are trademarks belonging to Berkley Publishing Corporation.

PRINTED IN THE UNITED STATES OF AMERICA

10 9 8 7 6 5 4 3 2

PART I

THE COUNCIL HOUSE MASSACRE

☆ Chapter ☆

1

The two riders wore the same stamp—that of the Lewis clan. Both were lanky, with searching blue eyes and powerful, square jaws. Nothing in the manner of these lean, raw-boned men indicated retreat or looking back, only a restless reaching for the horizon beyond. For them and the rest of their kin this broad land answered their needs as did few other places on earth. It didn't matter that dark-skinned foreigners or painted savages had staked a claim to it first. They were in Texas to stay, and neither Mexicans nor Comanche would ever root them out. For now, the Mexicans had been beaten south; the Comanches, however, were proving to be a different matter entirely. But sooner or later, however long it took and no matter how much blood and heartache the struggle generated, the frontiersmen knew they would prevail or die. For such men there was no turning back.

The older of the riders, a man in his early thirties and already a widower, was James Lewis. His companion was his nephew Mordecai, a young man not yet twenty whose bearing belied his youth. Unlike his uncle, he had been brought up in Texas and sat astride his mount with an infinite ease, as casual as any horse Indian.

There were on the way back to the Lewis compound along the Colorado River after a fruitless scout for a Comanche band rumored to be in the vicinity. James, already a member of the Texas Rangers, had returned home six months before after the brutal murder of his brother Michael at the hands of a Comanche band. Now weary and saddle sore, both men were looking forward to a straw mattress, home cooking, the comforting voices of their womenfolk, and even the shrill, heedless piping of children.

As Mordecai crested a grassy knoll, his restless eyes narrowed and he pulled his horse up, doing so with the barest motion of his knees against his big chestnut's flanks.

"Look over there, James," he said, pointing. "Beyond that clump of cottonwood."

"I see it," James replied, halting also and leaning over his saddle's pommel, a grim cast to his face. "I hope it ain't what I think it is."

A thin, black tracer of smoke was lifting into the sky. A column of smoke capable of carrying that far and that high could only be one thing—a burning building. More accurately, someone's barn or cabin.

"How far would you say?" James asked.

"Ten, maybe fifteen miles."

"Comanche?"

"No reason for a body to burn his own house down that I can see. Looks like we missed the savages."

They could see close to a dozen miles in every direction. Yet they knew how deceptive the faint roll of the prairie could be to the naked eye. A host of mounted warriors could be moving toward them only a thousand yards away and yet remain completely hidden in the grassland's deceptive swales.

"We better have a look-see," said James.

They had been heading northwest. Turning their mounts, they headed due north toward the black plume that hung on the horizon like an exclamation point. Without needing to speak of it, they knew they were probably too late to be of much help, yet they could not let that stop them from doing what they could.

James was a few yards ahead of Mordecai when he crested a ridge and caught sight of the Comanche. He pulled his mount around and swept back off the ridge so sharply that it slammed into Mordecai's mount, almost knocking it from under him.

"What the hell!" Mordecai cried as his horse recovered.

"We done found them blamed Comanche!" James yelled.

They had just crossed a stream. They galloped back down the long swale to its willow-choked bank and dismounted. Leaving their mounts among the willows, they moved back to a high cutbank and unlimbered their rifles, checked the loads, then brought out their Paterson Colts.

James counted eight Comanche warriors in all. Each warrior was loaded with booty, and most of them were so drunk they were having difficulty staying on their ponies. In a barbarous procession—some resplendent in bison-horn headdresses and buffalo capes—they moved steadily along the crest of a distant ridge. Their finery had a wild eccentricity about it—a white man's vest here, a frock coat there. Pants they had confiscated no longer had seats in them. One barbarian had wrapped a bolt of red cloth around his naked chest; another had tied pink and red ribbons to his pony's tail. A few of the savages wore stovepipe hats and one of them had an eagle feather stuck in his headband.

Lately, the usual tack of the Comanche was to slip down the rivers by night, hide by day, strike at sunset, then ride back to their northern strongholds before dawn. Yet here was this war party, drunk as lords, riding in the full light of day not a mile from the Colorado. The explanation for this was disheartening. Despite Lamar's fine words and the labors of the Ranger companies, these Indians had little to fear. After all, the Rangers were but a handful measured against the thousands of hostile warriors now descending from the high plains to pick the bones of Texan settlers moving into the wooded hill country.

"They're drunk as Irishmen," Mordecai said, his anger building at the sight of the prancing savages, images of his father's death twisting inside him like a knife. "Let's cut them down, James."

"Hold on, Mordecai. Hold your bile now and lay low."

"But there's only eight of 'em."

"You forgettin what put us on this track in the first place? A burning homestead. More'an likely there's survivers needin' help."

"Dealin' with them drunken heathens shouldn't take us no time at all."

"I always thought you was older than you looked, Mordecai. Maybe I got it backwards. Right now you remind me of my own fool bravado when I first came out here. I surely can sympathize, but I swear this ain't no time for showin' off your new pistols. Now, hush up and keep your backside down."

Coming from James, a man he had always admired deeply, this measured censure immediately sobered Mordecai. Of course James was right. That line of smoke on the horizon indicated the worst kind of trouble for a settler's family. This was no time for foolhardy heroics.

James patted him gently on the shoulder. "Don't take no offense, Mordecai," he said. "We'll just let these savages go this time. But bet on it, before we're done, we'll get a lot more chances to even the score."

Grateful for James's words, Mordecai straightened up and watched soberly as the Comanche, still following the ridge's crest, vanished to the northeast.

After a judicious wait to make sure there were no stragglers in the Comanche's war party, Mordecai and James mounted up again and continued north to the burning cabin. There was no doubt in either man's mind what they were likely to find when they got there.

II

The smoke had vanished into a cloudless blue sky and a good piece of the afternoon was gone when they topped a grassy knoll and reined in their nearly spent mounts. Below them, sitting in the gentle embrace of a meandering stream was what remained of the settlers' ranch. The main cabin was still standing; the barn and its stock of loose hay had sent the heavy plumes of smoke into the July sky. Tiny, flickering tongues of fire still lived in the blackened ruins.

They spurred their mounts down the long sweep of grassland and dismounted about twenty yards from the ranch house beside the sprawled body of a settler. He could not have been more than forty. He was lying on his back, his throat slit, and what looked like lance wounds in his chest. But the savages hadn't left it at that. They seemed to have an abominable fascination with a white man's genitals.

There was nothing either of them could do for the man. James drew his Colt and started for the house, Mordecai keeping pace, his own sidearm drawn and cocked. With close-in fighting, the Colts offered them more of an advantage. They did not expect any Comanche to be lying in wait, but it never hurt to be ready for the unexpected.

As the two men got closer to the cabin, they saw blackened shingles and noted the spent torchs and arrows that had been used in a half-hearted attempt to set fire to the roof. The damp sod underneath the shingles had held back the flames, eventually extinguishing them. The door was splintered and broken in, more than likely by a Comanche pony backed up to it, and what remained of the door hung askew on a single leather hinge.

They stepped inside expecting to find more bodies. There were none. The window shutters were smashed in. The kitchen table had been sliced in half by a single blow from a war club. In the center of the kitchen, a steamer trunk was hacked open. Any blankets or sheets it might have contained were gone, but the floor was strewn with a youngster's outgrown clothing. Above the stove, the hooks that had held the woman's pots and kettles hung empty.

Mordecai could almost smell the terror, the hot stench of savage bodies as they whooped and *ki-yi-ed* through the cabin. He followed James from the kitchen down a narrow hallway. At the end of it they found a smashed door and stepped through it into a small bedroom.

A boy not more than fourteen sat in one corner, his knees drawn up to his chin, his sightless eyes wide. Most of his scalp was gone. Blood had dried on his forehead and cheeks where it had flowed freely from the open wound. Mordecai walked over and stared down at the dead boy, his mouth dry with fury. From the neck down, the dead lad's shirt was caked with blood. A single stroke of a Comanche knife had severed his jugular. Usually the Comanche took children captive to make them their own, but at this age, Mordecai knew, the boy would not easily assimilate into the tribe and would make an intractible, uncooperative slave.

So they had cut his throat.

"Give me a hand," James said softly.

Sticking his Colt into his belt, James grabbed the boy's feet. Mordecai took him under his arms and together they lifted the blood-soaked body onto his narrow bed.

"See if you can find anyone else," James told him gently.

Mordecai ducked out of the bedroom. James found a blanket and sheet on the parent's bed and folded them over his arm for shrouds. He went back into the boy's bedroom, wrapped the dead boy in the sheet, and carried him outside. He located a charred but serviceable long-handled spade on the ground behind the ruined barn and selected a gravesite on a slight rise overlooking the ranch. He was digging the second grave when Mordecai called to him from the yard.

"I found a trail! Someone escaped, looks like!"

James dropped the spade and hurried down the slope.

The trail led away from a root cellar behind the house. They had little difficulty following the blood-stained path through the grass leading to the bank of the stream. There they found a dead woman. She had been in her late thirties. Judging from the cut of her chin, she was the mother of the boy they had found. Her dark chestnut hair had been shaken loose and was so thick that at first James did not realize she had been scalped. Her breasts had been sliced open and there were deep knife wounds in her waist. Her dress and undergarments had been sliced up the middle and flung aside. Lying spread-eagle on her back, naked, she stared up at them mutely, her face slightly contorted.

"Look," Mordecai said. "Over here."

He was down behind the riverbank. James joined him. Without a word, Mordecai pointed to the woman's small, naked footprints in the damp soil and the buckshot casings scattered on the ground around them. They told most of the story.

The woman had not let the Comanche take her without a fight. There were six casings in all; though she had been seriously wounded, she had managed to reload and empty the shotgun at least three times before the Comanche overcame her. Moving back up onto the grass, they saw the trampled grass and bloodstains ten or fifteen yards from the embankment. She had wounded or killed at least one of the attackers.

Mordecai felt a tightening in his throat and tears welling in his eyes. He turned away from James and sat down with his back to the embankment, hoping James would not notice. The sight of the butchered father and son, this woman so brutally violated, was a powerful, shattering reminder of his own father's death, a sight he knew he could never banish: his father pulled from his horse, the lunging lances, the blood-stained savages bending over his prostrate body. Now, the horror and pain of that moment was flooding back over him.

James stood beside him for a moment without a word, then rested his hand momentarily on his shoulder. Mordecai swallowed, fought back the tears, and stood up. He did not try to say anything. He knew that would not be possible now, not with this intolerable ache in his throat.

They buried the woman alongside her husband and son. James fashioned crude crosses for their graves while Mordecai picked wildflowers and set them down beside each one. Later, as James rode out with Mordecai, heading once again toward the Lewis compound, Mordecai's somber face gave mute testimony to the inchoate rage he felt. Rage and determination.

He was a true son of Texas and would do all he could to redress these murders—and the growing number of savage atrocities staining the soil of this Texas borderland.

III

Two days later, the Lewis clan gathered in Michael's house for supper. Marie, Hope, Petra, and Annie all helped in preparing the meal, with Angeline helping to serve and joining in with the clean-up afterward. Mordecai served as host, doing his best to fill his father's shoes. The rest of the children were bedded down in Mordecai and Angeline's bedroom.

Once the dinner table was cleared, the men were left with

their coffee and pipes while the womanfolk washed the dishes and scoured the pots and pans in the kitchen, doing so quietly so as not to disturb the men as they settled into their discussion. But though they kept in the kitchen, they were not far from the dining room and listened intently to the men, their eyes betraying their concern.

Andrew had put aside his congressional duties. Holding Petra gently in his arms the night he returned from Austin a week before, he had confided to her that, as far as he was concerned, these Indian raids could no longer be ignored. At a time like this, he was useless holed up in a boarding house in Austin. Frank, James, Sly Shipman, and Mordecai made up the rest of what had become the Lewis clan's unofficial council of elders.

James had just finished describing the Indians he and Mordecai had sighted from the stream bank and had wondered aloud if that war party could have been the same one that hit the settlers' place. Andrew did not think so.

"Looks to me like this was a different band," he said.

"I agree," said Sly Shipman. "Remember, James, you say there were no wounded warriors in that war party, and yet this woman had wounded or killed several of the savages."

"She put up a fight, that's for sure."

Mordecai added, "I figure she musta killed or wounded one of them, at least. She got off six rounds."

"Another thing," Frank added. "Those Comanche were sportin' top hats and frock coats. They sure wouldn't've found such fancy garments in that steamer trunk you described."

"Agreed," said James.

"Which means," said Andrew, leaning back in his chair and sweeping the seated men with a grim glance, "there were two Comanche bands—not just one—roaming through this here country. It appears to me these blamed savages are gettin' as thick as fleas on a hound dog.''

"I wish I could say I saw this coming," said Frank, shaking his head in sorrow. "But I didn't. Not until Michael's death did I wake up. I guess we all thought with the Cherokees gone our troubles would be over. And so did Lamar, I think. But these Comanche aren't a bit like the Cherokees.''

"That's right," said Sly. "They're a whole new breed of cat. They're marching straight out of hell on Mexican horseflesh—and nobody in east Texas gives a damn.''

"No matter what Houston says about Lamar," said Andrew. "He put it square in his inaugural when he said the white man and the red man cannot dwell in harmony together. He said Nature forbids it. After what James and Mordecai have just told us, I think I agree.''

"It's too bad we have to think that," said Frank, his gentle eyes troubled, "but I am afraid that doesn't make it any less true.''

"Trouble is," said James, "Lamar's not backin' us with anything more than talk.''

"I hate to remind you," said Andrew, "but the Republic of Texas has shot its bolt. Cooke's expedition up the Red River and over to Cross Timbers cost us three hundred thousand dollars. The republic is now broke. No one wants our paper money, and that's a fact. We can't pay for any more military campaigns. Not now, we can't.''

"And when Houston gets back in," James reminded everybody, "there'll be conferences and commisioners and Indian agents and treaties, and not one of 'em will be worth a pound of coon snuff.''

"I wish Houston would talk to the Mexicans," Frank said. "They've been fighting these Comanche for generations.''

"The Mexicans don't fight," James said contemptuously.

"They barter. They trade, they buy off the Comanche any way they can. Pay tribute is what they do. But it hasn't done them any good. I heard tell of one Mexican rancher two years ago who let a Comanche chief ride in and take his entire horse herd. He just sat back and did nothing while the Comanche took what horseflesh pleased them. He thought he would gain the Comanche chief's friendship. Instead, he earned only his contempt. When the Comanche were done selecting the horses they wanted, the Comanche chief showed his appreciation by killing the Mexican and raping his wife and carrying off his children. I say—"

Frank stopped James by reaching over and resting his hand on James's arm. Frowning, James glanced at him. Frank put a finger to his mouth and with a quick nod of his head indicated the women at the far end of the kitchen. They were cleaning the dishes still, but they had grown as silent as moths and were hanging on every word, Frank had no doubt.

Leaning forward, James continued, his voice lower, "I say we can't deal with these savages. They don't ask for gifts, they demand them as their right. They're like spoiled children. They take any kindness as weakness—and atop their mounts they see themselves as lords of the Universe."

"Up until now, that's what they've been," Sly reminded him. "It was the Comanche who drove the Apache into New Mexico. Think that over. Where the Comanche now roam as free as the wind, the Apaches once called home. Any tribe that can drive out the Apaches must be a cruel and resourceful enemy."

"I am afraid the problem is not one we can solve with peaceful overtures," Frank said. "To the Comanche, there is little difference between us and the Mexicans. And they will treat us as they have treated the Mexicans until we stop them. As I see it, this clash is inevitable. No Texan will let a painted, lice-ridden savage ride into his compound and take what he wants.''

''Maybe not,'' Sly said, ''but don't forget Parker's Fort.''

Sly's quiet reminder sent a pall over the men. During the moment of reflective silence that followed, everyone sitting at the table recalled the hideous outrage at Parker's Fort. During the three years since, the grim and terrible knowledge of what had happened to the Parkers on that fateful day hung over the frontier like a curse and a terrible warning.

James was the first to break the silence. ''I say its time we organize a band of Rangers,'' he said, his voice resolute. ''And soon. I know there's still trouble at the Mexican border—and I've seen enough of it with Captain Rush. But this is a borderland as well, and after what we've just heard, I say we got to do something before things get a good deal bloodier. Like Lamar said, we got to handle these savages with steel and lead.''

''A Ranger company up here?'' Andrew asked. ''Who'd lead them?''

''I'd be willing,'' said James. ''I'll ask Captain Rush to see to it. I've had enough experience. Last week he was talking about making me a captain.''

''You forgetting what I just said? There's no cash left in our coffers.''

''Andrew, do you know what it costs to mount a company of Rangers? Practically nothing. We provide our own mounts, our own shot, our own arms. We have no surgeons, no flag, none of the folderal of a military company. We travel light and at a minimum expense. We're volunteers. Irregulars. We come cheap. Our sweat is all it costs the Republic of Texas.''

Sly chuckled and clapped James on the back. ''Well said, James. I'm proud of you.''

''All right,'' said Andrew, giving in easily to the inescapable logic of James's argument. ''I'll ride with you to Austin.

I might be able to help. I still have some influence in the Lamar administration—while it lasts, that is.''

James seemed relieved for the first time that evening. "I'd appreciate that, Andrew. Thanks.''

That ended the discussion. The men retired from the table, all of them intent on what lay ahead, with James thinking of the trip he and Andrew would be commencing come sunrise.

IV

That night, lying in her lonely bed, Marie could not rid her mind of the conversation she and the rest of the women had overheard. What had truly riveted her was mention of Parker's Fort. For Marie, having lost her Michael to these same savages, she could not help wonder if the Parker Fort massacre was a foretaste of what might lie ahead.

She knew the facts of the incident well. It was seared into her mind as it must be in the minds of every man and woman on this borderland. The Parker clan had built a log stockade on the Navasota enclosing several frontier families, of which the Parkers were predominent. To travelers in that land, it was known as Parker's Fort. The families had found themselves a beautiful, oak-studded country of rolling plains, well watered and teeming with wild game. The soil was rich for corn, and the stream bottoms thick with deer and turkey.

On a bright summer morning, while most of the men were outside the fort at work in the cornfields, a large party of mounted Indians appeared outside the walls. One of them was waving a dirty white flag.

The men inside were the eldest John Parker, his sons Silas and Benjamin, and Samuel Frost and his son. Since the Indians appeared to be friendly, the men inside the stockade agreed to parley with the Indians without standing to arms.

Benjamin Parker went outside to deal with the Indians

while Silas stood at the gate. Benjamin and the Indians began talking in a mixture of pidgin English and sign language; the Indians remained on their horses. Back inside the fort, Silas's four young children remained with the Frosts and John Parker who were standing with the families of those men outside in the fields. After a brief parley, Benjamin walked back to the gate to inform Silas that the Indians wanted directions to a water hole and also some beef to eat. Benjamin stated that the Indians did not seem very friendly when he had refused to give them the beef, but said he would go back out and do what he could to avoid a fight.

Despite Silas's protests, Benjamin returned to the mounted Indians and was immediately surrounded by them. There was a momentary struggle. He tried to return to the fort, but several Indians drove their lances into him while the rest rode for the gate, cut down Silas, and poured into the fort. The two Frosts, father and son, died in front of the women. Elder John Parker and his wife tried to flee, but were ridden down by the mounted Indians. Several warriors seized the elder Parker and his wife, Granny. Parker was pinned to the ground, scalped, and his genitals ripped off. Then he was killed and mutilated still further. Granny Parker was stripped and fixed to the earth with a lance driven through her flesh. While she screamed in terror and fury, several warriors raped her. The remaining women were seized and attacked as well. In the fearsome struggles, two women were seriously injured and left for dead with gaping wounds.

Silas Parker's wife Lucy fled through the gate, shepherding her small children, but the Comanche overtook her near the river. They threw her and the children over their horses, preparing to abduct them. By this time, however, men were running from the fields with rifles. One of them forced the warriors to drop Lucy and two of her children, but another

Comanche made off with Cynthia Ann and John Parker, aged nine and six. Inside the stockade, as more Parker men arrived at the fort, the Comanche warriors leaped astride their horses, galloped out of the stockade, and headed north with three more captives—Elizabeth Kellogg, Rachel Plummer, and Rachel's fifteen-month-old son, James.

The Comanche war party had killed five men and mauled several women, leaving them for dead. When the settlers entered the fort, Granny Parker was crawling blindly toward the gate after having pulled herself free of the Comanche lance. Granny survived, but that night two of the other women died.

The fate of Rachel Plummer haunted every frontier woman. Eighteen months later Rachel Plummer was ransomed but died within a year after her return, the object of scorn and abhorrence, suffering as much shame and humiliation among her own people as she had among the Comanche. No woman on the Texas frontier could not be sure that such a fate did not await her.

Marie shuddered as she thought of what captivity would mean for her or her children in the hands of these marauding beasts—rape, torture, humiliation, terrible suffering, and privation, and even more terrible to contemplate, the loss of her children to these hellish fiends. If that were not enough, in the event of her captivity and eventual return, she would likely suffer a stigma so unforgiving and terrible that death, as it must have for Rachel Plummer, would come as a blessed relief.

Marie flung aside her bedsheet, lit a candle, and stole softly into Mordecai's bedroom. Halting in the doorway, she gazed down on his sleeping form. There was so much of Michael in his face; her throat tightened and tears stung her eyes. Would Mordecai turn on her, she wondered, if she were abducted by these devils?

She dared not answer her own question and returned to her bed, murmuring the same prayer she had whén six months before she had watched Mordecai lead the Lewis clan out onto the plains to recover her husband's body. *God help us all*, she thought.

☆ Chapter ☆

2

Atop their ponies, the fourteen Comanche cantered along the ridge for a hundred yards or so, then stopped. The warriors watched the covered wagon ramble across the grassland below, the iron tips of their fourteen foot lances gleaming in the setting sun, the bright feathers woven into their ponies' manes and tails tugging in the gentle breeze.

The chief of the war party wore a headdress fashioned from the head of a buffalo, the horns pointing up in an arc. All the way to the tops of his thighs his legs were encased in buckskin leggings. From the seams hung brass beads and fringes. On his left arm was his sacred shield and his bow was strung across his broad chest. He was naked except for his breechclout and leggings, his face was framed by straight black hair and splashed with war paint.

The wagon's destination was soon clear to the watching Comanche. It was heading for a thick patch of oak trees bordering a riverbank. With a nudge of his inner thigh, the war chief turned his pony and rode back off the rise, his war party following.

II

Pulled by two mules and a milch cow trailing behind, the wagon halted under an oak in the midst of the grove. The river that flowed below was the Colorado, and they had traveled along it since leaving Coleman's Fort at dawn and were now about a mile above the river's junction with the Llano. Riding strong Kentucky-bred horses, Sam Thompson and his son Will pulled up and dismounted. The young man was nearly seventeen, a husky, strapping replica of his father, and was two years older than his sister, Clara, who now climbed quickly down from the wagon with her mother. Their mother's name was Faith. She was still pretty at thirty-five, with blond hair, blueberry eyes, and a ready smile.

The family had journeyed all the way from Kentucky. Sam Thompson had fought with the Texans against the Mexicans, and on his return to Kentucky, he had told all who would listen of the fertile land of rolling prairies and thick woodlands he had happened upon. As soon as he was able to sell his own cabin and fields, he had returned with his family to this bountiful land.

Working as fast as they could in the fading daylight, the Thompsons set about making camp in the pleasant oak-studded knoll. A wolf howled in the distance. The lonely sound caused Faith to glance nervously over at her husband, who was leading the mules to a pasture near the wagon. Sam appeared to take no notice of the howling wolf, so she continued feeding the campfire with the twigs she had gathered from under the trees. Will led the two saddle horses down through the oaks, through a line of willows hugging the riverbank, to a lush field beyond. He hobbled the horses and started back to the encampment, glancing over in astonishment at the brilliant moon already poised on the horizon. The moon's brilliant light was almost bright enough for him to read his lessons by. He did not know that the West Texans called this brilliant silver dollar that would soon be poised overhead the Comanche Moon.

After supper Sam Thompson reminded his son to check on the horses, then went off himself to see to the mules. Will scurried down through the timber, saw that the hobbled horses, content with the lush pasture provided for them, had not moved far from the stream.

Will stopped suddenly. He thought he noticed movement below him in the trees, shadowy forms captured in the moonlight. It was deer, he told himself to quiet his thumping heart. This was a rich land; they had been seeing game everywhere since they left Coleman's Fort. From his left came what sounded like the short, high-pitched bark of a wolf. For a moment, he was almost certain he saw a pair of eyes gleaming in the darkness. *The wolves were getting closer!* he thought. A black dread fell over him.

But when he looked more closely, he saw no shadows and no gleaming eyes. Instead, there came from above him in the grove the echoing call of a meadow lark, as if to reprove him for his runaway imagination. Chiding himself, Will shrugged off the feeling of dread and continued on up through the trees toward the comforting glow of his family's campfire.

Near the wagon, Will's father and mother were talking softly. Choosing not to disturb them, Will sat down before the fire's warmth. His parents were discussing this spot as a possible homesite; he could tell from the excited way his father waved his arms as he talked, his sweeping gestures taking in the grove and the lush country around. Will saw his mother lean close to her husband and say something, her voice soft, soothing. Will's father replied, and she laughed softly and prodded him in a playful way.

Will's father reached into the wagon and took out the family Bible. Will was not surprised. He'd been expecting his father to read to them from it from the moment they stopped in this beautiful oak grove. Abruptly the cow blatted. Will glanced over at it. Tethered to the wagon's tailgate, she had stopped chewing her cud, but was holding her head up alertly, her tail drooping straight down. It was those wolves calling in the distance, Will figured. They unsettled her.

Clara stepped down from the wagon to join her mother and father. She had been combing out her hair while she sang, and now it hung down her back, gleaming in the bright moon.

Will's father glanced over at Will and beckoned him closer. "Get over here, son."

He got up and joined his family.

"Guess what, Will," his mother said, smiling warmly at him. "We're thinking of settling right here."

"We'll build on this knoll," Sam said, his voice filled with happiness. "It should give us a real fine view of the river and the cornfields we'll plant beyond."

"I suppose so," said Clara, "but it will sure be lonely until we get neighbors."

"Not for long," said her mother. "Coleman's Fort isn't that far."

"I didn't much like that place," said Clara. "It wasn't really a fort, just a wooden wall around some poor log cabins."

Her father laughed, "But did you see those cornfields along the river? And the fat cattle in that hip-high grass? It's a poor-lookin' fort now, but in a few years it will be a thriving community—and this lush land about us will be dotted with prosperous farms. Mark my words."

"Besides," said Will's mother. "Aren't you both tired of this journey? Think of the house we can build from this oak!"

"And think of the work that will take!" Will retorted with a smile. "Oh, my."

"Those families from the fort will help," said Will's

father. "I spoke to Bob Coleman. He was right optimistic."

"And I spoke with his wife," Faith added. "She was very friendly and said she wanted as many neighbors as she had back in Kentucky and was hopeful we'd plant ourselves close by. And isn't this a lovely spot?"

Gazing around him, Will certainly could not deny that. Clara shrugged and said she hoped they would visit the fort often, and that maybe on Saturday nights they'd have dances as well. She had heard a fiddler the night they camped outside the fort and would love to sing for them. And so it was settled. Here they would stay.

"And now, children," Sam said, "it seems to me that this would be a good time to study the word of God and to give thanks to Him for getting us safely to this bountiful land."

Sam guided them over to the fire. Will sat down in the grass next to Clara, and the three of them waited for Sam to find a suitable passage. Flipping the pages, he held the Bible up so that its pages could catch both the light from the fire and the brightness of the moon.

"What're you goin' to read, Pa?" Will asked.

"Try Proverbs, Pa," said Clara.

Frowning in concentration, Sam leaned closer to the fire to read over silently the passage he had selected. As he did so, a wolf howled from the timber just beyond the wagon. Sam glanced up in some annoyance, then looked over at Will.

"That wolf sounds pretty close, Will."

"I think I saw a couple when I came up from the river," Will said.

"Guess we'd better bring the stock in closer—and keep this fire going."

As his father turned his attention back to the Good Book, an arrow thumped hollowly into his back, slamming him forward into the fire. Sparks leapt up in a sudden shower as he fell into the blazing embers. At the same moment the night came alive with cries so shrill and terrifying they chilled Will's soul and caused the hair on the back of his neck to lift.

He jumped to his feet to see a warrior not five feet away coming at him full tilt. The Indian could not have been much older than Will. He flung himself through the air, knocking Will backward. Flat on the grass, Will struggled with the damned savage who held a tomahawk in his right hand. Slashing down with it repeatedly, he tried to crush in Will's skull. Twice the blade slammed off the side of Will's head. Wincing from the pain, Will snapped his head back and reached up to grab the brave's right wrist. Once he held it, he wrenched it to the side and rolled over onto the startled Indian's body. Pulling the tomahawk from the Indian's grasp, Will flung it aside. With a grunt, the Indian scrambled to his feet and reached back for the knife in his belt. Without waiting for him to draw it, Will bowled the Indian over and fled past him for the protection of the wagon, the Indian hot on his heels.

As he felt the Indian closing on him from behind, Will dropped to all fours. The Indian tripped over him and went cartwheeling to the ground. Will leaped astride the savage and closed both his hands about his throat, his thumbs crunching down on the Indian's windpipe. The Indian struggled fiercely, then tried to wrest Will's hands from around his throat. When that failed, he tried to pry each finger loose, but Will leaned forward with all his weight, increasing his pressure on the savage's throat until the brave's thrashing grew fainter. Abruptly, his eyes seemed to pop from their sockets and in a terrible gurgling sound of despair, the Indian settled into the ground under Will.

Will glanced up, the sound of his mother's screams suddenly flowed in on him with terrible clarity. He found that he was completely behind the wagon out of sight of the Indians. He peered under the wagon and what he saw froze his blood. His mother was spread-eagled on the ground, her clothes ripped off her, two Comanche warriors pinning her with their lances while a third was dropping his breechclout. Beyond his mother Clara was in the hands of two younger braves, who were dragging her screaming across the campsite.

As he jumped up to go to their aid, a greased, painted body hurtled out of the wagon and caught him shoulder high with such force that the two of them were sent tumbling down through the oaks, locked in a fierce, murderous embrace. They both came to a jarring halt athwart an oak tree trunk. The Indian struck first, the side of his head crunching against the tree. Dazed, the brave tried to recover in time to deal with Will, but he was too late. With a coolness born of pure fury, Will stood up and kicked the Indian in the side of his head. He saw the skull slam back against the tree, and when it sagged forward, he kicked it again, this time harder, the tip of his boot breaking through the Indian's skull just above his ear. His mouth open, his eyes staring blindly up at Will, the Indian sagged and rolled away from the tree.

An Indian's war cry came from above Will, a high, shrill yell meant to chill the blood in his veins. This time, however, it only served to warn Will. Turning, he saw an Indian plunging down through the trees toward him. Will did not hesitate a minute. He grabbed the knife from the dead Indian's scabbard and crouched in wait for the Indian rushing him. As soon as he was within a few feet, Will drove off the ground to meet him. Keeping low, he drove his shoulder into the Indian's legs just above the knees, sending him flying. The savage landed on his back behind Will. Will turned and fell astride him, his right hand driving the knife deep into his gut, cutting off the Indian's war cry as suddenly as if his throat had been slit. Twice more he plunged the knife hilt-deep into the Indian's belly, then rolled quickly off the savage and glanced up the slope, expecting more Indians to come plunging down through the trees after him.

But none came. And as he waited, he heard, more clearly than before, his mother's screams and realized that these filthy beasts were too busy with their raping and plundering to worry about him. He crept back up the slope to the encampment.

A cold, calculating intelligence drove him now as he took cover behind a thick bush at the border of the oak grove and peered at the half-naked savages. Across their hairless faces and foreheads, the savages had painted broad, black stripes. One brave had black rings around his eyes. Another had accented the hollows in his cheeks, giving him a frightening, skull-like look. Another brave had woven a single yellow feather into his scalp lock. As he peered out at these devils from hell, he told himself it would be foolish for him to expose himself, that he had best keep himself alive so that he could go for help and come back after them to destroy as many of them as God would allow.

Some of the savages were prancing about in the light of the campfire, while the rest, in a frenzy of destruction, were demolishing the wagon as they threw its contents to the ground, chopped open the trunks, and pulled forth the drawers from the bureaus and sideboards, spewing their contents out onto the grass. One found a mirror and was immediately forced to relinquish it to a more powerful brave. The small spinet piano was hurled from the rear of the wagon by two Indians and immediately hacked to pieces.

Keeping behind the bushes, Will crept away from the wagon and immediately came in sight of his sister. Tears of rage coursed down his cheeks when he saw her sitting on the ground with her head bowed, her wrists tied behind her. Her long, golden hair was matted with her own blood, and though she seemed conscious, she seemed barely aware of what was happening around her, and for that Will was grateful.

He kept moving until his mother came in sight. She was still pinned to the ground, but was no longer screaming. Her head was turned toward him, her face frozen in shame and horror as the Indian war chief, a warrior in a buffalo headdress, raped her; squatting naked beside them, two grinning savages waited their turn. Abruptly Will's mother came alive, and she began to scream again. It lasted for no more than a few moments as the warrior silenced her with two powerful, brutal blows.

Unable to take any more, Will eased himself away from the bushes and back down the slope. He had never scalped a man, but he had heard enough about it to know what to do. Using the knife he had taken from the Indian, he set about scalping both Indians. The first scalp he took was not a clean job, but with the second scalp he took more care. Grabbing a fistful of the Indian's black, greasy hair with his left hand, he dug the tip of the knife into the Indian's scalp, circled the head with a steady, even pressure, then yanked the scalp free. Tucking both bloody trophies and the knife into his belt, he kept on down through the oaks, slipped into the water and headed downstream for Coleman's Fort.

III

Rumors of a war party in the vicinity of Coleman's Fort had brought James and his newly formed Ranger company to the fort the evening before. The afternoon of the next day, Mordecai and Jonathan, on a patrol north of the fort, saw the figure struggling in the Colorado's swift current. The night before they had heard thunderstorms in the hills and canyons north of the fort, and the resulting downpour had been swelling the river since morning. They turned their mounts and headed for the riverbank. As they neared the river, they could see that the swimmer was being swept along as much by the current as by his own uncoordinated efforts to remain afloat. He was not far from shore, but was obviously close to exhaustion and was in danger of being swept back out into the main stream.

James and Jonathan dismounted and waded out into the shallows to intercept the struggling swimmer. When he saw the two men crouched in the water waiting to grab him, he waved one arm, floundered for a moment longer, then appeared to lose what strength remained in his thrashing arms. Crying out feebly, he sank beneath the surface. Mordecai ducked under the water and grabbed the man about the shoulders and kicked for shore. Jonathan kept close behind Mordecai and helped both regain the riverbank. When the three finally clambered safely onto it, their clothes plastered to them, the swimmer was gasping for breath and nearly unconscious.

"Thank you," he managed finally.

Mordecai figured him to be about seventeen, perhaps eighteen. He was big and powerful in the shoulders, which probably accounted for his being able to survive in that swift current.

"What happened?" Jonathan asked.

"Indians!" the young man gasped, his eyes wild. "Indians! They got my mother and my sister!"

That was when Mordecai and Jonathan noticed the dripping scalps tucked into the young man's belt alongside a Comanche knife.

"What's your name?" Mordecai asked.

"Will," he told him. "Will Thompson." He grabbed Mordecai's shirt front. "We got to go back there! We got to get them back from those savages."

"Back where?"

"Up the river. An oak grove. It was just past the junction of another river."

"The Llano?"

"I don't know its name."

"We can find it," Jonathan assured him. "We'll stick to the Colorado and keep on past the Llano. We know that country."

"How many in the war party?" Mordecai asked.

"I . . . don't know. They came out of the night. They . . . didn't give us any warning. I thought they were wolves. I mean that's what I kept hearing . . ."

"What about your Pa?"

Will's face went pale, and looking suddenly away from them, he bowed his face in his hands and began to sob.

☆ **Chapter** ☆

3

James and his Ranger company did not waste time. Two hours after Will Thompson was pulled from the water, they were riding upriver at a quick lope. The twelve-man outfit had no surgeon and was without the usual Lipan or Tonkawa brave to act as scout; they had instead Abe Goldthwaite, a mountain man of indeterminate age from New Mexico who had settled in Coleman's Fort. He had already established a local reputation as a Comanche tracker, and if any proof were needed of his competence in this regard, it could be found in his saddle bag, where he kept a grisly assortment of eleven Comanche scalps.

Slung over his right shoulder was a buckskin sack containing his pipe, flints, awl, bullet-mold, and other assorted tools of his trade. Over his left shoulder hung his powder horn. His principle weapon was his .60-caliber Hawken plains rifle, its barrel thirty-six inches long, its effective range well over two hundred yards. It fired a long, heavy lead bullet, and as James had noticed on a hunt for fresh game with Abe earlier that day, it used two to four times as much powder as a Kentucky rifle. Despite this prodigious expenditure of powder, however, there was not a man in the company that did not envy the fabled Hawken firepower.

In addition to the two horse pistols in his belt, Abe carried a scalping knife and a tomahawk. James had seen him practice throwing the knife the evening before and was astonished at the man's skill with this weapon. He could bury its blade into a tree from twenty or more feet with uncanny accuracy. And James had no doubt that he could throw his tomahawk with the same skill. He rode now just ahead of James, his bearded face grim with resolve, his eagerness to close with this Comanche war party evident in the single-minded concentration he directed at the trail ahead.

Will Thompson was riding alongside Jonathan, and Mordecai was keeping just behind James. Despite his exhaustion from his trip downriver, Will Thompson had shaken off his fatigue and was intent on only thing: overtaking the savages that had carried off his mother and sister and killed his father. James had no difficulty understanding how Will felt, but he was uneasy with the young man, nevertheless. He had caught something vaguely unsettling in his eyes—a frightening reflection of the near-demented hate he now felt for this Comanche war party. But what was truly unsettling to James and every other Ranger were the two bloody scalps that hung from Will's belt, trophies he refused to clean or put out of sight. Locked in mortal combat with these Comanche savages, lucky to have survived, and forced to flee for his life, this young man had somehow contrived to rip these bloody scalps from the skulls of two of the Comanche raiders.

It was soon dark. Unwilling to take the chance of losing the trail in the darkness, Abe suggested they halt beside the river and make camp to wait for daylight. At Abe's further suggestion, they gathered only dry aspen kindling for the campfire, explaining that it burned without smoke. Come morning, they did not want to give the Comanche any warning of their presence.

As Will Thompson paced, impatient of this delay, the Rangers gathered around the campfire to discuss their situation. What concerned all of them was whether or not they would be able to cut the war party's trail come daylight. More important, would they then be able to overtake the savages?

It was Mordecai who voiced this concern to Abe. The mountain man was smoking his clay pipe, his back resting against a deadfall. After a quick glance over at Will Thompson pacing impatiently beyond the campfire's light, he looked squarely at Mordecai and closed one eye.

"If we cut their trail," he told Mordecai, "we'll overtake the devils."

"You sure?"

"When it comes to hostiles, ain't no man sure. And that's a fact. But these here Comanche devils are real fond of celebratin' their great victories. Just about now I'd say they're dancin' and screamin' around their fire, tellin' each other what fine braves they are, what noble deeds they just done, and how they're as fierce as mountain lions and as swift as antelopes. They'll keep that up through the night, dancin' an' yippin' till they drop off. Yep, we'll catch up to them—if we can cut their trail tomorrow."

"What I don't understand," said Jonathan, "is why they take captives like they do. Women, children. It just ain't Christian."

"Ain't never hear tell they were Christian. You got to see the world through a Comanche's eyes, that's all."

"What do you mean?" a Ranger asked, leaning close.

"Why, these devils don't see nothin' wrong with takin' women and children captives. They figger a woman or a child is just more booty—like a fine mount or a rifle or a mirror. We buy our slaves at the market, the Comanche wins 'em in battle."

"Slaves?" Mordecai asked, frowning. "That's why they take children?"

"That's one of the reasons. But that ain't the only one.

Thing is they need children. Their women don't produce many cause they're always in the saddle tryin' to keep up with their masters. Children is real valuable to a Comanche, not only as a slave, but as a replacement for them braves lost in battle. And once they adopt a captive manchild, they just figure he's a Comanche like they are. If these adopted captives grow up and lose their scalp in battle, they mourn 'em just like they was blood kin.''

"All these boys they take, they end up as Comanche warriors?'' Jonathan asked, outraged at the thought.

"Not of all 'em. If they're too young to keep up on the trail goin' back, the Comanche kill 'em and leave 'em for the buzzards. If they're too old, they might not convert, and they light out as soon as they get the chance, so these the Comanche sometimes make fight each other to the death soon as they reach their village. That's great sport for them. And if one of them captives acts like a coward or tries to run, they kill him or castrate him and keep him as a slave. The Comanche have huge horse herds. They need slaves to look after them.''

Mordecai spoke up then, his face grim. "I can't believe a white boy or girl would turn into an Indian. It just ain't Christian.''

"Maybe it ain't, but I seen it. Most captives become blamed good Comanche, an' it don't take long. The boys take to the wild life pretty quick. An' the young girls learn soon enough to do what they're told—and considerin' the alternative, I don't much blame them. Before long, they're adopted into a Comanche family and pretty soon pickin' out a likely brave.''

"I find that hard to believe,'' said James.

"Mebbe so, but it's the truth. This ain't Kentucky—it's the plains, and this here's a different world, I reckon.''

He paused to pull on his pipe. Then started up again. "Let

me tell you about one ten-year-old Mexican girl I took back from a Comanche village ten years ago. A Comanche raidin' party deep in Mexico killed her kin while she watched. She was next on the list, but a Mexican Comanche threw her onto the back of his horse and took her back with him. He told her he was goin' to keep her until she was old enough to marry him. The thing is when it came to killin' Mexicans, this warrior had more Mex scalps than a true Comanche.''

James shook his head in wonder. ''Why? Why would they turn on their own kind?''

''I think I know why,'' broke in Clyde Bonner, an old timer who had been listening intently. ''I reckon this Mex wanted every Comanche to know he was a true Comanche, even if he was a full-blooded Mex.''

Abe nodded. ''That's the reason, Clyde. Pure and simple. And it ain't only Mexicans who convert and turn on their own kind. White men and women do it, too. I seen it.''

There was a troubled silence then as each man around the campfire digested this disturbing intelligence. It aroused in them a deep sense of impotence. How did they fight such ruthless, unrelenting heathens who could turn their own kind against them?

''What happened to that Mexican girl?'' Jonathan asked.

''She took up with an Apache chief—one who led a war party on her Comanche village.''

''How'd you get to know her?'' Clyde asked.

''I was with that Apache war party.''

''You mean you fought with Apaches?'' another Ranger asked in astonishment.

Abe fixed the Ranger with his cold, blue eyes. ''This child will ride with the devil hisself to make war on them bow-legged bastards,'' he said. ''Damn their eyes. Near fifteen years ago they staked out my Flathead woman on an anthill. Tearin' out their livers is the purest joy I know.''

The casual bloodthirstiness of Abe's remark sobered the men. Without any further discussion, they left the fire and retired to their blankets. James set out the pickets and sent Jonathan to remind Will Thompson that if he didn't get any sleep, he wouldn't be much help the next day. A moment later, on his way to his own blanket, Jonathan passed James and told him that Will Thompson had not needed much convincing.

II

It was mid-morning when Abe's buckskin-clad figure appeared on a distant ridge to the northwest. They had cut the Comanche's trail that morning, and Abe had been scouting ahead. As the Rangers pulled up to peer at him, the mountain man waved his rifle slowly from left to right. James turned his horse and headed for the ridge, the Rangers trailing after him. Before anyone knew what he was about, Will Thompson broke from the line and headed at full gallop for the distant figure. For a brief moment James considered calling him back.

When they reached Abe, the Rangers learned that the Comanche were not more than an hour's ride ahead. But it was Abe's contention that they should not be in too much of a hurry to close the gap until the Comanche war party reached the broken escarpment looming ahead. The Indians would camp in one of the canyons, and this would give the Rangers a better chance to surprise them. The debate that followed was intense, but not acrimonious. A few were for overtaking the Comanche and taking them on the run until Abe reminded them that Comanche horses were faster than their own stock, at least for short distances, and that if they did not succeed in overtaking the war party, their precipitate action would only alert the war party that it was being pursued. One more point that James brought up settled matters: since they were now deep in Comanche territory, a smoke signal from the alerted war party might bring a storm of Comanche warriors down on them.

Abe's and James's counsel prevailed, and with the mountain man scouting ahead to keep track of the war party, they kept on, keeping to a steady, ground-devouring trot.

As they rode, James could not help but notice the bountiful lushness of the land. Ahead were cedar-studded hills, while on all sides of them stretched undulating grasslands. Clumps of oak appeared like floating islands in the distance. It was a land of small, clear streams and gentle beauty, closed to Texan settlement by these savage horse Indians, but surely, James thought, not closed forever.

III

It was nearly dusk when Abe crested a distant knoll and headed directly toward them. James held up the Rangers and dismounted to wait for the mountain man to reach them. A moment later, Abe dismounted in their midst.

"They're just ahead," he told James, pointing to a low line of hills fronting a distant plateau. "In a canyon below that ridge. Right now they're setting up camp alongside a stream. They're pretty sure of themselves—ain't even setting up any lookouts."

"No wonder," said Jim Tillman. "They figure they're safe now deep in their homeland."

"Yes. And that's our advantage," James reminded the men. "They won't be expecting any trouble, not now."

Abe nodded in agreement. "That's the way I see it."

"How far is it?"

"It ain't far. A half-hour ride, maybe less."

"Then let's move," said James.

Will spoke up then. "Abe," he said. "Did you see my people? My mother and sister? Are they all right?"

"Your mother ain't with 'em," Abe told the young man, his face grim. "They must've . . . left her back at the Colorado."

Will said nothing, but every man there saw his face lose its color. He was keeping his emotions in check, but not without cost.

"What about my sister?" he managed.

"She's with them, Will," Abe said. "I got close enough to see her."

"Mount up," said James.

IV

The Comanche Moon was already well up in the sky. In its bright wash, the Rangers had no difficulty making out the members of the Comanche war party. In all, they counted nine blanketed Comanche lying around three campfires. They saw no sign of Will's sister, but that didn't trouble them. If Abe said she was with the Comanche, that was good enough for them. Farther down the canyon, James glimpsed the Comanche's pony herd.

Beside him, Abe nudged James. "You know what's more helpless than a turtle on its back?"

"Maybe you'll tell me."

"A Comanche afoot."

"So?"

"Might be a good idea for you to circle around behind that pony herd and stampede it right through the encampment. By the time them devils figure what hit them, the rest of us'll be on them. And without their ponies, them devils will be gone beaver."

"Sounds good, Abe."

"You want me to take the rest down to the canyon?"

"What about Will Thompson. Is he armed?"

"I'll give him one of my pistols," Abe said.

James pulled back from the canyon rim and explained the plan to the rest of the men. Not a man voiced any objection to the plan, and most seemed to think it was a good one.

"Give Jonathan and me a half-hour to reach the pony herd," James told them. "When we start the stampede, move—and move fast."

"You figure you two are going to be enough?" Mordecai asked. It was obvious Mordecai would have preferred to be the one to go with James.

"Two's plenty," said James.

Then James pulled Mordecai aside so he could speak to him in private.

"I know you want to go with me, Mordecai, but I need you to stay back here and keep an eye on Will Thompson. If he catches a glimpse of his sister before we make our move, he might jump the gun and ruin everything."

"All right, James," Mordecai said. "But you be careful, hear?"

"You be careful, too, Mordecai."

V

James and Jonathan led their horses along the canyon rim until they found a game trail beyond the Indian encampment and followed it down to the floor of the canyon. They swung back toward the Comanche encampment, keeping close in under the canyon rim until they could see the backs of the Comanche ponies ahead of them. They tethered their mounts and moved closer on foot, keeping to the brush at the base of the canyon wall until they caught sight of the loose rope corral holding the ponies. James peered cautiously out from a clump of juniper, looking for sign of any Comanche braves who might be guarding the ponies.

"There's one," said Jonathan.

"Where?"

Jonathan pointed. "Over there, near the trees."

James saw him. Wrapped in his blanket, the Indian was sprawled under a cottonwood, apparently asleep. It was obvious that this Comanche, at least, did not think he or his ponies were in any danger. As Jim Tillman had said, the Comanche figured they were safe in their homeland.

It reminded James of what Captain Hal Rush had pointed out to all of his men. The Comanche had been safe in the high plains for so long they could not conceive of any enemy daring to challenge them deep in their own hunting lands. Another trait of the Comanche that worked against them was their tendency to chase an enemy band only until they lost interest, after which they would simply give up the chase, like children tired of playing the same game. What this meant was that the Comanche had no conception of the white man's tenacity in pursuit, or of his deadly singleness of purpose when it came to going after what was his. In this case, it was a captured white woman.

James lifted his head to peer over the backs of the ponies. A narrow stream was just beyond and to the left. Straight ahead on this side of the stream, between it and the canyon wall, was the Comanche camp.

"I'll get that guard," James told Jonathan. "Go back to our horses and wait for me there."

Jonathan nodded.

James vanished into the canyon's shadows. Jonathan moved back the hundred yards or more into the timber where they had tethered their mounts. He waited beside them for what seemed like forever and was getting somewhat nervous when his horse shook its head and took a step back. As he reached out to pat the horse's neck, he heard a moccasined foot crushing the pine-needle ground behind him. He whirled and brought up his Paterson Colt. The Comanche's war club came down just as quickly, knocking the gun away. As Jonathan reached back for his knife, the Comanche bowled into him and sent him flying.

His head struck the ground. Dazed, he felt the Indian grabbing his hair with one hand. He saw the Indian raising his hatchet. Something hard smacked into the Comanche's chest—the blade of James's bowie knife. The Comanche sagged to his knees, trying to tug the knife out from between his ribs until, eyes wide in surprise, he toppled forward onto its handle, driving the blade in still deeper. James moved swiftly, silently past Jonathan and kicked the dead Indian over onto his back. He withdrew the knife and wiped it on the grass.

Jonathan sat up, shaking his head.

"I should've figured there'd be another one out here," James told Jonathan. "I got back in time to see this son of a bitch stalking you. I didn't dare call out. Might've aroused the camp. You hurt?"

"Only my pride." Jonathan said, running his hand through his long hair. "I'm sure glad I still have this scalp. Thanks, James."

"Well, if you ever get the chance, just return the favor."

"I'll do that. What about the other one?"

"He's chasin' buffalo with his ancestors. I sliced through that rope corral. You ready to move out?"

"Wait'll I pick up my Colt."

James mounted up as Jonathan retrieved his Colt and dropped it back into his holster.

"Okay," Jonathan said, swinging up onto his horse. "Let's give them ponies a ride."

VI

The moon gave them plenty of light as they rode over the canyon floor. With Jonathan on his left and the ponies just ahead, James abruptly urged his horse to a hard gallop. Jonathan did the same. The sudden pounding of the horses' hooves alerted the ponies. They froze, heads lifting, ears flickering. James unlimbered his Paterson and sent a shot over their heads. Jonathan sent another bullet after it, then let out a war cry as fierce as any Comanche's.

Like a single animal, the ponies bolted headlong down the canyon, James and Jonathan on their heels. By the time the ponies reached the Comanche camp, some Indians were on their feet, waving their arms frantically, trying to halt or turn aside the stampeding ponies, but the spooked horses were too much for them. One brave tried to catch and mount a pony charging past him, but succeeded only in getting himself dragged about ten yards. Meanwhile, just beyond the encampment, Abe and the rest of the Rangers had broken from the timber at the base of the canyon wall and were charging across the canyon floor toward the encampment.

By then, James and Jonathan were already inside it. A Comanche darted out of the night and reached up to grab James's thigh. James flung himself from his horse and crushed the warrior's skull with a chopping blow from the barrel of his Colt, then sent a quick bullet into the face of another. A third Comanche came at him from the side and flung an arm around his neck. As James was dragged backward, he saw the Comanche's knife gleaming in the moonlight as he prepared to plunge it into James's chest. As James tried to twist away, something hard smashed into the Indian, driving him to his knees. The Comanche dropped his knife and sagged forward to the ground, a gaping bullet hole in his back.

Clyde Bonner swept past James, yelling like a Saturday night drunk, his Paterson smoking. Above the gunfire, the high, unsettling war cry of the Comanche now rang out almost continuously. No warrior relished hand-to-hand combat more than a Comanche—and not one of them gave quarter as they met each Ranger head on.

James saw Jim Tillman turn his mount to run down a Comanche. The Indian flung himself to the ground and as Tillman swept past him, he rose from the grass and loosed an arrow at Jim. It caught the Ranger under his shoulder. He ripped it out, turned his horse and ran down the Comanche.

A Ranger behind James shouted a warning to him. He spun about in time to see a naked warrior charging him. James fired, but the shot went high, and the Comanche caught him on the side of the head with his war club. The blow staggered him, but he managed to keep on his feet and fling up his forearm as the war club came down a second time. The force of this second blow nearly shattered James's forearm and sent him tumbling backward to the ground.

He cocked and fired up at the Comanche. Again his shot went wild. A Ranger rode out of the night, pouring a stream of bullets into the Comanche's back. With a tremendous leap, his horse cleared James, and the Ranger vanished beyond him. James jumped to his feet to see another Ranger being pulled out of his saddle by a Comanche. James leaped forward, grabbed the savage, and yanked him off the Ranger. The Indian stayed on his feet and, swinging around, struck James a glancing blow on the chest with his war club. James thrust his Colt deep into the Comanche's stomach and pulled the trigger. The Indian sagged, hung for a moment on the end of the gunbarrel, then dropped to the ground.

VII

Mordecai did his best to keep track of Will Thompson, but as soon as he and rest of the Ranger company surged out of the timber, Will Thompson left Mordecai at a hard gallop and plunged heedlessly ahead of him into the Indian camp. For a few moments, Mordecai lost track of him as the Comanche's ponies, nostrils quivering, eyes wild, plunged past his mount. When he caught sight of Will, the young man was running across the moonlit ground toward a white girl racing to meet him, an Indian blanket falling from her shoulders. Mordecai turned his mount and galloped over to them. Oblivious to the danger all around them, Will and his sister were embracing in the midst of the battle fiercely raging on all sides of them. Mordecai leaped from his horse and rushed toward them.

"Get down, you two!" he yelled. "Get down!"

Will turned, alarmed, Mordecai's shout having alerted him to the danger. As he grabbed his sister's shoulders to pull her to the ground, she uttered a small, stifled gasp. Her face went slack. Will cried out her name and caught her as she sagged forward into his arms. It was then that Mordecai saw the hatchet's blade buried in the back of her neck.

With a terrible cry Will rushed at the Comanche who had thrown the hatchet. He had Abe's pistol in his hand, but instead of firing it, he swung it like a club at the Comanche, who dodged nimbly aside and brought his war club down on Will's shoulder. The blow was enough to stagger him, but he still managed to drag the Comanche to the ground. Mordecai leapt astride the two and managed to get one arm around the Comanche's neck. Reaching back for his bowie, he plunged the long blade deep into the Indian's chest. The Comanche bucked once, then sagged lifeless to the ground. Sprawled beside the dead Comanche, Will looked past Mordecai, his eyes wide.

''Behind you!'' he cried.

Mordecai swung around. A Comanche, his lance hip-high, was rushing at him. James reached back for his Colt, but before he could bring it up, the Comanche stumbled and went down as suddenly as if his legs had been cut out from under him. Astride his mount, Abe loomed out of the night, jumped to the ground and withdrew his scalping knife from the dead Comanche's back.

VIII

On the other side of the encampment James, panting slightly, stepped back from the Comanche he had just shot and looked about. A sudden, awesome silence had fallen over the moonlit battlefield, the only sound that of a single horse blowing. James could not see one Comanche brave still on his feet. But where was Will's sister?

James glanced quickly about, searching the dark encampment, waiting for the sight of a girl's slim figure rising uncertainly from the ground. His hope was that when the battle erupted, she'd been able to keep down or maybe break away from her captors. But as he scanned the eerily quiet battleground, he saw no sign of the girl. Then he caught sight of Abe standing with Mordecai. He hurried across the encampment. A moment before he reached them, he caught sight of Will Thompson on the ground before the two men, cradling in his arms a girl with long, blond hair.

Mordecai took James by the arm and drew him aside. ''It just happened,'' he said. ''She's dead.''

''Damn,'' James muttered. ''Damn it all to hell.''

IX

That night, sleeping under another Comanche Moon, James awoke suddenly to the sound of pounding hooves.

Snatching up his rifle, he flung off his blanket and jumped to his feet. A lone horseman was galloping away from the camp. The other Rangers were also on their feet, rifles at the ready. As they gathered nervously around James, peering after the rider, Mordecai strode over from his picket post with Clyde Bonner and Abe Goldthwaite.

"Relax, boys," drawled Abe. "That ain't no Comanche. It's young Will Thompson."

"Will?" James said. "Where the hell's he goin'?"

"He's headin' back into them hills—to find more Co-manches, I reckon."

"Alone?"

Mordecai nodded. "He borrowed Clyde's rifle and enough balls and powder from me to last him a long time. He took plenty of dried beef and beans, too."

"You mean you didn't try to stop him?"

"What's the sense o' that? Ain't no reason why he should go back with us. He's lost all his kin—his Ma and Pa and sister. The way I look at it, he'll be joinin' them soon enough in the hereafter—and maybe sendin' a few o' them savages on ahead of him."

"It won't be an easy death if those Comanche catch him alive."

Mordecai spoke up then. "Abe told him what to do about that, James. Told him to keep that pistol Abe gave him loaded to use on himself when the time came."

James took a deep breath and peered into the night. He could no longer see Will Thompson, and the pound of his horse's hooves was fading rapidly. After a moment or two, the night swallowed up all traces of the young rider. Perhaps Abe was right. Since the burial of his sister, Will had not been a pleasant companion. His eyes had remained wild with grief, his face a mask of such raw hatred he was unsettling to look upon. And now he had become a one-way campaign of retribution, seeking more Comanche scalps to go with the two he had already taken. And he'd get them, James had no doubt.

But not many and not for long.

James looked back to his men and reminded them that they had a long ride ahead of them come daybreak—and all of it through Comanche territory. Then he and the rest of the Rangers went back to their blankets.

Bone weary though he was, James found it difficult to fall asleep. Staring up at the moonlit sky, his thoughts went from that lone figure riding off into the night to the sad memory of Libby and the son he had held in his arms for so brief a time. They at least were now safe from the random terror of this bloody borderland, and he took grim consolation from this knowledge. Until he reminded himself that others of his kin, the women especially—Marie, Annie, Petra, and young Angeline—were not really safe at all, not while these Comanche roamed the plains as free as the wind. With this realization James felt a terrible apprehension.

☆ Chapter ☆

4

Early in 1840, before James Lewis and his men pursued that Comanche war party past the Llano, Captain Jack Hays and his fourteen-man Ranger company found themselves riding beside the Pedernales River northwest of San Antonio when over a slight knoll ahead of them swept a large Comanche war party. The Rangers were armed with Colt revolving pistols, and instead of running for cover, Hays wheeled and led his men in a charge directly at the onrushing war party. Through a blizzard of shafts they rode, engaging the Comanche knee-to-knee, their Colt Revolvers blazing. Hays lost several men to arrows, but his company's devastating fire struck down at least a dozen warriors. Startled, then terrified by the awesome medicine of men who charged in the face of superior numbers and fired guns which seemed inexhaustible, the Comanche war party broke and fled. Keeping close on their tails, the pursuing Rangers managed to bring down nearly thirty warriors all together.

Only a few days afterward, Hays's company ran into a vastly superior force of Pehnahterkuh Comanche in the Nueces Canyon west of San Antonio. This time Hays allowed the warriors to charge and—as was the Indians's custom—to completely surround the Rangers. Hays calmly directed his men to dismount and discharge their rifles at the circling

Indians. They did so and with deadly effect, after which the Comanches, certain the Rangers were now at their mercy, swooped in for the kill. Hays directed his men to mount up, then led them in a point blank assault on the charging Indians. In keeping with Hays's orders, each Ranger singled out a Comanche warrior and rode directly for him, guns blazing. This tactic so amazed the Indians that the Texans were on them before they could react. Through the Comanche circle Hays led his men, cutting down warriors left and right. Once past the Comanche, Hays and his company rode on, apparently in full flight.

Certain that the *tejanos* had only empty weapons left, the enraged Comanche rode after them. Abruptly, Hays wheeled his force about and charged back to meet the amazed Indians, the Rangers's revolvers once again spitting death. Thrown into utter confusion, the Comanche milled about in a growing panic as each Ranger singled out an Indian, rode close beside him and fired point-blank. As more and more of the Comanche were cut down by guns that never emptied, the warriors flung aside their useless weapons and shields and rode off howling, bent low over their ponies, suffering greater loss of life in this headlong flight than they would have if they had stood their ground and fought.

Colt six-shooters had given the Rangers an advantage they were quick to exploit. In the weeks that followed, Hays and other Ranger captains pressed their advantage relentlessly, driving deep in Comancheria, attacking camps whose warriors were off raiding deep into Mexico, and following tactics encouraged by Lamar, burned the Comanche's food stocks and drove off their vast pony herds. Though many of the Pehnahterkuh Comanche were not defeated in this fashion, and the band's numbers as a whole were in no sense exhausted, this warfare with the *tejanos* had suddenly ceased to be sport. By this time, they had lost their superstitious terror of the miraculous revolvers and had come to understand that they were simply guns of a new and better kind fashioned in the white man's awesome forges. As a result, their chiefs decided they needed a truce to gain new provisions, restock their pony herds, and perhaps obtain from white traders those devastating new sidearms for themselves.

Accordingly, early in March, three Pehnahterkuh chiefs rode into San Antonio and asked for a council. Commander Henry Karnes, in charge of the southern frontier region, met with the chiefs and agreed to the parley. He had only one condition. The bands must return all white captives before serious talks could begin. The three chiefs accepted this condition and promised to return with the band's principal chiefs within twenty days.

Immediately, James and his small band of volunteers, along with Hays and the other Ranger companies patrolling the fringes of Comancheria were told to cease operations and return to San Antonio. Karnes was anxious that there should be no more forays against the Indians until the parley, a wise precaution. He did not want to ruin any chance they might have of regaining the abducted whites now held by the Comanche, for by this time some two hundred Texans had been carried off by Comanche raiders.

News of the upcoming parley and the possible return of the white captives aroused the frontier with a desperate hope, especially for those bereaved families who had seen their loved ones carried off. Soon, members of the captives' families began streaming into San Antonio to await the exchange of prisoners.

II

James and Mordecai were crossing the plaza in San Antonio when Mordecai caught sight of Manuel walking past a cantina. With a hoop loud enough to turn every head in the plaza, he waved his hat at Manuel and called out his name. Manuel turned and caught sight of the two men. At once his handsome, bearded face creased into a pleased grin. A moment later the three were standing in front of the cantina, embracing warmly as they exchanged excited greetings. The Anglos shouldering past them into the cantina did not look favorably upon the undisciplined warmth of this greeting between two white men and a Mexican, but this did not bother James or Mordecai in the least. And Manuel, Mordecai noted with some relief, had developed a hide tough enough to ignore their reactions. He was perhaps learning that not all Anglos were alike.

Stepping back and shaking his head with undisguised pleasure, Mordecai said, "I was just hopin' I'd find you here."

"I am glad you saw me," Manuel said. "I have a surprise for you."

"For me?"

"There are visitors at my place."

"Visitors?" James asked.

Manuel grinned broadly. "Marie and Angeline."

"That's wonderful!" said James. "What are they doing here?"

"With this truce, they think maybe now would be a good time to get some shopping done. I am proud to have them. And my mother, she is more than pleased to have someone to share the gossip with."

"They didn't come over here alone, did they?"

"Frank and Hope came with them. They expect Andrew to join them later. Frank says Lamar wants Andrew to be on hand when the parley begins."

"Frank bring the boys?"

"No. Sly and Annie are takin' care of them back at the compound."

James glanced at Mordecai. "You're too young to get drunk, Mordecai, but maybe we can wet our whistle inside this cantina and get us some visitin' done. Then I think maybe we should ride out to Manuel's place."

"Suits me," said Mordecai, grinning at the thought.

Mordecai was still a young man but in James's eyes, this tall, bronzed son of Texas, growing rapidly into the spitting image of his late father, had already proven his manhood in the toughest crucible of all—the heat of battle. Letting Mordecai join him in a drink was his way of acknowledging that. Mordecai understood perfectly and was more than pleased.

The three men strode into the cantina, found a rough-hewn slab table close to one wall, and ordered beers. Shoving their hats back off their foreheads, they leaned back and looked around. Mordecai was pleased to get out of the blazing sun, even if the cantina did stink of sweaty feet and unwashed bodies. The sawdust on the floor was stained black with chewing tobacco, spilled drinks, and God knew what else. Their suds arrived, warm but wet. Mordecai gulped his a little too fast and began to cough. Manuel grinned and pounded him helpfully on the back. Mordecai put the glass back down and shook his head.

"Hey, it ain't the beer," he protested. "It just went down the wrong way."

"So take it slow and easy, Mordecai," James advised with a grin. Then he glanced across the table at Manuel. "We just got in, Manuel. What do you know about this parley?"

"Not much. But things are heating up."

"How so?"

"Lamar has appointed Colonels Cooke and McLeod as commissioners, along with Colonel Bill Fisher. Fisher's brought in three companies of the 1st Texas Regiment to keep order in case of any trouble.''

"Which means he expects it,'' said Mordecai.

"I say it's a wise move,'' said James. "The Comanche won't make trouble when they see we're prepared for it. And Fisher and Colonel Cooke are not men they'll want to cross, I'm thinking.''

"I still do not like it,'' said Manuel.

"Why not?''

Manuel sipped his beer and shrugged. "I am sorry, *amigo*, but I do not know for sure. I just smell trouble.''

Mordecai nodded uneasily. "Well, I think you're right, Manuel. With the Comanche you never can be sure.''

A shadow loomed over them. James looked up to see Abe Goldthwaite's powerful figure standing beside the table, a pleased Jonathan at his side.

"This here a private party?'' Abe asked, "or can me and this young buck join in?''

"Join in,'' said James, grinning up at the mountain man. "And welcome.''

As the two newcomers sat down, James introduced Manuel to Abe. The mountain man greeted Manuel with a hearty smile and extended his hand, his huge paw swallowing Manuel's in his. It looked to James as if the two were going to be good friends from the start, judging from the friendly gleam that lit both men's eyes.

"Abe just got in,'' Jonathan explained. "We spent the past hour lookin' for you.''

"We weren't tryin' to keep our whereabouts a secret,'' said James, waving over the bargirl. "We were on our way back to the hotel when Mordecai spied Manuel.''

"We been jawin' about the parley,'' Mordecai told Abe.

"Feels like trouble to me,'' said Abe ominously.

"That's the same tune Manuel's been singin'.''

The bargirl took their order for two more beers. As she left, Abe looked shrewdly at Manuel. "And why are you worried, *amigo*?"

"I do not think Cooke and Fisher understand the Comanche."

"That's a fact," said Abe emphatically. "A pure and simple fact."

"You mean you don't think the Comanche will keep their word?" James asked. "After all, they're the ones who asked for this council."

"Of course they did. But that don't mean what everybody thinks it means. It sure as hell ain't a peace treaty they're after."

Abe's and Jonathan's beer arrived. Abe picked his up and took a gulp, then smacked his lips and wiped the suds off his beard.

"All right, Abe," James said. "So what are the Comanche up to?"

"The way I see it, we been buzzin' them pretty good, driving off their ponies and killin' their braves. So they figure they need time and maybe a chance to trade. They need gunpowder, bullets, and maybe a few o' them newfangled revolving pistols that've been raisin' such havoc with them. They're partial to our saddle horses, too, I reckon."

"They couldn't be that foolish," said James, "ridin' in here and using them captives to bargain for trade goods."

"I keep tellin' you, Hoss. You gotta think like a Comanche if you're gonna deal with him. To a Comanche, them white captives they got ain't people—they're just trade bait like their women, or their horses, or a new trade blanket."

"There is something else," said Manuel, "I have been hearing what the Commissioners' terms are for a treaty."

"What are they?" asked James.

"They are very stiff. The Pehnahterkuh must remain west

of a line drawn through central Texas. Never again can they approach settlements or white communities. And they must not interfere with any white men settling in vacant lands anywhere in Texas.''

James frowned. ''I don't see how we could possibly enforce such terms. And for sure, the Comanche would never agree to them.''

''I am not finished, *amigo*,'' Manuel said grimly. ''There is more.''

''Let's hear it,'' said James wearily.

''The custom of giving presents to any Comanche who rides up to a cabin or settlement is to be done away with. And there must be no more taking or ransoming of captives. Furthermore, if during this council the captives they are holding are not freely given up, Fisher and his troops will seize the chiefs and hold them as hostages until all the white captives have been released.''

Abe snorted in derision at the pure absurdity of expecting the Comanche to accept such harsh terms—or to allow their chiefs to be held as hostages. He looked gloomily at James.

''It's like me and Manuel said, Hoss. These here commissioners just don't know the Comanche. There'll be trouble.''

Abe pulled his glass toward him.

Before he could lift it to his mouth, two men materialized beside their table. One of them was a burly, raw-faced fellow wearing a black, high-peaked sombrero. His companion had a scar that ran from his right cheekbone clear down to the corner of his mouth. Both men's eyes were redrimmed, the raw stench emanating from them eloquent testimony to the amount of whiskey they had consumed. Three other worthies moved up behind these two, apparently to back their play as soon as things got interesting.

Abe tossed down the rest of his beer and glanced up at the two men.

"Take a load off, gents," he said mildly, "and join us."

"We don't drink with no greaser," said the big fellow in the black sombrero, his mean eyes resting on Manuel.

"Yeah," said his companion. "This goddamm Mex ought to haul his ass out of here so decent Texans can drink in peace."

Mordecai saw Manuel's face go cold with fury. But before Manuel could react to this insult, James grabbed his beer glass and, jumping up, smashed it into the big one's face. The man staggered back, blood streaming from his shattered nose, as he grabbed the pistol in his belt. James snatched the pistol from him and kicked the man in the groin. The fellow's face went slack with pain as he crumpled to the sawdust. James flung the pistol to the floor and kicked it into a corner.

On his feet the instant James slammed the big fellow with his beer glass, Abe grabbed the scar-faced one around the waist and lifted him over his head. Abe spun around twice, still holding the terrified man above his head like some oversized rag doll, then hurled him at the other three men. The four went down like ten-pins, all arms and legs and cries of outrage. Stepping back, Abe drew both of his pistols and surveyed the cantina.

"Step forward all you pure-blooded Texans!" Abe drawled. "Now's your chance! Proclaim your intentions."

Meanwhile Mordecai kept his own pistol trained on the writhing men struggling in the befouled sawdust. Beside him, Jonathan and Manuel stood ready, obviously not the least bit reluctant to tangle with any comers. But not a single man in the cantina stepped forward to accept Abe's challenge. Each one remained where he sat or had been standing when the fracas began; they stared at the five men like startled deer waiting to see which way to jump.

"Hey there, James Lewis!" cried the barkeep. "No need to wreck the place." His bung starter in hand, he rushed out from behind the bar and stepped over the bloodied fellow James had left facedown in the sawdust. "Hell, these here buffalo chips ain't Texans no how. They hail from Oklahoma, and I never seen a critter from that state worth a pinch of coon shit."

"Then get them out of here, Ben," James told the barkeep. "We want to drink in peace!"

The barkeep spun about. "Milton! Hugh! Throw these here troublemakers out—and anyone else wants to argue with this here Texas Ranger and his friends."

The two troublemakers were promptly dragged to the door and booted unceremoniously out through the batwings. The barkeep picked up the big one's pistol and flung it out into the street after them. As the five sat back down at the table, the bargirl hurried over with drinks—on the house.

"That barkeep knows you, eh?" Abe said to James.

"We rode together last year on the brasada. He near got his ass shot off, so he excused himself from combat. I didn't recognize him until he jumped out from behind the bar with that bung starter."

"He didn't recognize you neither—not till the fun started."

James grinned sardonically. "You noticed that, did you?"

The fracas had put an end to their discussion, if not their concern. Finishing their drinks, the five men paid up and left. Outside in the square, as they paused a moment to get their bearings, two officers with the 1st Texas pulled up beside them.

"Would you be Abe Goldthwaite?" one of them asked the mountain man.

"That's me, sonny."

He was a very young officer and obviously pleased he had

managed to find Abe. "Colonel Fisher's compliments, sir. He'd like to see you in his quarters."

"Now?"

"If it's convenient."

Abe turned to James. "You'll be off to your kinfolk, I reckon."

"That's right," said James. "You're welcome to join us, Abe."

"Much obliged, James, but I better see what ol' Fisher wants first. Maybe he heard we was tearing up the town."

"Pardon me, sir," said the officer, "but you ain't under arrest or nothin'. Its this business with the Comanche. I think the colonel wants you to act as an interpreter. People been sayin' you speak Comanche."

"Not near as good as I do Apache and Kiowa," Abe told him. With a nod to James and the others, the mountain man strode off with the two soldiers.

III

Two days later, twelve Comanche war chiefs of the Pehnahterkuh, dressed in their finest attire and painted for ceremonial occasion, rode into San Antonio. They were led by an old bald chief, Mook-war-ruh. He was their Spirit Talker and had been selected by the other chiefs to be their spokesman. The Comanche had attended many councils with enemies, both European and Amerindian, and were not the slightest bit concerned for their safety. For as long as such councils had been held, it was a sacred pledge among all the plains Indians that no act of violence, no matter how minor, would be tolerated. Since the councils were usually lengthy affairs, the chiefs had brought with them their wives and families. All in all, close to sixty-five Comanche rode into San Antonio that bright March day.

As they waited for the council to begin, the chiefs sat cross-legged in the dust of the main plaza outside San Antonio's small, one-story limestone courthouse and smoked their pipes. The Comanche women, painted and dressed in costumes as bright as the chiefs, also squatted on the ground, but at a discreet distance from the men. In and out among the patient women, their boys raced, playing war games. A large crowd of curious townsmen and spectators who had been streaming into San Antonio for days gathered to watch. Soon the men began tossing coins into the air for the Comanche boys to use as targets for their miniature arrows. The mood of the onlookers was not overtly hostile. Everyone was simply eager to see—many for the first time—the strange and dreaded horse Indians.

And with those twelve Comanche chiefs came two captives.

IV

Angeline and Marie, visiting for the day with Mary Maverick, were among the very first to see the two returned captives. Andrew and Mary's husband Sam both men visibly furious, brought the female captive and a Mexican boy to the Maverick house. Manuel, who had ridden in with Marie and Angeline, was sent for at once, since it was hoped he might be able to calm the decidedly hostile Mexican youngster.

Angeline, peeling potatoes in the kitchen with Marie, was the first to hear the commotion coming from the front of the house. Putting down her paring knife, she lifted her head. What she was hearing were the angry cries of a young boy and finally the slamming of a door. A moment later Mary Maverick's distraught face appeared in the kitchen doorway.

"Marie, Angeline, you must help me. Please."

Angeline put the bowl of half-peeled potatoes hastily down

on the table and started from the kitchen. Marie lifted a pot of stew off the stove and, hastily wiping her hands on her apron, followed Angeline into the dining room.

"I've never seen Sam this angry," Mary confided to Marie. "And I don't blame him!"

"What is it?"

"The Indians just brought in two captives. The Mexican boy we've had to lock in the pantry, but it's the girl . . . Matilda Lockhart . . . !"

By that time Marie and Angeline could hear someone kicking furiously at a door somewhere. Confused, they followed Mary Maverick into the living room.

Andrew was sitting on the sofa beside a girl who could not have been more than sixteen. She was dressed in torn fragments of a dress and was as filthy as some rag doll abandoned by the road. Andrew was holding both of the girl's hands in his, while Sam Maverick stood over her, his face white with fury. As Marie and Angeline entered the living room, Sam Maverick stepped away from the sofa as his wife hurried up to join him; both were obviously so distraught they were completely at a loss as to what to do. Marie and Angeline hurried closer to the girl on the sofa. The girl, tears streaming down her cheeks, lifted her face to them.

Marie groaned and in a quick, reflexive action, covered her mouth with her apron. Confused and dismayed, Angeline pulled up hastily, her feet rooted to the floor as she gazed in horror at what the Indians had done to Matilda Lockhart.

Sores covered the girl's thin, bruised face, but it was what had been done to the girl's nose that truly horrified Angeline. It had been completely burnt off, leaving not a single scrap of flesh left to cover the nostrils. These two gaping holes in the girl's face imparted to it a hideous, skull-like aspect. And if that were not enough, her thin frame had obviously been beaten repeatedly, leaving bruises on her face, head, and arms. In addition to this, Angeline recognized what could only have been fresh burns on almost every exposed bit of flesh, only a few of which had begun to heal.

With a tiny cry, Marie rushed to the sofa and enclosed the girl in her arms. At once the girl, her head buried in Marie's breast, began sobbing uncontrollably, as if all the terror of her capture and torment were coming out at last in one anguished flood of despair. Angeline stole closer, tears now coursing down her own cheeks. Andrew got to his feet and stepped away from the sofa to give Angeline a chance to sit beside the girl. As soon as she sat down, Angeline reached out and took Matilda's hands in hers.

At this, the girl's sobs subsided somewhat and after a short while she lifted her head slightly and pleaded that no one be allowed to see her.

"There, there," Marie soothed. "We won't let anyone else near."

"But why?" Angeline asked.

"I am utterly degraded," the girl cried desparingly.

"Don't say that," Marie urged. "You're away from them now. You're back with your own people. We'll send for them."

"No! Please don't do that!"

"But why not?"

"They would not take me back."

"But of course they would," Angeline protested.

"No! Don't you see? I can never hold my head up again. I will bring only shame to my people now. It would have been better if the savages had killed me."

"Now, you musn't talk like that," Marie told her softly, stroking the girl's filthy, matted hair.

Matilda flung up her face. "Look at me," she cried pitifully. "I am disfigured. And I am no longer a virgin. Diseased savages have taken me at will, and I gave birth to a diseased infant. She was torn from my breast and her head shattered against a tree. I am ruined. There is nothing left for me now. I want only to find a place to hide. You must help me. Please!''

''We'll talk about it later,'' Marie told her soothingly. ''For now, we'll bathe you and get you into a clean dress. I'm sure you'll feel differently then.''

Andrew walked closer to the sofa.

''Matilda,'' he said softly, leaning over the girl, ''do the Comanche have any more captives?''

Matilda looked up at Andrew and nodded. ''Yes, there are more,'' she told him

''How many.''

''At least fifteen.''

''Where are they?''

''They are being held in the Comanche encampment outside San Antonio.''

''Did you learn much of the Comanche language?''

Matilda nodded.

''Can you tell us the Comanche's intentions?''

''Yes. I overheard them planning for this council.''

''Will they return all the captives as they promised?''

''No. Not all at once.''

''What do you mean?''

''They plan to bring in only one or two at a time. In return for each captive they expect many new weapons, gunpowder, vermilion, and other trade goods. One chief is certain his band will come away with many fine horses. They regard this as an opportunity to bargain for much of the trade goods they require.''

Andrew frowned in bitter fury. But he could not say he was surprised. The night before, at Manuel's place, he had heard Abe Goldthwaite argue that this was exactly what the Comanche intended. No doubt about it—Abe knew the

Comanche. They were hoping to use this council to gain trade goods and were not at all bashful at using the humans they had mutilated and utterly degraded as their medium of exchange. As Abe had put it, to the Comanches abducted men and women were no more than chattels to be bought and sold like so many bolts of cloth.

"Matilda," Sam Maverick asked gently, "those burns on your body. Who put them there?"

Matilda seemed to wince as she recalled. "It was the women of the tribe. They delighted in tormenting me. They held torches to my face to make me scream. It was they who burnt off my nose."

Sam flung about furiously to face Andrew.

"My God, Andrew," he cried. "These Comanche women are no better than devils incarnate. What manner of filth are we dealing with? How can Sam Houston talk of conciliation with such heathen? Lamar is right! They must be wiped from the face of this planet!"

Mary reached out to calm her husband, but she said nothing to contradict him.

It was clear to Angeline that Mary felt as her husband did. And, God help her, so did Angeline. Sitting beside this poor disfigured creature, she vowed that if ever she were captured by these savages, she would kill herself rather than let herself be used in this fashion. But then came a terrible thought: Would she be *able* to kill herself? Surely Matilda must have wanted to do the same thing, yet here she was, still living, suffering the shame and disgrace of what had been done to her. If Matilda had not been able to end her torment, what assurance did Angeline have that she would be able to do so?

This unnerving thought sent a terrible chill through her.

V

Mordecai arrived at the Maverick house with Manuel half an hour later. Mary answered the door and let them in.

"Is Andrew here?" Mordecai asked her.

"You just missed him."

"Well, he sent word," Mordecai explained, "about a Mexican captive the Comanche brought back."

"Yes, your mother suggested Manuel might want to take him out to the ranch until his people can be found."

"How old is he?" Manuel asked.

"He could not be more than ten."

"I would be glad to take the boy."

"Oh, that would be such a relief to us," Mary told him.

Marie and Angeline appeared from the kitchen. With a tiny cry of delight, Angeline ran to Mordecai. He put his arm around her and hugged her in greeting. Marie, untying her apron, hurried closer, her face beaming at sight of her son. Mordecai could not help noticing the way Angeline's eyes kept straying from him to feast on Manuel and how Manuel could not seem to take his eyes off her. It was clear enough to anyone with eyes or a heart that these two were meant for each other.

"Has the council started yet?" Marie asked Mordecai.

"Not that I know of. You two been all right here?"

"We've been pretty busy with the Mexican boy and the girl captive."

"Then they *are* going to return them?" Manuel asked, obviously surprised.

"Not exactly, Manuel," Marie told him unhappily. "But Andrew can tell you more. He and Sam Maverick left a few minutes ago for the courthouse to speak to Colonel Fisher."

Manuel asked, "Where's the boy?"

"We had to lock him in the pantry," Mary Maverick told

Manuel nervously. "He's been most troublesome. I'll show you the way."

"Trouble? How come?" Mordecai asked as he and Manuel followed Mary down the hallway.

Mary frowned. "I don't know how it could be possible, but the boy apparently wants to return to the Comanches."

"What's his name?"

Mary pulled up in front of the pantry. "He wouldn't tell us. He insisted on speaking in Comanche—at least that's what it sounded like to Sam and me. He kicked Sam and even tried to bite him. Sam had no choice but to lock him in there. You'd best be careful, Manuel."

As she spoke, she inserted a key in the pantry door's lock and turned it. Pushing open the door, she moved aside to let Manuel and Mordecai step into the pantry. As they entered it, a small bundle of fury crouching in one corner uncoiled and burst past them like a thunderbolt. When Mary reached out to grab him, she was knocked brutally aside. Angeline had enough sense to pull Marie out of the boy's path as he ran down the hall, through the living room and out the front door. He leaped off the porch and was gone in an instant.

Standing in the open doorway a moment later, Manuel watched the boy disappear in the direction of the plaza.

"Let him go," Manuel said. "Nothing can make him return to his own people. He's a Comanche now."

☆ **Chapter** ☆

5

Inside the courthouse Colonel Fisher stared at Andrew and Sam Maverick, his eyes blazing with fury. Then he stepped out from behind his desk and approached them.

"Men," he said. "You must be exaggerating."

They were in the courthouse chambers, a hot, humid room with a few dust-laden law books slumped on three shelves in one corner. On the wall over the desk a massive buffalo head stared glassily out into space, completely dominating the room. Colonel Fisher had been at the desk going over some treaty documents when Andrew and Sam Maverick entered.

"I am afraid Sam's not exaggerating," Andrew said. "You might like to see for yourself what these savages have done to the Lockhart girl. But I warn you, it won't be pleasant."

The colonel, a tall broomhandle of a man with a tan so dark it gave him the look of an unusually tall Indian, strode to the door. He flung it open and bellowed at a soldier leaning against a corridor wall, ordering him to bring in Colonel Bill Cooke and Colonel McLeod, on the double.

Fisher slammed the door shut and strode back to Andrew and Sam. "I'm going to send Bill Cooke over to your house, Sam—if you don't mind. What I want is solid confirmation of that girl's condition, and I want Bill to see it for himself. He's been wondering if maybe Lamar's not a bit too hard on the Comanche. Maybe this will stiffen his spine some.''

A moment later, the summoned commissioners entered the room. Colonel Fisher asked Sam Maverick to repeat to them his description of Matilda Lockhart, then suggested to Cooke that it might be a good idea for him to visit Sam Maverick's residence to verify the girl's condition. As Cooke started for the door, McLeod started after him, telling Fisher he was going as well. Fisher offered no objection, and a moment later the two men vanished out the door.

As the door closed behind them, Andrew said to Fisher, ''I think you should know what the girl told us, Colonel.''

''What do you mean?''

''She is apparently a very intelligent girl, more's the pity. Evidently she's learned the Comanche tongue—she has overheard what the Comanche chiefs are planning for this council.''

''All right, Andrew,'' Fisher said. ''Let's have it.''

From what the girl had told them, Andrew said, the Comanche had no intention of bringing in all the captives. Instead, they were going to deal their prisoners one at a time in an effort to gain as many trade goods as they could. Peace, apparently, was the least important item on their agenda.

Fisher moved back behind his desk and slumped into his chair. ''Karnes was right. He wrote Lamar he had no faith in these savages, said the only reason he didn't arrest those three chiefs when they rode in asking for this council was because it would still leave most of the other chiefs free. Three were not enough. But if what you say is true, Andrew, we'll have enough of these butchers this time. More than enough!''

''You mean you won't deal with them?'' Maverick asked, his eyes gleaming.

''Well now, Sam, before I slam the door on them, I just

might want to verify what that girl told Andrew here.'' Fisher
looked at Andrew. ''Tell me, how many captives do these
savages still hold? Did the girl say?''

''Fifteen, at least.''

''Then we'll just make sure that the Lockhart girl heard
correctly. There still might be a chance the Comanche will
bring the captives in.''

''Colonel,'' Sam said, ''that poor girl was not lying, and
these devils must be taught a lesson!''

''Simmer down, Sam. You know damn well what my
intentions are. I just want to do this right. No sense in alerting
the chiefs before we're ready to make our move.'' Fisher
looked at Andrew. ''What do you say, Andrew?''

''I agree, Colonel. It won't hurt to make sure. We don't
want to show our hand too soon. These Comanche are like
children. They probably have no idea how we view their
treatment of Matilda Lockhart. They see nothing wrong in
their behavior. For them, this council is just one more fine
opportunity to trade for goods.''

''And that's the pure and simple horror of it,'' Sam said,
agreeing with Andrew. ''They can loot and murder and
rape—and to them it is all a fine game. But they are not
children. They are brutal, murdering savages, and it's time
they learned just who they're dealing with.''

''So what are your plans, Colonel?'' Andrew asked.

''You know well enough, Andrew. And Lamar is in
agreement. Unless the chiefs agree to bring in every hostage
without bickering about trade goods in exchange, we'll hold
these chiefs hostage until every single one of those captives
have been returned to us.''

''The chiefs are not likely to stand still for that.''

''I don't expect they will. But we've got the 1st Texas on
hand to back our play. That force should be more than
sufficient. Damn it, Andrew, we want those hostages back.''

The door opened. Cooke and McLeod burst in, their faces raw with outrage. Andrew realized at once that they were about to verify emphatically what he and Sam had already told the colonel. They crowded Fisher's desk, their faces pale with fury, and began their outraged report. Andrew left the room. He was already familiar with Matilda Lockhart's fearful condition and had no stomach for hearing it described again.

As he left the courthouse and gazed out across the plaza at the waiting Comanche chiefs, resplendent in their ceremonial robes and painted faces, he could not suppress a growing sense of foreboding. The council would begin within the hour, and he was sure now it could only lead to a deadly, even bloody confrontation. But there was nothing he or anyone else could do to prevent it. There were no longer any cool heads to help deal with this situation. When the chiefs allowed that pitifully disfigured Matilda Lockhart to be brought in that morning, they committed a terrible blunder.

II

James and Abe Goldthwaite, arms folded, stood behind the courtroom's high benches and watched the twelve chiefs file in. Copper-hued savages in buckskins, their faces were painted gaudily for this important council. In a few cases, their long, boot-like moccasins were painted a bright blue. Into the seams of their buckskin shirts were sewn beads and silver coins. Two chiefs had tiny bells sewn into their leggings' seams that chinked melodiously as they strode in. The chiefs' long hair, greased with bear fat and buffalo dung, was carefully braided and decorated with silver bits, scraps of colored cloth, beads, and glass.

Without their grim buffalo-horned headdresses, and no longer astride their war ponies, these chiefs were considerably less terrible in aspect than those mounted warriors that James and Sam had been fighting in the past months. But the chiefs' calm confidence and dignity as they strode into the room—even their arrogance—was difficult not to admire. They were men who had never known subordination or slavery, who took no orders except by choice, lords of the plains, living as they pleased across the land, dark-eyed hunters who stood for violence, cruelty, and blood courage. James grudgingly admired these men, even as he hated them.

The courtroom's wooden chairs had been folded and stored in the jailhouse next door, giving the chiefs plenty of room. They squatted patiently on the dirt floor, facing the three commissioners who had come in earlier and had been waiting for them behind the three high benches that had been brought in especially for this council.

On one side of the room Andrew stood beside the door. Captain Jack Hays stood across the room. Jack Hays was a surprisingly young man, with a lithe, almost womanish figure. His hawk-like eyes did not miss a thing, however, and his square jaw was set grimly as he watched this barbaric procession file past him into the room. A few of Hays's fully armed Rangers were strung out along the wall beside him. Close beside Andrew stood Mordecai, watching the chiefs file in with eyes that were easily as cold and hard as Jack Hays's. This young son of Texas saw nothing noble in these lice-ridden savages.

When all the chiefs had finally entered and made themselves comfortable, Colonel Fisher turned to Abe and beckoned to the mountain man. Without comment to James, Abe took up his Hawken and strode over to the commissioner. James pushed himself away from the wall and sat down in a wooden chair next to Colonel Bill Cooke, who was sitting at the bench on Fisher's left.

"Ask them if they are ready to begin," Fisher told Abe, his powerful voice booming through the courtroom.

Abe relayed the message, addressing the seated chiefs. One of them answered with a nod of his powerful head, then got to his feet with great dignity.

"This here's chief Mook-war-ruh," Abe told Fisher. "He's all ready to go, Colonel."

"Fine," said Fisher grimly. "Why don't you thank him for returning the two captives."

There was a hint of suppressed fury in Fisher's voice, but this was completely lost on the old chief. His impassive face showed no emotion as he accepted Fisher's thanks, then folded his arms and leaned back, his obsidian eyes surveying the three commissioners with a proud, imperious glance. The old chief was ready for the bargaining to begin, obviously having no idea how Matilda's pitiful condition had infuriated these commissioners as well as the townsmen who had learned of it soon afterward. In fact, a description of Matilda Lockhart had already swept like a grass fire through San Antonio, causing a seething resentment that James saw visible now on each Ranger's face as he peered coldly at the squatting chiefs.

"Now ask him," Fisher rumbled, "why he's come in here without returning any more of the captives."

Abe asked Mook-war-ruh about the other captives.

Mook-war-ruh pushed himself to his full height and launched into a fine oration, his arms moving gracefully, his voice filling the room, his head turning slightly so as to take in each one of the three commissioners. At last the oration subsided and came to an abrupt end. He folded his arms and waited.

Abe cleared his throat and turned to Colonel Fisher. "The chief admits there are more captives, but they are in the camps of other bands. The chief has no power over these bands."

Colonel Cooke glanced at James, his eyes gleaming with anger. "That old son of a bitch," he muttered. "The girl's already told us they've got fifteen captives out there, maybe more."

At the sound of Cooke's voice, Mook-war-ruh glanced in his direction, as did Colonel Fisher.

"Keep it down, Bill," said Fisher. "Let me handle this."

"Then handle it," Cooke replied testily. "That old bastard is lying in his teeth."

Fisher looked back at the chief and nodded grimly, then asked him why they had come in for this council if they couldn't bring in the captives. After all, that was the condition of this parley.

After Abe's translation, the old chief answered without a moment's pause, his voice filling the courtroom, obviously enjoying his prominence as spokesman hugely. When he had finished his reply to Fisher's question, Abe spoke directly to Fisher.

"Mook-war-ruh says he don't doubt that you'll be able to ransom all the captives."

"At what price?" demanded Fisher.

Abe asked the chief and got another long, involved oration.

"This old fox has a long list. Colonel," Abe told Fisher. "What he's after in exchange is a great store of food goods: salt, flour, sugar, tobacco. He'd like some gunpowder and ammunition, too."

"Is that all?" Fisher asked, his voice laced with bitter sarcasm.

"They sure is, Colonel. Blankets, vermilion—and a case of those famous revolvin' pistols. I reckon that's what they really want. And Mook-war-ruh's ready to bargain."

"Is he now?"

"Yes he is, Colonel. And Mook-war-ruh's wants to know how you liked his answer."

"How I liked his answer?"

"That's right, Colonel."

His patience at an end, Fisher got to his feet and nodded quickly at Jack Hays. The captain opened the door and said something to a soldier standing in the corridor, then stepped back into the courtroom as a file of soldiers entered the room. As they took up positions along the walls, the squatting chiefs frowned in some concern and talked nervously among themselves. Mook-war-ruh, however, remained impassive, secure in the knowledge that nothing untoward could happen at a peace council.

Fisher turned to Abe.

"Tell the old fraud this, Abe," he said. "Tell him he and the other chiefs are not going to use those pitiful captives they've raped and mutilated as bargaining pawns. Tell him that he and the other chiefs will be held in the jailhouse next door as hostages until every one of those captives have been returned to us."

"Hold it, there, Colonel," Abe said nervously. "You mean you want me to tell these Comanche chiefs we're goin' to throw them in prison?"

"You heard me, Abe."

"I can't tell 'em that, Colonel! They wouldn't stand for it. They'd fight to the death before allowing themselves to be made captive. Besides, they're here under a truce, a sacred truce as far as they're concerned."

"What's the matter with you Abe?" Fisher demanded. "Are you their advocate or an interpreter?"

"Colonel, I'm just trying to tell you it won't work. I know these people."

"Dammit, Abe. Will you please translate my demand?"

Abe turned away from Fisher and cleared his throat. At the same time, he lifted his Hawken and rested it in the crook of his right arm, a move that did not go unnoticed by the chiefs.

Two of them in the back of the room got to their feet. Abe cleared his throat and addressed Mook-war-ruh directly. He spoke quickly, bluntly—and as soon as he had finished, the rest of the chiefs jumped to their feet, instantly filling the room with their war cries.

James saw a chief rush to the doorway and thrust a knife into a soldier who attempted to bar his way. Jack Hays clubbed the chief to the floor, then poured two quick shots from his Colt into the man's body. Fisher stood up behind the bench, his voice thundering above the uproar.

"Soldiers! Protect yourselves! Fire on these savages! Cut them down!"

At once the room was filled with the rattle of gunfire, smoke and the whine of ricocheting balls. James, his own gun out, saw a chief heading directly for him. Almost without thinking, he raised his gun and punched a hole in the savage's chest. But still he came on and not until Abe's thrown knife caught him in the throat did he drop. Turning, James saw old Mook-war-ruh catch a Ranger near the wall and bury his hatchet in the man's skull before a soldier cut him down with a gunshot that blew his head apart.

One of the chiefs attacked another soldier, ripping the musket from his arms and discharging it into the man's gut. As James dashed toward the door behind Abe, he saw Andrew snatch the rifle from the chief's hands and club him to the ground with it, hitting the chief repeatedly about the head and shoulders with a wild, unthinking frenzy as if the chief were a rattlesnake he had found in his bedroom. Another chief charged from the back, heading directly for Abe.

"Abe!" James called. "Look out."

"Let the son of a bitch come!" Abe cried as he turned to face the chief.

Swinging from his heels, Abe brought the full force of his

Hawken's barrel around, catching the chief on the side of his head. It collapsed like a rotten melon. James looked away, then ducked quickly as a thrown knife narrowly missed him. He saw the chief who threw it and took after him. A dying Comanche sprawled on the floor reached up and grabbed one of James's feet. James went down so fast he was more surprised than hurt. He clubbed the Indian senseless with his revolver and scrambled to his feet in time to see the chief he had been pursuing succeed in fighting his way to the door, then push himself outside.

James could hear the chief's cries to those waiting in the courtyard. Other chiefs broke out after him, shouting a warning to their families. James heard the Comanche women screaming. He stumbled out through the door himself and managed to bring down with a single shot the chief he was after. Then something struck him on the right shoulder, and he went plunging to the ground as four or five other chiefs swept past him into the courtyard, the soldiers streaming out after them. James rolled out of the way as the pursuing soldiers discharged their muskets at the fleeing chiefs.

Flat on the ground, his head reeling, James watched, dumbfounded, as the courtyard erupted into a scene out of hell. The Comanche women who had been squatting patiently in the courtyard had become thoroughly aroused furies, fighting with a ferocity that belied their sex, wielding hatchets and knives with deadly skill. Some had bows and were sending shafts into the chests of soldiers, while beside them, their young warriors—who were entertaining the townsmen a few moments before with the accuracy of their toy bows and arrows—were loosing shaft after shaft at soldiers and startled townsmen.

James saw one small Comanche boy send one, then two arrows into the chest of Judge Prescott, a circuit judge with whom James had spoken for a brief while before entering the courthouse. The judge had been on his way through San Antonio and had stopped to watch the Indians ride in, the way he would have done if a traveling circus had come to town. Without a cry, the judge sank to the ground as a townman emptied his shotgun at the Indian boy, cutting him nearly in half.

James tried to get to his feet, but could not get his right arm to support him. He sagged back to the ground and momentarily lost track of time until he felt someone shaking him urgently. He opened his eyes to see Andrew bending over him, a stricken look on his face.

"You hurt bad, James?"

"I don't know. My shoulder feels numb. I think I took a slug."

"Let me see."

Andrew went behind James and, as gently as possible, examined the bullet wound. After a few moments of probing, he smiled at James, obviously very much relieved.

"A ball grazed you," he said. "Looks like you lost some blood, but you'll be all right. You're one lucky man. We got soldiers and Rangers back in there wounded real bad—some dying. These Indians sure as hell ain't Cherokees."

"No, Andrew. They sure as hell aren't. These here are horse Indians. True savages."

"Where's Abe?" Andrew looked around, hoping to spy the mountain man. "I don't see him anywhere."

"Last I saw he was using that Hawken like a war club," James told him. "I hope he keeps his scalp. I need that old reprobate."

"Yeah. Too bad Fisher didn't listen to him."

"In the state he was in, I don't think Fisher would've listened to God himself."

"Come on. I'll help you over to Maverick's house. This town is going wild."

As Andrew helped James to his feet, Jonathan and Mordecai ran up, obviously concerned. Once assured James was in no immediate danger, the two young men ran off to join the hunt, like hounds on the scent. The Indians had been driven from the courtyard by this time, leaving it littered with the bodies of dead Comanche women and children, and more than one Ranger or soldier with hatchets in their backs or small arrows sticking from their torsos like porcupine quills. In the distance James could see soldiers and townsmen racing off after the fleeing Indians.

"Let's get the hell out of this," said Andrew.

"Lead the way, brother," said James.

They were almost to Maverick's house when they turned a corner and saw a mob of angry men soaking down a bakery with kerosene. Before they reached it, the bakery was up in flames. From inside came the cries of the two Comanche trapped inside. Abruptly, driven by the flames, the Indians broke out through the front door. The first one to emerge, already wounded, staggered a few feet, obviously blinded by the smoke. A townsman with an axe split open his skull. The other Comanche got as far as the middle of the street before a fusilade of shots brought him down.

All James could think of was how glad he was that neither Mordecai nor Jonathan were part of this mob. And then James recalled his own part in the slaughter.

III

That night, James visited the church where Hans Morgenthau, the only doctor in San Antonio, worked frantically to save the severely wounded whites. James was almost ashamed to take the harried doctor's time, but the man uttered not a word of reproach as he patiently examined the superficial wound in James's shoulder, cleaned it out thoroughly, bandaged it, and sent James on his way.

Mordecai had accompanied him to see the doctor. On the way back to Maverick's house, they passed the jail and could hear coming from within it the wailing and lamentations of the Comanche women and children who had been captured and thrown into cells. Hearing their wails was more than distressing; to James it presaged bloody days ahead for the entire sweep of this borderland. It would be a cold day in hell before the Comanche nation forgot this outrage. The council house fight would be seen by the Comanche as pure treachery, the dishonoring of a solemn truce, a crime almost beyond their comprehension.

When he and Mordecai reached Maverick's house, they found Abe Goldthwaite already there with Colonel Fisher. James was relieved to see them both healthy, neither one with a single scratch. Andrew was on hand as well. A heated discussion was in progress, and as James strode into the living room, he caught enough of it to know they were discussing what course they should take to accomplish the safe return of those captives the Comanche still held. Though Andrew and Sam Maverick were a part of the discussion, it seemed that Abe and the colonel were the ones doing most of the talking.

As James and Mordecai entered the room, Colonel Fisher acknowledged their presence with a perfunctory nod. Too intent even to acknowledge James and Mordecai, Abe leaned forward in his chair and jabbed his pipestem at the colonel.

"It won't work, Colonel. Ain't no way you goin' to make any deals with these red devils now. That's all done."

"Not necessarily," said Fisher.

"Colonel, forget about swapping them hostages you got for the captives. Them chiefs are dead. Altold, we got thirty-three dead Comanche, and that's includin' women and children. With their principal chiefs gone, this Comanche band is goin' to need a while to mourn their dead and elect new chiefs, and when they do, we'll hear about it. But right now, they sure as hell ain't about to make any deal for them captives they still got."

James spoke up. "I agree with Abe. If we still had the chiefs alive, we could deal. But not now."

"You just walked in, James," the colonel snapped testily, "so you don't know what this is all about. I say we still got cards to deal. We are holding as hostage the widow of one of their greatest chiefs. I'm going to put her on a horse tomorrow and send her out to her people to tell them that the survivors of this here council house fight will be put to death unless the band releases all the white captives."

"How much time are you going to give them?"

"Twelve days should be sufficient."

"Twelve centuries won't be long enough, Colonel," Abe said. "No more deals. Not with these people."

"I say it's worth a try," said Andrew wearily. "Besides, what are we going to do with these hostages? We can't put them to death. If we're going to let them go, we might as well get some use out of them, make whatever deal we can."

Standing close beside James, Mordecai muttered softly, "Maybe we should've thought of all this before."

The Colonel's ears were sharp. He looked at Mordecai. "We don't need your two cents, young man," he growled.

Mordecai shrugged. "Well, Colonel, looks like you got it anyway."

The colonel's face revealed a sudden weariness and a growing frustration. He turned back to Abe.

"Abe," he said, "I'm going to send that chief's squaw out tomorrow, and what I want you to do is check on what happens when she gets back to that encampment."

"You mean you want me to go with her?" Abe asked, incredulous.

"Of course not. Wouldn't be at all healthy."

"Then what've you got in mind, Colonel?"

"I understand you've got a pretty good idea where the rest of the band is camped."

"I do."

"Take someone and ride out tonight, so you'll be on hand when the chief's widow arrives. If you're the scout James here says you are, you should be able to get close enough to the encampment to see what happens."

Abe cocked an eyebrow at James. "How about it, James? I guess you'll be ridin' out with me."

"Me?"

"Why not? It's your big mouth got me into this."

"And I'll go too," said Mordecai.

Abe glanced quickly at Mordecai. "Two's company, three's a crowd," he said.

"But James is wounded," Mordecai said. "His shoulder's all banged up."

James laughed. "You saw Morgenthau fix it up fine, Mordecai. Hell, I can hardly feel it."

From the direction of the kitchen, Marie and Angeline came rushing into the living room, their silken skirts rustling. They must have been standing in the kitchen doorway, listening. Sam Maverick's wife was not with them. James guessed she was upstairs with the Lockhart girl. The poor creature had been terrified when he heard the gunfire that afternoon and looked out the window to see Comanche running past the house, fighting off the soldiers and Rangers, sometimes in hand-to-hand combat with townsmen.

"Mordecai," said Marie, her face pale with concern. "You are not going with James. I won't have it."

"Please, Mordecai," pleaded Angeline, "stay here with us."

"No need to worry about that," said Abe, getting quickly to his feet. "You can rest assured, Angie. I already said three's a crowd. James and me, we'll do just fine. Besides, Mordecai should stay on hand in case them Comanche out there decide to ride in here and let off a little steam."

"Mother of God," Marie gasped. "Do you think they would?"

"Well, ma'am, this town's got a pretty good wall around it, but there's a passle of angry Comanche out there. Like I told the colonel this afternoon, he'd better make sure every man here keeps his powder dry and his eyes open. We just poked a stick into a hornet's nest, and them hornets is looking for someone to sting."

Angeline rushed to Mordecai's side. "You heard him, Mordecai. You're needed here. Stay with us."

Mordecai was obviously embarrassed by all this concern for his safety on the part of his mother and sister, and he did not want to back down in front of the men, but looking into Angeline's imploring eyes, he was helpless.

"No need to get all upset," he told her. "I reckon as how James can do just fine without me tagging along."

The look on Marie's and Angeline's faces was reward enough for Mordecai. He forgot his embarrassment and dropped an arm over his sister's shoulder, hugging her affectionately.

Then he turned to James. "You and Abe be careful."

James slapped Mordecai heartily on the back. "Ease up, boy. No need for you to fret."

Colonel Fisher was on his feet as well. He reached out and shook Abe's hand, then James's. "Good luck, you two. Find out what you can, then get back here."

Abe started for the door. "Let's go, James. We better get our gear set. Looks like we got a ride ahead of us."

With a wave to the others, James moved out after the mountain man, grateful he was leaving no wife behind to worry. He guessed that was what made him and Abe such a good choice for scouting a Comanche camp.

☆ Chapter ☆

6

As usual the Comanche encampment was marked by the buzzards circling overhead. Since no word had yet arrived of the fate of the chiefs in San Antonio, the Comanche had set out no sentries, and in fact, the Comanche camp was wide open. Their encampment was in a deep canyon that cut through the Balcones Escarpment. A broad, shallow stream meandered through it, its banks lined with cottonwoods and willow that were only now leafing out.

Tethering their mounts in a narrow gully well to the back of the canyon, Abe and James descended into the canyon, waited until nightfall, then crept to the edge of the stream. Keeping to the willows, they worked themselves upstream until they were directly opposite the Indian encampment, then hunkered down to wait for daylight.

Halfway through the next morning, a covey of half-naked Comanche women just past their teens splashed into the stream and began throwing water at each other. One of them, laughing excitedly, ran across the shallow stream, the water never once reaching above her bared waist, while two others, slapping handfuls of water at her, kept in laughing pursuit. The play was natural and light-hearted, a delight to watch. James found it difficult not to smile as the three girls continued to splash and tease each other. They drifted so close to the spot in the willows where he and Abe were crouching that at one point James was almost tempted to reach out and yank playfully one girl's long black hair, but he caught himself and grinned at Abe, as if Abe might have had the same crazy impulse.

Their laughter like music in the clear air, they splashed back across the stream and vanished in the encampment along the far bank. Pushing back into the willows, James found himself wondering how creatures seemingly as innocent and as full of laughter as those Indian women could have been roused to burn off the nose of a captive white girl and then, not content with that barbarity, continue to devil her with flaming brands, scarring almost every inch of her body.

It was something James just could not fathom.

He turned to Abe. "They seemed harmless, didn't they. Like a bunch of silly young ladies at a picnic."

"Just don't turn your back on 'em."

"Yeah. Look what some of them did to that Lockhart girl. How do you figure it, Abe?"

"Ain't no way you can—lessn' you're a Comanche."

James had no doubt Abe was right. A Comanche might look and talk like a normal human being, but in no way did he resemble the white or red men James had known. The Comanche's culture made him as alien as if he had dropped from the sky. Something terrible in it made them cruel beyond pity to outsiders—white or red. Perhaps it was because for so long they had lived on these plains unopposed. Any whim could be a command. Here they knew no master, no fear. They came and went as they pleased. This was their realm, and it had been for so long as they cared to remember; no other tribe dared to venture into it, not even the Apache.

Abe had already told James how the Comanche had swept down from the northern Rockies at least a century before to drive the Apache from these open plains. The Apache! A crueler, more fearsome tribe James could hardly imagine, judging from the tales he had heard. Since their exile from these plains, they had fought off every attempt by the Mexicans to drive them back still farther, preventing the Mexicans from establishing much more than a few scattered settlements. With relentless fury, the Apache raided the Mexican ranches over and over, burning them out, carrying off horse herds and captives. In their unrelenting warfare on the Mexicans, they were as pitiless, as ruthless as any Tartar. Single-handedly, according to Abe, they had stopped the Spanish from advancing north and conquering these lands as they had the lands of the Inca.

Yet, as fearsome as were the Apache, they had met their match in the Comanche, who had driven them from their ancestral home. The question now was whether or not the Texans could drive the Comanche from this land in turn. For this was what the Texans were about. James had no illusions about that. Neither did Lamar. James suspected they could do it, but it would be a long and terrible conflict. The Comanche would not go easily. And yesterday's perfidy would seal their terrible resolve, brand into each warrior's soul an everlasting enmity for the hated, treacherous *tejanos*.

II

It was an hour or so before dusk when the Comanche chief's widow reached the canyon. Astride a horse she had used cruelly, her head hanging wearily over its neck, her wailing began before she reached the stream. She cut through the willows less than a hundred yards from where the two men crouched and splashed across the stream to the camp, her shrieking wails reaching a climax as she rode into the Comanche crowding the far bank.

Beating her breast and tearing at her hair, she flung herself in reckless abandon from the mount. As she told of the deaths of her husband and the other chiefs, a groan, sounding like wind moaning through trees, swept through the listeners. Then came the screams and after that—coming from everywhere, it seemed—the long, terrible, keening wails. Peering across the stream at the encampment, it appeared to James that every Comanche had gone insane.

The wives, daughters, and mothers of the dead chiefs flung themselves about in a mindless frenzy, punishing themselves terribly as they screamed out their anguish. Some of the barbarities they inflicted on themselves were clearly visible to James and Abe. They saw women ripping open their faces and breasts with long knives. Some chopped off fingers. A few appeared to injure themselves fatally and lay where they fell, ignored by all those around them who were dancing about in a veritable orgy of wild, inconsolable grief. Wrapped in their robes, the men rocked and moaned, some chopping off their hair. Then, as darkness descended, the mourning went to an incredible extreme. Great fires were built, and in their blazing maws, horse herds belonging to the dead chiefs were immolated. The maddened whinnying of the terrified horses and the stench of their burning flesh filled the night.

Abe nudged James. James turned to him, and saw that the mountain man appeared to be as drained as he himself was by this show of savage grief.

"What are you thinkin', Abe?"

"That widow woman didn't spend much time discussing Colonel Fisher's offer." He said this drily, his voice making no effort to hide the scorn he had felt for the Colonel's idea from the beginning.

"You're right, Abe. All she did was wail."

"Which means them hostages are in bad danger now."

"You sure, Abe?"

"If you was a Comanche over there right now, what would

you do when you found out you had some defenseless Texans handy you could punish?''

''Jesus, Abe. Those poor devils.''

''Only thing is, we don't know for sure.''

''You mean we should wait?''

''I think mebbe we ought to duck low in the water and get over there, see what we can find out. Maybe save one or two of them.''

''I'm game if you are, Abe. But I think you're crazy.''

Abe spat out a long dart of tobacco juice. ''Not as crazy as you think, Hoss. We got the element of surprise in our favor. You think any Comanche is goin' to expect a white man to be crazy enough to enter this camp now?''

Without replying, James pursed his lips and looked out across the stream, studying the camp. Every now and then an Indian darted past a campfire. Abe was right. The Comanche were so crazed by their grief, so taken up by their wild mourning rituals, they wouldn't be expecting two crazy Texans to walk in and join them.

''You can stay here if you want,'' Abe said.

''No need to shame me into it, Abe,'' James told him with a grin. ''I'm ready. Even if this *is* the craziest stunt I ever heard of.''

''Before we cross, we better take off our gunbelts and hold them out of the water. And keep your ass down, Hoss. All we need is our heads above water to see where we're goin'.''

James unbuckled his gun belt. A moment later, a yard or so behind Abe, James slipped into the water after him. In less time than he would have wanted, he found himself running up onto the far bank, following close behind Abe as the mountain man headed for the rear of a lodge crowding the river bank.

Pulling up behind it, the two men paused. Abe looked quickly around, then told James to follow him. The two men slipped around the lodge, then moved across a small clearing and into a clump of alder. They cut through it, peered out, and found themselves close enough to see a good portion of the huge Comanche encampment. From their spot across the stream, they had not realized just how large a camp it was. The night was lit with the garish light from roaring campfires, and Comanche men, women, and children were still running in and out among the shadows with the panicked frenzy of ants whose anthill has just been stomped on.

Their wailing and moaning filled the air—but another cry, more chilling still, assaulted James's ears. They were screams, not of grief, but of terrible, soul-wrenching pain.

"Hear it?" said Abe, his eyes above his tanned cheekbones bleak with anger.

"Yes."

"The hostages."

James felt sick.

"Over there," Abe said, pointing.

About fifty yards distant, four Comanche women were prancing about something staked out on the ground beside a leaping campfire. James peered more closely and saw a boy's small head thrashing as he screamed. The knives in the women's hands flashed in the firelight as they cut and ripped with expert care. They were in no hurry to kill their victim, and were bending all their resources and fiendish skill to keeping the boy alive long enough to wring the last shriek and convulsion from his tormented body.

It seemed the Comanche's grief had turned to fury now, and as Abe had predicted, they were venting it on the Texans they still had in their midst. From the sounds of other screams James could hear now, there were many others staked out under this high plains moon. Their deaths, too, would be long in coming as they were skinned, sliced, horribly mutilated, and finally roasted alive. What had happened to Matilda

Lockhart was nothing compared to what these remaining captives were facing.

"Ain't nothin' we can do now, Hoss," Abe said. "We better get back across that stream. And let me be the one to tell Colonel Fisher."

They left the alders. With Abe in the lead, James trailed cautiously behind him. As he darted out from behind a cottonwood, a Comanche warrior, hair shorn and eyes wild, stumbled out of the night and slammed full into him. The warrior jumped back, startled. Then, enraged at the sight of a white man, he reached for his knife and rushed James. James ducked low and danced nimbly to one side, slashing at the warrior with his bowie, laying open the Comanche's right side. Jumping away from James, the savage saw Abe rushing out of the night toward him and swung around, apparently ready to alert the camp with a war cry. Before he could utter a sound, Abe took out the savage's windpipe with a single brutal slash of his tomahawk. The warrior crumpled to the ground, gurgling.

"I think we've worn out our welcome," Abe said, heading back for the stream.

They were almost on the other side of the stream when James heard Comanche women yelling angrily. Splashing into the willows, they looked back and saw a woman on a Comanche war pony riding into the stream, two Indian women racing after her. The woman rider appeared to be hugging something to her breast as she rode.

"It's a white woman!" Abe said. "She's making a run for it."

James left the trees and beckoned to the rider. The darkness made it impossible for her to see that James was a white man. Fearful he was a Comanche, she turned the pony downstream. Abe stepped out beside James.

"Over here!" he called to her. "Over here!"

The woman turned the pony again and headed straight across the stream toward them, the two Comanche women, shrilling their fury, hard on her heels. Before the woman on the pony could reach them, one of the Comanche women grabbed one of her ankles and attempted to pull her off the horse while the other one snatched the horse's bridle and halted the horse. James waded swiftly out to the three women, grabbed the one holding onto the white woman's ankle and flung her into the water. Abe caught the other one and found himself battling a wild cat. But only for a minute. As she let out a scream and plunged toward him with hooked talons, he buried his fist into her belly. The woman doubled over. He grabbed her hair, spun her about and bent her neck back over his knee, snapping it. The sound echoed sharply in the night. Abe released the woman's hair, reached back for his knife and sent it at James.

James ducked and heard the knife slam into flesh just behind him. He turned and saw the Comanche woman he had flung from the horse sinking into the stream, Abe's knife protruding from one breast, a war club slipping from her fingers.

"She was comin' at you, James," Abe said by way of explanation. "I told you. Never turn your back on a Comanche woman."

The white woman on the horse gaped down at them. She was cradling an infant in one arm.

Abe looked up at her. "Who're you, ma'am?"

"Janet Webster."

"Get goin', woman. This ain't no time to hang around here."

"My son, Booker. He's still back there."

"Too late to think of that now, ma'am."

She nodded grimly, dug her heels into the pony's sides,

splashed past them to the bank, and vanished into the night, heading up the canyon.

James and Abe moved after her swiftly on foot, left the canyon and retrieved their mounts. At dawn the next day, they caught sight of the Webster woman at least a mile ahead of them. When she saw two riders overtaking her, she was too frightened to look carefully and veered sharply to the east, managing to boot the Indian pony into a half-hearted gallop.

"She keep going that way she'll miss San Antonio," Abe said.

"I'll overtake her."

"Okay, hoss. See you in San Antonio."

PART II

PLUM CREEK

7

The next day the aroused Comanche warriors stormed from their encampment and rode hard for San Antonio, intent on avenging the massacre of their chiefs. But shorn of their great war chiefs and uncertain of their medicine, they milled about helplessly in the hills northwest of San Antonio. With no single prestigious warrior or chief capable of mobilizing them, their councils divided, they could not muster the force nor make the decision required to storm and take San Antonio, something they could easily have accomplished, considering their numbers.

The Comanches, as always, were wary of assaulting or fighting within closed places, and San Antonio was protected by high limestone walls. Eventually, when they learned that their hostages were being kept in the Mission San Jose, at least three hundred Comanche rode up to the mission walls, challenging the soldiers guarding the hostages to come out and fight. But the truce Fisher had promised the Comanche chief's widow still had three more days to run, and the officer in charge of the troops refused to engage the Indians.

Furious, aware that now they had no *tejano* captives to exchange for their people, the warriors circled the walls, shouting insults and challenges, but never daring to directly assault the riflemen secure behind the high walls. At last, frustrated, howling out their defiance, the Comanche rode off. When the deadline passed, Fisher gave orders to allow the Comanche women and children to escape, since nothing could be accomplished by holding them. The Texans knew by that time that all the captives held by the Comanche had been killed.

In the weeks that followed, the furious Comanche swarmed about the frontier settlements like maddened hornets, raiding, murdering, burning out homesteads, and carrying off screaming women and children. Jack Hays and the other Ranger captains organized in each village or settlement what came to be known as minutemen—posses of volunteers who kept horses, arms, and provisions ready for instant action. In San Antonio, the minutemen were mustered by the raising of a flag over the courthouse and the pealing of the San Fernando church bell. In other settlements, the burst of a cannon or the pealing of a church bell accomplished the same purpose.

But for the most part, all these companies could manage was to ride in the wake of the Comanche war parties, helpless to do little more than bury the dead and mutilated bodies they found in the smoldering ruins of their cabins or ranchhouses.

II

Though the Lewis clan homesteads along the Colorado seemed to be a relatively safe distance from the wide-ranging Comanche war parties, a meeting was held to debate the issue. It was decided to leave nothing to chance. Accordingly, they designated Marie's ranchhouse a central gathering place in time of trouble and made the decision to transform what had been her and Michael's home into a fort.

More logs and adobe were added to the house walls until they reached a thickness of three, and in some places four, feet. To protect the roof from the Comanche's fire arrows they laid down a shale roof over two feet of sod. The doors were reinforced with massive oak logs designed to absorb bullets as well as arrows, and the windows were fitted with heavy battle shutters. While the men worked, neighbors rode up to watch the building of the fort, joking about what they called the Lewis Fort, pointing out weaknesses as they saw it in this or that item of construction—but most of them stayed to help and returned to their own homesteads to build similar forts.

Almost as if the construction of the Lewis fort was a signal of some kind to the marauding Comanche, by early summer their fearsome raids slackened. The borderland's horizon was no longer smudged continuously with the smoke of burning fields and cabins. The weary Rangers and the local minutemen began to breathe more easily as night after night passed with no fresh reports of Comanche depradations.

Perhaps, they hoped fervently, the Indians had lost their taste for further warfare and had departed the region to seek out the great buffalo herds to the north. The people of the frontier took a deep breath, hoping that at last they had seen the end of that bloody fiasco at the San Antonio Council House.

III

A few days into August, riding point for Captain Ben McCulloch's Ranger company, Abe reined in his mount and dismounted. Frowning intently, he went down on one knee to examine the ground more closely. A quick glance told him what he had suspected the moment he spotted the trampled earth from his saddle. Thousands of unshod ponies had beaten a broad trail into the ground, and the passage had been recent, within a few days at least.

Mordecai rode up.

"What is it, Abe?" he asked, reining in.

"Trouble, looks like," Abe said. "Bad trouble."

Mordecai dismounted swiftly and standing beside Abe studied the ground, taking in the significance of the tracks with one swift glance.

"Comanche!" he muttered. "And a God-awful lot of them."

"A host," Abe said grimly. "Like it says in the bible. They must have sneaked past San Antonio in the night."

"I'd say we're about two days behind them."

"And they're headin' right for Victoria."

Swiftly, Mordecai and Abe remounted and headed back to McCulloch and the Ranger company. When Ben McCulloch saw them pounding toward him, he halted his men, then spurred forward to join Abe and Mordecai.

"Ben," Abe greeted him. "We just come upon the track of a Comanche war party."

"More like an army," said Mordecai.

"Army?"

"He's right, Ben. A horde. Better than a thousand Comanche, I'd say, heading south toward Victoria."

"Show me."

Abe and Mordecai rode back with the captain to the edge of the trail they had cut. Off their mounts, the three men examined the beaten ground. It was Mordecai who pointed out the gouges in the ground left by the Indians's travois. Ben McCulloch straightened up and stared off in the direction the Comanche were taking.

"My God," he muttered. "We've got only two dozen men."

"You won't do no good attacking this column, Ben. All you can do is get help, round up every man can carry a gun, and stay on these savages' trail until you can take them."

"We've got to warn Victoria," said Mordecai.

"It may be too late for that," Abe told him.

"But they ain't movin' all that fast," Mordecai pointed out. "It looks like each warrior's got his own remuda, and I saw plenty of travois tracks. They're taking their women and children with them."

"He's right, Ben," Abe said, turning to the Ranger captain. "Looks like half the southern Comanche are on the warpath."

"I can skirt the Comanche," Mordecai said, "and maybe get ahead of them in time to warn Victoria."

Ben McCulloch never took too much time to make up his mind. He nodded quickly to Mordecai. "Then do it, Mordecai," he said. "Get on your horse and ride hard. And you go with him, Abe. There's a better chance of two getting through than one. I'll follow this trail and send out riders for re-enforcements, as you suggested. We can't do a thing until we get more men."

Abe mounted up. "Just be careful, Ben," he cautioned. "Hang back. If the Comanche see you followin', they'll cut back and eat your company alive for the sheer sport of it."

"You be careful, too. Both of you."

Mordecai mounted up and, with Abe in the lead, rode off. Skirting the broad Comanche trail, they headed almost due east.

IV

The two men rode almost without relief through the night and the next day. Forced to save their mounts, finally, they dismounted and led them the remaining miles to Victoria. As they neared the town, they saw smoke darkening the horizon ahead of them. Both men sagged with disappointment. They were too late. Nevertheless, they kept on, and an hour or so before dusk they slipped into an oak stand on a rise overlooking the Guadalupe River and the town of Victoria beyond.

It appeared to be still intact. The smoke they had seen earlier, must have come from outlying barns and homesteads that had been surprised by scouting Indians. On a ridge on the far side of Victoria, the Comanche had set up their lodges, forming a massive semi-circle that nearly ringed the town. Fires winked in the night, and even from this distance, Mordecai could hear the throb of drums as the warriors danced their war dances in preparation for the next day's assault on Victoria.

"Looks like them townsmen're pretty well forted up," Abe said. "And I don't see no houses burnin'. Looks good, so far."

"We ain't goin' to do them much good out here."

"Or ourselves, I'm thinkin'."

"So let's go," said Mordecai, pulling his mount close and stepping into the saddle.

Abe mounted up also and rode out of the grove, spurring ahead of Mordecai. Glancing back at the young man, he said, "Keep your head down, hoss."

Mordecai nodded. Abe lifted his weary animal to a lope and, staying in front of Mordecai, led the way to the river. It was low enough for them to ford easily, but when they gained the far bank, two Comanche rose out of the tall grass lining it. One warrior reached up and grabbed the mountain man's thigh and yanked him from his horse. Ignoring the other Comanche, Mordecai leapt from his horse and landed on the Comanche's back, ripping him off Abe. He and the Indian struck the ground together. The impact caused Mordecai to lose his grip on the Indian. He rolled away and reached back for his bowie. The Comanche sprang to his feet, head low, a wicked-looking skinning knife gleaming in his hand. But before he could attack, Abe buried the barrel of his Hawken into his skull.

Behind Abe the second Comanche was racing for him.

"Abe!" Mordecai cried. "Behind you!"

Abe ducked down onto all fours. The Comanche, running hard, tripped over the mountain man and went tumbling, coming to rest on his back a few feet in front of Mordecai. With not the slightest hesitation, he plunged his knife into the Comanche's chest. Still panting hard, he drew back, the Comanche's hot blood dripping from the bowie's blade.

"Thanks," Abe told him, slapping him hard on the back.

Mordecai spun around, looking for his horse. Without mounts they'd never make it to the town. Fortunately both horses were so spent they hadn't gone far. Retrieving them, they mounted up and charged out of the brush lining the banks. Off to their right, two mounted Comanche in full warpaint, screeching like banshees, rose out of a swale and took after them. Ahead of Mordecai and Abe were two warehouses and a line of other buildings. In the alley between the warehouses, besieged townsmen crouched behind a barricade of overturned wagons and tables. Abe and Mordecai headed directly for the barricade.

As they neared it, the townsmen opened up on the Comanche. Mordecai kept his head down and urged his stumbling horse on. He could feel it trembling under him and knew the animal was close to foundering, but he did not let up as he dug his heels into the horse's flanks. About a hundred yards from the barricade, Mordecai glanced back in time to see the nearest Comanche peel off his pony as one of the riflemen picked him off. Those manning the barricade broke into a cheer and, in response, Abe let out a Comanche yell and waved his hat. A second fusilade erupted from the barricade directed at the remaining Comanche. Abruptly, the warrior wheeled, plucked his wounded comrade off the ground, and galloped off.

Abe and Mordecai clattered up to the barricade, dismounted, and led their lathered mounts into the street behind it; they were immediately surrounded by anxious townsmen. One big fellow, his shoulders massive, his broad face as brown and wrinkled as old leather, pushed his way through the press of townsmen and shook both Abe's and Mordecai's hand.

"I'm Jim Travers," he announced. "Who be you?"

"Abe Goldthwaite," Abe replied. "This here's Mordecai Lewis."

"Looks like you two just went and jumped from the frying pan into the fire."

"Is there a Ranger captain here?" Abe asked him.

"You're talking to him. What can I do for you?"

"Well, first off, we're as dry as bleached bones. You got any place where we can wet our whistle and rest up?"

"Go over to my hotel," spoke up a man standing behind Jim Travers. He was a short, stocky fellow in a white shirt and vest. His rifle was an ancient flintlock, but he carried it with authority. "Tell the cook Jock sent you."

"Much obliged," said Abe.

Jim Travers escorted Abe and Mordecai to the hotel, where they found a table in a corner of the dining room. When a shotgun-toting cook poked his head out of the kitchen door, Travers told him Jock had sent them over and asked the man to bring out a meal for his two guests, explaining that they had dropped in unexpected. The cook peered in some perplexity at Abe and Mordecai, then shrugged and vanished back into the kitchen.

"We rode here to warn you," Abe told Travers, "but it looks like we got here too late."

"We were just too far behind," Mordecai said.

"Much obliged for the effort, anyway," Travers said. "You did your best. But we sure as hell could've used some warning. Them Comanche just showed up out of nowhere. Never saw so many redskins come so sudden.''

"How are your people holding up?'' Abe asked.

"You saw that at the barricade. We're ready for the red devils now. But they could've charged right in here and taken us with our pants down. Instead, they circled the town like we was a stand of bison, seizing mules and horses and spearing our cattle.'' He shook his head in wonderment. "They been havin' a real holiday since they got here, dismembering in plain sight them poor devils they caught outside town when they first rode up.''

"Ben McCulloch's on their tail, and he's sending out riders to arouse the countryside. But there's still too many of them and too little of us.''

"How many Comanche do you figure there are, altold?''

"Close to a thousand warriors—and that's not includin' their women and children.''

Travers frowned. "We're goin' to need some help, I'm thinking.''

"All you're going to get is what you already have—plus the two of us. Ben won't dare try anything, not yet. But if you'll take advice, I got some.''

"I'm listenin'.''

"The Comanche are goin' to get tired of playin' games. They'll be in here first thing tomorrow. I say let 'em in.''

"Through the barricades?'' Travers was astonished.

"That's right.''

"They'll burn us out.''

"I reckon they'll try. And maybe they'll burn down a few houses; but if you put your people on roofs and behind windows and scotch their asses, you'll be rid of 'em soon's they lose their stomach for house-to-house fighting. I ain't seen a Comanche yet take heavy losses without pullin' out.

They just can't afford it—leastway's that's the way they figure it.''

"You sure that'll satisfy them? Just ride in and burn a few homes, then pull out? Why, Abe, there be enough Comanche out there to chew us up and spit us out, then wipe the plate clean.''

"I know that, but mister, the thing is, you gotta remember—you're dealin' with the Comanche.''

Mordecai spoke up then. "And that means you got to think like 'em.''

"That's right,'' said Abe, slapping Mordecai on the shoulder. He turned back to the Ranger captain. "Now, you say these hostiles been roundin' up your ponies and mules?''

"They got close to two thousand, I'd say.''

"Well, now, that should satisfy the red devils, and it'll sure as hell slow them down on the trail.''

"Dammit, Abe, this is going to cost us.''

"I ain't sayin' it won't. But when it's done most of you'll still have your scalps, and your women won't be ridin' off to comfort no Comanche's bed, and that'd be a pure blessin', I'm thinking.''

"Yes, yes. Of course it would.''

"And when they're gone, look for McCulloch's men. They won't be far behind the Comanche. You and your townsmen can join his command. We ain't goin' to let these Comanche out of this without makin' them pay. But that means we're goin' to need every able-bodied man—includin' any on crutches.''

Their food arrived, and Mordecai and Abe ate heartily. When the meal was done, the cook brought them both full steins of beer to wash it down. Abe paid no attention as Mordecai downed his beer almost without pause.

"So what's your next move, Abe?'' Jim asked.

Abe looked at Mordecai. "What do you think, Mordecai? You're in this, too."

Mordecai did not hesitate. "I say we leave here and get ahead of this horde, warn the settlers. Looks like they're headin' for the gulf, Linnville, maybe. We got to warn all them people."

"Getting out of Victoria won't be easy," Jim told him. "Not tonight, it won't."

"Never thought it would be easy."

Abe said, "Jim, we'll need fresh horseflesh. We just about run ours into the ground gettin' here. Anythin' in the livery?"

"Don't you worry," Jim said. "We'll fix you up. We got some prime horseflesh. Rather you two take 'em than let those heathen get hold of 'em."

A few hours after midnight, Abe and Mordecai slipped into the river beside their horses. Holding onto their saddlehorns, they swam downstream. When they could no longer hear the throb of the Comanche drums, they crossed to the far bank, mounted up, and headed south.

They had napped in the hotel until midnight, the beer and exhaustion giving them a brief but solid sleep. Now they rode through the moonlit night without pause, in a steady, ground-devouring lope. When day broke they found themselves pounding over a hot, dry, harsh country of gently rolling prairies which occasionally took them into blessedly cool, fertile river bottoms. This vast, open country was dotted with farms and tiny settlements, and they took the time to arouse every settler in their path. In more than a few cases, they rode far out of their way to warn isolated ranchers others told them about. They were once again on their way due south, heading for Linnville, when they noticed a thin column of smoke lifting into the northern sky.

Abe reined in his mount. Mordecai halted also, and both sat on their horses, intently studying this ominous sign. It was the first smoke they had seen since leaving Victoria. Mordecai knew what was bothering Abe. It gave him concern as well. Had the Indians already swept past Victoria? Could that vast horde be circling around and coming at Linnville from the north?

"Maybe we better go take a look-see," Abe muttered.

After about three miles they topped a gentle, oak-studded knoll and found themselves looking down at what was left of a ranch house and barn. The only thing left standing was the cabin's wall and its fieldstone chimney. The barn was a smoldering ruin. The fence posts and rails had been pulled up, and there were no horses left in the lush, stream-fed pasture. Even the rancher's privy had been roped and apparently dragged about the front yard for sport.

"There maybe survivors," said Abe. "Let's get down there."

When they got to within a quarter mile of the ranch, they caught sight of the speared cattle lying in the tall grass, some of them still twitching. They kept on and dismounted in the cabin's front yard. They were about to inspect the cabin's ruins when they heard a groan coming from the direction of the barn. They found the rancher lying in the tall grass bordering it. A raw-boned fellow with straw-colored hair, he had lost his scalp, his face was swollen from countless bruises, his torso was a bloody mess. The Indians had sliced off the bottom of his feet and had then apparently made him run about on the bloody stumps until he had collapsed. Then they had shot him, disemboweled him, and scalped him.

And he was still alive.

His grey-flecked entrails had spilled out onto the grass. His long bony fingers cradled them as if they were alive and he was trying to comfort them. His eyes flickered open and he turned his head just enough to see Mordecai bending over him. His swollen lips moved and his voice—coming from the remotest region of hell—whispered hoarsely, "For the love of God . . . kill me! Kill me!"

Appalled, Mordecai backed off and glanced at Abe. "I can't do that, Abe."

Abe leveled his pistol at the man's head and blew a hole in the center of his forehead, instantly ending the rancher's torment.

"I'd do the same for a horse," Abe told Mordecai. "Simple mercy, I say."

"Those bastards," Mordecai said, trembling.

"Call 'em anything you want," Abe responded. "I won't argue. But keep your eyes open. They ain't far behind us, I'm thinking."

Abe was right. As Mordecai turned from the torn figure on the ground, he saw a long line of Comanche appear on a distant ridge behind them. Caught in the golden rays of the setting sun, they stood out clearly.

"Turn around, Abe."

Abe turned. "Yep. Here come's the main body. This here pillage was done by Comanche war parties scoutin' ahead."

Mordecai's eyes swept the horizon. To his astonishment still other Comanches rode into view until their numbers seemed to enclose them in a vast semi-circle. They must have made only a token assault on Victoria or, as Abe had predicted, lost heart completely after a few hours of house-to-house fighting.

"We got ourselves trouble, hoss," Abe said. "It's too late for us to make a run for it. We'd better cache up."

Abe started for the cabin, Mordecai following him, wondering what kind of shelter they could find in what was now only a smoldering ruin. Abe crouched down behind the cabin's remaining wall, as did Mordecai.

"This here wall ain't goin' to help us much," Abe said, peering out at the distant line of Indians moving closer. A great cloud of dust rose into the sky behind them, and from where Mordecai stood, it appeared that the Comanche's ranks seemed well nigh inexhaustible.

Abe did not respond to Mordecai's remark. Mordecai turned to see Abe lifting the trap door that led to the cabin's root cellar. Abe peered down into it, then glanced at Mordecai.

"Well, hoss, there's room down here."

"What about the horses?"

"We'll take our gear off and send them out of here."

They left the ruins and hurriedly off-saddled the horses, then slapped them on the rump and sent them off at a gallop into the pasture. They lugged their gear back to the cabin. Abe dropped his into the root cellar, then followed down after it. Mordecai handed him his own saddle and gear, then jumped down beside Abe.

That was when he saw the woman and child.

"Didn't want to say nothin' about them, hoss," Abe explained. "I think mebbe we better just leave them there."

"My God, Abe, why?"

"Give the Comanch' somethin' to consider. Might keep them from investigatin' this here root cellar too close."

With a shudder Mordecai slipped past the two mutilated bodies and followed Abe deeper into the root cellar. There were barrels of apples, bags of carrots and huge, ungainly sacks of potatoes. Abe lugged his gear behind the potatoes and Mordecai followed.

"Keep your head down, hoss," Abe told him. "Case them devils ain't scared by the spirit of that woman and her child."

"You ain't so sure, huh, Abe?"

"Never can tell about these devils. Put your saddle in front of you. It'll stop an arrow sure enough."

"I don't like this, Abe, trapped down here with two . . . dead bodies."

"You can go back up and make a run for it if you want."

Abe said, as he returned to the opening, reached up and pulled the trap door down. The sudden darkness gave little comfort to Mordecai, and he was sure he could smell the two corpses. He swallowed hard and tried to convince himself that he could not smell a thing.

II

It was not long before the horde of Comanche reached the ruined cabin. Both men expected the Comanche to continue on, but such was not the case. Night had fallen, and from the sounds that filtered down to them, it was clear that the Comanches were halting their march in order to make camp.

Mordecai was hoping the Indians were going to avoid the burnt-out cabin for fear of disturbing the spirits of the dead, or some fool notion along that line, when he heard the unshod hooves of a Comanche warrior's pony pounding across the cabin's floor. A shout from the warrior brought others and for a moment Mordecai was afraid the assembled ponies pounding up onto the cabin floor might break through the charred, weakened planks. Then came the sound of the Indians' moccasined feet as they dropped from their mounts.

"What'll we do if they come down here?" Mordecai whispered to Abe.

"Don't get your balls in an uproar. Keep down and hold your fire until they find you."

"You think they will?"

"How in tarnation would I know that, hoss?"

Mordecai cursed himself for asking such a stupid question and realized he was sweating so bad his palms were wet. He rubbed the moisture off them onto his britches and gritted his teeth as he listened to the Comanche's hideous, incomprehensible jabber as they stomped about above his head.

"Get down, hoss," Abe whispered. "They're at the trap door."

Abruptly, the door was flung open, and a Comanche with a torch in his hand leapt into the root cellar. At the sight of the mutilated mother and daughter, the Comanche yipped like a startled dog and jumped back, almost dropping his torch. He came to a halt less than two feet from the potato sacks behind which Mordecai and Abe were crouching. From above came the laughter of the other Comanche. One of them leaned over and poked his torch into the cellar to take a closer look at the two corpses, illuminating their mutilated features with such clarity that the first Comanche, uttering a quick howl, darted back to the opening and leapt out of the cellar. As soon as his legs vanished, the trap door was slammed down, and in a moment the Indians rode their mounts off the cabin floor.

The silence that followed was a blessing.

Mordecai wriggled out from behind the sacks.

"Where you goin', hoss?" Abe asked.

"I want to get that door open. To let some air in. To get out of here!"

"Stay right where you are, hoss," Abe warned. "We ain't goin' nowhere—not for a while anyway."

"Abe—!"

"You heard me, hoss. We're cachin' here until this horde pulls out."

"I'll get sick."

"Get sick, then. Only remember, if you do, you'll have to sit right in it."

Suddenly, the insistent, rhythmic pound of Comanche drums came from all sides. Jubilant Comanche were dancing about their fires, celebrating their triumphs, boasting of their prowess in the art of rape and plunder. As their yipping howls and *ki-yi*'s filled the night, Mordecai settled back against the potato sacks.

Abe was right. They weren't goin' nowhere. And if Mordecai knew what was good for him, he wasn't going to get sick.

III

In the tiny port of Linnville, James and Manuel were working up a powerful sweat as they loaded crates onto Manuel's flatbed. Two of Manuel's finest work horses, big chestnuts with broad, powerful chests, were standing in the wagon's traces. The wooden crates contained the new revolving pistols that had been shipped all the way from the factory in Paterson, New Jersey, and they were earmarked for the Ranger companies still ranging the borderland. Back in the States, these new-fangled revolving pistols still had not caught on, it seemed, but here in Texas, Jack Hays, Sam Walker, and other ranger captains recognized these pistols for what they were—an equalizer that made a Texan more than a match for any Comanche in close combat.

The two men had been sweating under the hot sun since noon, having arrived in town only that morning. They had come straight down the Colorado, bypassing San Antonio; their intention was to take the weapons to San Antonio, where Jack Hays was waiting eagerly to distribute them.

After they finished lugging the last crate from the warehouse onto the wagon, James left Manuel to tie down the heavy crates while he walked into the customs office to pay the duty to Major Watts. The major left his desk and walked up to the counter. In his office to the rear, Watt's wife, a fair-haired, handsome woman, glanced up at James and smiled. Wearing a green eyeshade, she was hard at work, pouring over bills of lading. James thought she looked rather cute in the eyeshade.

Major Watts placed the customs slip down on the counter. "You all loaded up?" he asked.

"Yep," James said, noting the duty required. "We'll be pulling out now."

James was relieved. The amount was less than Captain Hays had thought it would be, which meant that the struggling Republic of Texas would be spending less of its hard-earned currency on this transaction than the unhappy treasurer had been told to expect.

"Why not stay awhile?" the major suggested, "Rest up some in the cantina across the street. You look like you could use a drink."

"I could that," James agreed, counting out the specie and pushing the coins across the counter to the major.

"And you just tell Gunther to put it on my tab," the major said, sweeping the coins off the counter into his palm. He stamped the bill of lading paid and handed it to James. "You just might call it my contribution to the Rangers," he said with a smile.

"Much obliged, Major," James replied, stepping to the door. "I guess Manuel and I will take you up on that."

Manuel had finished tying down the crates and was up on the wagon seat waiting to set off when James rounded the warehouse and told him they were going to drive down the street first and visit the cantina. He didn't expect any protest from Manuel, and he didn't get any. He jumped up onto the seat beside him, and a moment later they pulled up outside the cantina, hopped down, and went inside.

At the bar both men ordered whiskey.

"Your name Gunther?" James asked the barkeep.

"That's me, all right."

"Major Watts wants you to put this whiskey on his tab," James said as he pulled his drink toward him.

"So you say."

"You want to check, go on over."

"I ain't got the time." The barkeep was a florid-faced man as wide as he was tall with a few strands of black hair slicked back across his balding pate. His eyes were small and mean, and James saw his hand snaking under the counter for his bung starter.

"You mean the major doesn't have a tab here?"

"He has a tab."

"Then bring your hand back up onto the bar and fill our glasses again."

The barkeep hesitated for a moment, then brought up his hand and rested it on the bar. With his other hand, he lifted the bottle and refilled both glasses.

"Much obliged," said James.

"Good whiskey," said Manuel.

"I don't talk to greasers," the barkeep snarled, for the first time looking directly at Manuel.

Manuel flung the whiskey in the barkeep's face. James reached across the bar and grabbed Gunther's shirt front and dragged him up and over the bar, flinging him to the floor. The man struck a table. It tipped under his weight and spilled him onto the floor. He broke a chair as his heavy frame plunged through it to the floor. As the man scrambled to his feet, James stepped forward and buried his fist in the man's expansive midsection. The barkeep's eyes went glassy, and his mouth popped open as the breath exploded from his lungs. The other four or five patrons were on their feet in an instant, but instead of rushing James and Manuel, they moved cautiously back until their backs were against the wall.

James returned to the bar. Manuel did, also. Both men downed their drinks, and Manuel was reaching for the bottle when they heard the clatter of hooves in the street outside and a woman's scream. They looked to the door just as a woman rushed in through the batwings, eyes wide with terror.

"Indians!" she cried. "Indians!"

James and Manuel rushed to the door and peered out to see four Comanche warriors clattering up to the customs office, their faces slashed with black war paint. As they dismounted, Major Watts appeared in the office doorway, a shotgun in his hand. He raised the gun and cut one Comanche in half, but another Comanche sent a shaft into his chest. The man was dead before he toppled out of the doorway. The rest of the war party swarmed past the major's sprawled figure into the customs office. Immediately from within came the screams of the major's wife.

All this happened in a matter of seconds, taking that long for the significance of what was happening to penetrate. Incredibly, out of nowhere it seemed, a Comanche war party had ridden into town.

IV

The men in the cantina milled about in a panic, not a single one of them willing to leave it to rescue the screaming woman—which left it up to James and Manuel. They drew their Colts and rushed from the cantina just as the three savages burst out of the customs office. One was carrying bags of gold, another had flung the major's wife over his shoulder. Raising his Colt, James picked off the Comanche carrying the gold. Beside him Manuel cut down the other Indian before he could reach his pony. The Comanche carrying Watt's wife remained unscathed as he flung the woman over his pony's neck, mounted up and rode out of town. Neither James nor Manuel had dared risk a shot for fear of hitting the woman.

James hurried out into the middle of the broad street and peered out of town at the coastal plain beyond. What he saw made him catch his breath. A long, seemingly inexhaustible line of Indians covered the horizon, a great cloud of dust lifting into the air behind them. Other townspeople left their stores and businesses and crowded around the two men to peer out at the prairie. At sight of this massive host of barbarians descending on them, a great moan of fear and apprehension swept through the crowd. Some men and women, overcome with panic, broke off and started running back to their stores or houses, reminding James of chickens in a barnyard scattering before a clattering horseman.

He could understand their dismay, however, and felt it himself.

"My God," he muttered to Manuel. "It's an army."

"James!" Manuel said. "These guns! We must not let the Comanche have them."

Manuel's remark galvanized James. Manuel was right. But how could they keep these weapons from the Indians? They would soon own this port—and everything in it. All around them townsmen were calling out to each other to make for the docks. Someone cried out that they must all take to the boats and abandon the town.

As a barber rushed past him, James reached out and halted him. "We need your help," he told him. "We've got crates of Colt revolving pistols in this wagon. We can't let the Comanche get them. We have to get them onto a boat."

The barber understood at once. He called out urgently to someone across the street and beckoned him over. The man came promptly. He was wearing a black jacket and a cap with a dark visor; one look at his nut-brown, weather-beaten features and James knew him to be a seafaring man.

"I'm James Lewis," James told him. "I've come down here to pick up these crates of revolving pistols for Jack Hays. We got Rangers in San Antonio waiting for them. We can't let the Comanche get them."

"Yes, I know those crates," the seaman replied, his voice

powerful. "It was my ship brought them in. I'm Captain Harmon. Looks like we'll have to get them back onboard."

He turned and bellowed in a foghorn voice to three sailors darting out of a cantina down the street. They halted in mid-stride and looked back.

"Get over here, you lubbers!" Harmon cried.

A distant rattle of gunfire erupted from the plains surrounding the town as advance elements of the Comanche horde galloped closer, unnerving the townspeople still further, especially the three sailors hurrying over to them. But the captain paid the distant gunfire no heed as he directed his three crewmen to climb onto the wagon. As soon as they had done so, James and Manuel stepped up onto the seat. Manuel grabbed the reins as the captain stepped calmly up onto the wagon seat and seated himself beside James and proceeded to direct him.

In a few moments they were rattling out onto the dock, at the end of which the captain's sloop was tied up. The sailors hopped down from the wagon and, with James and Manuel's help, began the task of lugging the crates back onto the ship. They stored them above the hold, hard against the ship's rail.

While the five men labored to transfer the crates, a frantic, unruly crowd of townspeople, including women, children, and babes in arms, poured out onto the dock, hoping to find refuge on the two barks tied up there and on the captain's sloop. As he worked, James could see beyond the dock and down the shore, other townspeople pushing dinghys and rowboats through the surf out into the bay, the tiny, crowded boats threatening to capsize at any moment in the treacherous surf.

With the crates loaded back onto the sloop, Manuel and James drove the wagon back off the dock and unharnessed the horses. With a sharp slap on each rump, they sent them down the street and watched them gallop out of town.

"The Comanche will give them a long life," Manuel remarked sadly, "but it won't be an easy one."

"I hate to leave the wagon here for these savages."

"Nothin' we can do about that, James," Manuel told him soberly. "We got our own scalps to think about now."

They joined the crowd of townsmen still charging down the dock. Some dropped into rowboats, others into sailboats, but most of them clambered aboard the sloop with James and Manuel. The two other, smaller barks, loaded to a dangerous level with fleeing townspeople, had already left the dock. As soon as Captain Harmon decided that his sloop could handle no more passengers, he sang out to the helmsman, and his ship pulled away from the dock.

Not long after, standing on the deck, their rifles at the ready, James and Manuel watched the Indians pour into town. Whooping and yelling in sheer deviltry, they smashed windows and broke into the shops and stores lining the waterfront. With their women at their sides, they rushed into dress shops to emerge and prance about in the garish costumes they found inside.

A few Comanche galloped down the dock, brandishing lances and howling defiance at the people in the boats. A few arrows thudded into the sloop's oak sides. James and Manuel hefted their rifles, but held their fire. They were well out of range by this time, and the Comanche's arrows were soon falling short of the ship. There was no sense in wasting good lead.

Soon the sloop was tacking about in the harbor, a safe distance from the shore, the passengers crowding the deck watching in growing dismay at the Comanches rampaging through their town. It was like watching a wild opera in which mounted clowns were the main actors. The barbaric, painted horde crowded the small port's streets, howling and screaming their defiance to the skies, while a few warriors rode out into the surf, sending arrows at those in rowboats. Some men in the boats discharged their rifles at the Indians, but the rocking boats made accurate aim impossible. Screaming and yelping like maddened coyotes, the surf washing sometimes as high as their naked thighs, the Comanche brandished their lances, challenging those in the boats to battle.

James nudged Manuel. "There goes our wagon," he said.

Manuel's black, newly painted wagon stood out clearly. It was piled high with sacks of flour and other provisions and was now being pulled by a pair of mules, one of which had a bright green ribbon tied to its tail.

"Over there," said Manuel urgently. "Look at that crazy old man!"

James followed Manuel's gaze and saw a tall, elderly man close to the beach who at that moment was stepping out of his rowboat, brandishing a shotgun. He was dressed in a black frock coat and hat and appeared to be a judge or a preacher. As the lanky figure strode toward the Indians through the surf, he was shouting and swearing furiously at the Comanche.

The elderly man had obviously let his fury at the rampaging Indians get the best of him. Suddenly he fired both barrels at the Comanche milling about him in the surf. Fortunately, the charge went wild. Then, to James's astonishment, the old man, now waving an empty shotgun, continued on toward the Comanche. Amazed, the Comanche failed to cut him down. Indeed, they rode around him, ignoring his wild, gesticulating figure, pretending they did not see him. It was clear to James they considered him either very courageous or a madman, in either case a man possessing very powerful medicine.

Crowding the ship's rail beside them other passengers were

watching the drama with baited breath. Like James, they were fully aware of the fearsome chance the old man was taking as he stumbled about in the surf, continuing to shout imprecations at the horse Indians.

"Why, that's Judge Hays!" a woman behind them gasped. "That poor man! He'll be killed."

"The Comanche consider his medicine too powerful to challenge," Manuel said, chuckling, his dark eyes focused on the old man.

"Well, he better get his ass out of there while he still can," James commented nervously, "or some young brave eager for a coup will come along to challenge that powerful medicine."

Abruptly, the judge came to his senses and apparently reached the same conclusion. Turning swiftly about, using his shotgun to stabilize himself in the rolling waves, he waded back to one of the boats circling close behind him. When he got near enough, he reached out and willing hands pulled him unceremoniously into the boat. The judge immediately sank out of sight beneath the gunwales. The townsmen manning the oars pulled frantically and soon put a great deal more open water between them and the Comanches.

"They're breaking into my warehouses!" someone cried.

"Better your warehouses than you, Jim," another told him.

James glanced around at the man who had just spoken and saw dark rage purpling the man's face as he watched the goods being dragged out of his warehouses and into the street. Looking back at the plundering savages, James could understand the man's impotent rage. The goods the warehouses held had obviously been earmarked for the shops and stores of San Antonio, but they were not going to get there.

Bolts of red, green, and bright blue cloth went rolling into the street as Indians eager for such treasures fought over them in quick, vicious tussles. Stovepipe hats appeared on the heads of warriors who mounted up and began galloping about trailing long ribbons and bolts of crimson cloth. Others found umbrellas and immediately snapped them open and rode about, looking as foolish as apes in a bathtub. The women were close on their warriors' heels, rushing into the warehouses to emerge with pots and pans and other household items, which they packed on mules. Barrels of gunpowder, flour, and a what appeared to be a shipment of iron for barrel hoops were loaded onto a string of mules; the iron would probably be used for forging arrowheads, James realized.

While all this was going on, a chief rode up and began ordering his warriors about. Though James could not understand his words, he could tell that the chief was unhappy at the wild, undisciplined looting and was doing his best to regain control of his warriors. But his words went unheeded as the braves and their women continued to carry out a steady stream of goods from the warehouses.

"Who's the chief," Manuel asked.

"I never saw him before," said James. "He wasn't at the council house."

"Which is a good thing for him," Manuel said grimly.

One of the passengers stepped up beside them. He was carrying a long Kentucky rifle; his powder horn hung from a leather thong about his neck. He was dressed in greasy buckskins and most of his face was hid behind a gray-streaked beard. His left eye had once been hit with something and didn't seem to be doing him much good; it was red-rimmed and angry-looking. If the man smelled of anything, it was horse. He spat a long line of tobacco juice over the side, then wiped his mouth.

"That there chief is Buffalo Hump," the mountain man said. "He's jest about the only chief the Honey Eaters got left."

Honey Eaters was a name the Tonkas used for the southern

Comanche, but it was one James seldom heard used by a white man.

"Where you from, mister?" James asked.

The stranger's one good eye looked James over coolly. "You don't need to know that, do you?"

"You're right. I don't."

The fellow shifted his feet and lost some of his edge. "I'm from north and west o' here," he drawled. "The Rocky Mountains, mostly. Come down here to trade my plews and thaw my froze feet." He grinned then. "Looks like you Texans done stirred up a hornet's nest."

"We did that," Manuel agreed.

"Well, hoss, you'd a had a bushel more trouble if Old Bent wasn't fixin' a treaty between the Northern Comanche and the Cheyenne and Arapaho. Right now the Comanche're busy smokin' the peace pipe and swappin' pony herds in the Arkansas."

"That so?"

"Yep. Course, that's gonna make trouble for you later, I'm thinkin'. With their northern flank secure, them bands might figure on comin' down to join this here Buffalo Hump's next campaign."

"That's likely," James acknowledged grimly, "if the son of a bitch gets away with this one."

The three men went silent then as they watched the looting. Wagons and mules were soon laden with plunder, while the younger braves, out of pure devilment, amused themselves lancing the livestock and roaring with savage humor as the domesticated beasts toppled over to kick their last. Meanwhile, other Comanche warriors had turned into comical dandies, festooned with ribbons and top hats as they galloped through town, setting it ablaze. From the way most of them were riding—in some cases tumbling ingloriously off their ponies—it was clear that among the many choice items the braves had found were barrels of whiskey.

"I like it," James said grimly.

"What do you mean?" Manuel asked, surprised at James's comment.

"Buffalo Hump rode in here with an army. He's ridin' out with a mob of drunken plunderers. He's lost control of his warriors. From now on, they'll be thinking of only one thing: returning with all their loot intact."

"And don't forget the horseflesh and mules they must have taken," Manuel reminded him.

The mountain man beside them nodded. "I guess you got that figured right," he remarked, sending another lance of tobacco juice into the sea. "Right now, them Comanche're like kids at Christmas time. All they want to do now is get back home to play with their new toys."

Manuel, his eyes watching the prancing Indians with grim intensity, remarked coldly. "Well, I'm hoping they won't get the chance to play with them."

James nodded. That was just what he was hoping as well.

By late afternoon Buffalo Hump's warriors had taken all the plunder they could carry and proceeded to head northwest out of Linnville, leaving behind a roaring conflagration as the fires they had set took hold of building after building and swept with the speed of a prairie fire through the rest of the town.

Watching from the sloop, James groaned inwardly at the hellish landscape that remained. Great plumes of smoke pumped into the heavens, darkening the sky above. Blazing shingles and shards of wood pumped high into the sky now plunged back to earth, landing with searing bursts of steam in the waters of the bay. A few came down dangerously close to the loaded boats. At last, when the savages were no longer in sight, the people in the boats began rowing back to the shore.

Captain Harmon gave an order to his helmsman; the sloop heeled over and headed for the dock.

At least, James thought wearily, the Comanche had not gotten hold of the items they would have given the most for—those crates of revolving pistols fresh from Colt's factory.

☆ Chapter ☆

9

Mordecai stirred with increasing uneasiness as the Comanche continued to clatter over the floor of the ruined cabin. It seemed to him that the pounding would never end, and he could not help but wonder what would happen if just one of the ponies broke through the weakened boards. But the steady thumping kept on, and in addition, soon there came the voices of the women and children calling to each other along with the bumping, scraping sound of their travois dragging across the flooring as they did their best to keep up with their warriors.

Abruptly the racket ceased as the last Comanche party clattered across the cabin floor. The morning sunlight showing through the cracks in the floor now gleamed with undiminished brightness, illuminating the root cellar with a dim, but steady light. Mordecai could still hear the Indians moving off in the distance, but the sound of their passage faded quickly. Anxious to be free of his underground prison, Mordecai clambered over the potato sacks and headed for the trap door. He was almost to it, reaching out to push it open when Abe caught him from behind.

"Hold it right there, hoss. We ain't out of this yet."

"But they're gone, Abe."

"Just hold yourself down and wait a bit."

"But I can't stand this smell, Abe."

"You'll have to. Any Indian camp this size always has a few stragglers. I'm thinkin' there's still a few old braves and crones out there doin' their best to keep up."

Almost as if to prove Abe's sagacity, there came the sound of a pony picking its way across the cabin floor and close after it the steady scratch of a single travois. A dog with this lone Comanche apparently smelled something interesting under the cabin floor and held back a while to sniff at the floor, barking nervously all the while. A sharp whistle brought him off the floor. He left, and silence reigned once more.

Pushing past Mordecai, Abe nudged the trap door open about an inch and peered out. Only with the greatest of care did he slowly push the door all the way open. This done, he peered cautiously about him in all directions, and when he saw no Comanche near enough to catch sight of him, he went back for his saddle and the rest of his gear, pushed it out ahead of him, then pulled himself out of the cellar. Mordecai grabbed his own saddle and gear and waited in the opening.

"Okay, hoss," Abe told him. "I can still see the red devils, but there's no more coming."

Mordecai heaved his saddle up onto the floor and boosted himself out of the cellar. Crouching beside Abe, he took deep gulps of the early morning air. It still stank of Indian, but it was big improvement on the stench of death he had been inhaling for so long. Following Abe's gaze, he could see the rear of the disappearing Comanche horde, though most of it was pretty well obscured by the massive cloud of dust their passage sent into the sky behind them.

"My God, Abe," Mordecai said, getting cautiously to his feet. "I never thought these floor boards would hold."

"I was thinkin' the same thing."

"Why did they do that? Why didn't they go around the cabin?"

"They were trampling on the bones of their *tejano* enemies."

Mordecai understood at once. "Yeah," he said. "I can see that. Like dancin' on someone's grave."

Abe glanced around. "Too bad," he said. "I was hoping mebbe I'd see some horseflesh left behind, but I don't see nary a one."

"No self respectin' Comanche would leave behind a good mount, Abe. It ain't in their nature."

Abe chuckled. "Now you're beginnin' to think like a real Comanche, hoss."

"So what do we do now?"

"Freshen up in that stream over there, then wait for Ben to get here. If he's still trailing this horde, he should be showin' up soon."

The two men took full advantage of the stream, drinking their fill and then taking a cold dip. It didn't do much to fill their stomachs, but it washed off the stench of death.

Pulling on his boots, Mordecai peered anxiously about him. "Where's Ben and that growing army of his, Abe? You sure they haven't missed us?"

"I ain't sure of nothin', hoss. So just relax. Less'n you want to sprout wings and take to the air."

"We may have to do that, Abe. I sure don't want to walk all the way to the gulf."

"I say we go on up to that knoll," Abe suggested. "It looks cool enough, and we can see pretty far from up there."

Mordecai immediately saw the wisdom of this course. They promptly lugged their weapons and the rest of their gear up onto the knoll and sprawled under a large oak, resting their backs against their saddles. As Abe had suggested, the knoll's elevation enabled them to see a great distance in all directions. From it, the distant cloud of dust raised by the Comanche war party was still visible. They concentrated their gaze on the expanse of prairie stretching to the northwest—the direction from which they felt Ben McCulloch would be coming. As the minutes passed without any sign of the Ranger captain and his men, Mordecai grew increasingly impatient, while Abe simply puffed on his pipe and waited calmly.

In less than an hour, a confused mass of floating dots and smudges appeared on the horizon, quivering in the heat waves building up on the prairie. At once Mordecai sprang to his feet. Abe calmly put his pipe away and got to his feet also. As the two men watched, the shimmering blobs became more solid and gradually began to resemble riders.

"It's Ben, all right," Abe said.

As McCulloch and his command got closer, they became a long, thin line extending across the horizon, a few riders bunched in the lead. Mordecai figured it to be at least a hundred riders all told, perhaps even more.

Mordecai took off his hat and waved it frantically at the approaching riders. To his disappointment, not a single rider responded to his wave or increased his pace.

"Wait a minute, hoss," Abe drawled. "They can't see us. Not at that distance."

"Do you see any extra mounts?"

"Now, how can I tell at that distance?"

Abe sounded a little exasperated at Mordecai's question, but Mordecai was too anxious to care. After a few moments, the line of riders dropped completely out of sight as they dipped into a long swale; when they reappeared a moment later, they were a distinct, clearly delineated line of riders.

This time it was Abe who waved his hat. Mordecai followed suit. At once two riders from the group in the lead spurred directly toward the knoll where Mordecai and Abe were standing.

"They seen us!" Mordecai cried, immensely relieved.

"That they have, hoss."

"Abe," Mordecai said hopefully, "it looks like Ben's got a small army with him."

"Small is right," Abe drawled. "It still ain't no match for that horde of savages just left here."

Reluctantly, Mordecai was forced to agree.

When the two riders got close enough for Mordecai to see them clearly, he started down the knoll, eager to join them. Abe, in not too much of a hurry, followed along with him. Before they reached the oncoming riders, they had to scramble across a draw rendered foul by the Indians's night soil. The Comanches had made no effort at all to cover any of it, as if fouling the *tejanos* land was a good part of their reason for being there.

On the other side of the draw Mordecai and Abe pulled up to await the riders. One of them was Ben McCulloch; the other was the Ranger captain they had left back at Victoria, Jim Travers. Mordecai was pleased to see that Travers had apparently been left unscathed by the Comanches.

"Glad to see you two again," Travers said, grinning down at Abe and Mordecai as he rode up. He pulled to a halt beside them and dismounted. Ben McCulloch dismounted also and walked wearily over to them.

"You two look none the worse for wear," he said. "Where's your mounts?"

"Hell, Ben. They don't need to tell us," said Travers. "The Comanche took 'em. Am I right, Abe?"

"We had no choice," Abe told him. "They were on us before we knew it. We cached under that burnt-out cabin and let the horses go."

"That's right," said Mordecai, "we spent the night in the cabin's root cellar. Us and two corpses."

"Two corpses, you say?"

"He's right," Abe admitted. "The wife and daughter of

the settler the Comanche burnt out. We'll need a detail to bury what's left of them.''

McCulloch sighed, his face sagging wearily. "That's all we been doin' lately."

"We still got our saddles and the rest of our gear," Mordecai said. "I sure hope you got some spare horses."

"We got some," McCulloch replied, mounting up. "But go easy on 'em. Our mounts are beginning to flag. We been on the trail now for too long, and we've just about run out of grain. And this land's pretty dry. Abe, is there a stream near here?"

Abe nodded. "In that pasture over yonder."

"I'll send someone forward with your mounts. Jim, you can give them a hand." He turned his horse. "I'll be wanting a full report, Abe, on what you found."

"I didn't find much," Abe told him. "Just lots of burnt-out cabins and a passle of frightened women and children. But we managed to warn a few settlements."

"I know that. The men from those settlements have already joined up. But I'll still want a full report."

McCulloch clapped spurs to his mount and loped back to his men.

"Where's your gear?" Jim asked Abe and Mordecai.

"On that knoll," Abe said, pointing.

"Let's go then."

The three men started back to the knoll, Jim leading his horse. The stench from the draw stifled any conversation until they had put it well behind them. Not until they reached the oaks crowning the knoll did Abe ask Jim Travers how it had gone at Victoria.

"Pretty much the way you said it would," Travers replied, slumping down onto the cool grass. "The morning after you two left, a few warriors rode into the streets. We didn't put up too much resistance until they were inside the town. Then we opened up on them from the roofs and windows, like you suggested. They set a few fires, but we didn't lose many buildings, and the savages lost heart pretty quick after we cut down five of them. It wasn't long after they rode out that the rest of the Comanche folded their lodges and pushed on past us.''

''How many did you lose?'' Abe asked, pulling out his pipe and lighting up.

''Fifteen all told. Some Mexican traders lost five hundred mules and horses they had just bought in town the day before.''

''That was all?''

''Don't forget our own mules and horses I mentioned before. At last count we all lost close to two thousand head.''

''Well, you still got your scalps,'' Mordecai reminded him. He was on his feet, slumped back against a tree. ''That's something.''

''It sure is, son. And a hundred men from Victoria are riding with Ben right now. We'll get them murderin' bastards. Soon's we find out what they're up to.''

''Why that's easy enough,'' drawled Abe, puffing on his pipe. ''They're up to lootin' and rapin' and havin' themselves one fine party.''

''I mean what's their plan? Where they headin'?''

''For the gulf, it looks like.''

''Good. We'll trap 'em down there and make them go for a swim.''

''It won't be that easy.''

''Our numbers are swelling, Abe. We got close to a hundred and fifty already.''

''That ain't near enough.''

''I know. I know,'' Travers said, reluctantly.

Travers had been doing his best to pump up his belief that they would soon be able to bring this Comanche war party to heel, but after what he had experienced in Victoria, it was clear to Mordecai that he was not at all sure this could be accomplished. And Abe's blunt response to his enthusiasm had just about deflated his optimism.

Fresh mounts were soon brought up to the bluff for Mordecai and Abe, and after the company had given themselves and their mounts a chance to refresh themselves at the stream and the remnants of the three settlers had been buried, they continued on after the Comanche war party. In the hours that followed, they rode past the speared cattle, the smoldering cabins and barns, and they buried the mutilated corpses that littered the prairie in the Comanches' wake; it was not a difficult trail to follow.

And with each passing hour the anger building in the hearts of these Texans built steadily into a cold, murderous rage.

II

Ten miles outside Linnville, on the banks of a narrow creek, James and Manuel came upon Ben McCulloch's growing force. The two men were driving a pretty poor excuse for a flatbed, which was drawn by mules too ornery to have remained within the Comanche's outsized remuda. After the Comanche pulled out of Linnville, they had repaired the wagon's bed with raw timber, and all six crates of Colt weapons the men had taken from the warehouse were tied securely in place.

There were broad smiles and shrill hoops when James and Manuel stood up in the wagon seat and called out to Mordecai and Abe. McCulloch was pleased to welcome this additional complement to his forces and took the opportunity to rest his men and their weary horses.

McCulloch settled down under a willow tree with James and Manuel. Abe and Mordecai, along with a good number of the other Rangers stood close by, eager for news of what happened in Linnville. Without much preamble, McCulloch asked James straightaway which direction the Comanche were taking.

"Northwest," James answered immediately.

"They ain't coming back this way then."

"No," said James. "They're heading northwest, following the Colorado."

"That's settled country."

"I know."

"Why would they risk that?"

"Two reasons," Manuel said, speaking up. "Number one, they want to get back to their home grounds with all that loot they took. And the other reason is Buffalo Hump no longer has a disciplined body. They're half crazy with liquor and trying to keep together the huge herd of horses and mules they've taken, not to mention the cart loads of supplies."

"Buffalo Hump, you say?"

"Yeah," said James. "A mountain man in Linnville told me it was him leading this Comanche war party."

"A mountain man," Abe asked, stepping closer, his face intent. "What was his name?"

"He wouldn't say, Abe," James said, addressing the mountain man. "But one thing was for certain, he was a damn sight uglier than you are."

"What'd he look like?"

"Like the devil himself," Manuel broke in, grinning. "He had a beard with a grey streak in it and a bloodshot eye that wasn't workin' all that well."

"Well now," said Abe, pleased. "That'd be ol' Red Eye hisself. His Christian name's Bill Williams. Used to be a preacher. A tough old nut if ever there was one."

"Then he'd know this chief's name?" McCulloch asked.

"Ol' Bill would if anyone would. He's lived with most of 'em. Last I heard he was with Bent on the Arkansas."

"That's the man," said James. "He said Bent was fixin' up a peace treaty between the northern Comanche and the Cheyenne and Arapaho."

"Where's ol' Bill at now?"

"Last I seen he was headin' back to the Rockies. Said he'd had enough of all this flat land. The way he talked about them mountains," James said, "I might've gone with him. But I had these here crates to get back to San Antonio."

"Not any more, you don't," McCulloch broke in, "not if them are Colt revolving pistols in them crates."

James grinned at McCulloch. "That's what I got, all right."

"I knew you were goin' after them. Coming on you like this is a stroke of luck. Leave 'em right here, James. We got use for them and any we got left over we'll be happy to distribute."

"Help yourself," James told him.

Immediately, McCulloch called over one of his men and directed him to unload the wagon and give out the guns and ammunition. As soon as the men learned they were about to be issued new Colts, the one who had been selected to unload the wagon found he had plenty of helpers. Once the guns were handed out, James and Manuel did their best to instruct the men in their use. This did not take long, since even if the men did not possess revolving Colt pistols, they were already familiar with its accomplishments and knew pretty well how to load them.

Once the revolvers had been distributed, McCulloch returned to his discussion with James and Manuel.

"Now let's get this straight, James," he said. "You say Buffalo Hump is retreating northwest—he's not going back the way he came."

"Yep. He's following the Colorado."

McCulloch nodded sagely. "I should've figured that. He's high-tailin' it out of here. We lost a man yesterday when we ran into a Comanche scouting party. They could've turned on us and ate us alive, but they broke off just as quick as we did. Looks like they don't want to fight now—just hang on to what they plundered."

"I know that country where they're heading," James said. "They will have to cross Plum Creek."

"Yeah, James. I know that country, too," McCulloch said.

"So why not stop them there?"

McCulloch frowned, considering this option. It didn't take him long to make up his ind. "We'll do it," he said, nodding decisively. "We'll alert the settlements on the Colorado, send word for every able-bodied man to head for Plum Creek. We'll be waiting there for this Buffalo Hump."

"You're forgetting one thing, Ben," James said soberly. "I've seen the condition of your horses. Most of them are in pretty bad shape. You'll never be able to get to Plum Creek in time."

"We'll take only the strongest horses and leave the rest. The men we leave behind can keep on harassing the Comanche, keep the savages fighting a rear-guard action."

Abe had moved closer to listen to the discussion. He nodded approvingly. "A good plan," he said. "That way the red devils won't be expectin' anyone to be waiting for them at Plum Creek."

McCulloch stood up. "That's the way I see it."

"So what are we waiting for," James said, getting to his feet also.

☆ Chapter ☆

10

Mordecai and Abe remained behind as McCulloch rode north for Plum Creek with James, Manuel, and about five others. Under the leadership of a member of the Texan Army who had recently joined them from Linnville, a lieutenant Owens, they resumed their pressure on the Comanche's flanks, continually firing upon the Indians, goading them to attack, fighting off their sporadic counterattacks with the withering fire from their newly acquired Colts, then resuming without pause their relentless pursuit.

Soon, however, the men's exhausted horses began to give out. They could no longer be ridden, only led. Nevertheless, the men continued to pursue and harry the Comanche without let-up, and as a result, Mordecai and the others began passing dead mules that'd been shot on the trail by the frustrated warriors, and not long afterward, the Comanche began abandoning much of the loot they had taken. Chests of ribbon and bolts of calico, dressers, and streamer trunks were soon littering the Texas plains.

Meanwhile, aroused by McCulloch's messengers, Ranger companies and local militia, and every Texan old enough to mount a horse and wield a gun had set out for Plum Creek from Gonzales, Lavaca, Cuero, and countless other isolated settlements. Brigadier General Felix Huston of the Texas

141

Army soon arrived at the rough bivouac, and as the ranking regular officer, he took command of all Ranger's companies, militias, and volunteers. The next day at the Bastrop militia, the largest single contingent, arrived. Meanwhile, James found himself in command of close to thirty men. The other Ranger captains were employed in the same fashion, acting more or less as advisors to the general, who recognized fully their experience in dealing with the Comanche.

When the Comanche column, preceded by Comanche scouts, came at last within a few miles of Plum Creek, the remnants of Ben McCulloch's original force, still led by Lieutenant Owens, managed to flank the Indian column and reach the Plum Creek bivouac. At once, Abe and Mordecai sought out James and Manuel and enjoyed their first real rest in two hard-driving days and nights. Finally, close to sundown, fourteen Tonkawa warriors, under their chief, Placido, arrived at Felix Huston's headquarters, their chests heaving. They had trotted thirty miles without pause to join the Texans in their fight against their traditional foes. Huston knew from experience what splendid scouts they would make and immediately directed that they tie white rags to their arms to identify them as scouts. He then gave them the task of scouting the approaching Comanche column on foot, urging them to bring him continuous reports.

II

Early the next day, with Abe acting as unofficial chief of the Tonka scouts, Mordecai and Manuel waited with James's company for orders to move. On the suggestion of Captain Hays, the men were ordered to dismount in order to rest their horses. Then their weapons were checked, and some of the greener volunteers were urged to discard useless impediments, such as extra powderhorns, canteens and heavy sabors, weapons Captain Hays pronounced more colorful than useful. When it was decided that the men were ready, the captains gave the order to lead their mounts at a walk out onto the plains before Plum Creek. There they formed two long, parallel lines and waited for the oncoming Comanche. Meanwhile, the inexhaustible Tonkas were bringing in steady intelligence on the Comanche's disposition, reports that James did not hesitate to share with his men.

Mordecai shaded his eyes as he watched the vast, roiling cloud of dust stirred up by the huge Comanche column lift into the sky. From the look of it, the Comanches were less than a mile from them, but they were moving steadily through the bright morning sunlight, apparently contemptuous of the grim ranks of Texans waiting them.

As he watched the darkening sky, Mordecai was aware of his pounding heart, but it was not fear he felt, only an eagerness for battle, as if he were a dog straining on a leash. He had seen too many Comanche depredations, too many mutilated bodies of men, women, and children, too many burnt-out ranches and fields in these last days—not to mention his own father's murder, a scene seared indelibly into his soul. Now he wanted nothing less than the total destruction of these hated, murderous savages.

Besides, if they did not succeed in stopping this enormous war party, none of those settlements north of Plum Creek would be safe, and that included the recently constructed Lewis Fort. Mordecai did not even like to think of what would happen to his mother and his sister and to any other members of the Lewis clan if these savages were allowed to survive this encounter.

''You look a mite grim,'' said Manuel.

Manuel was standing beside Mordecai, his mount's reins in his hand.

''Not grim,'' Mordecai replied. ''Determined.''

Manuel smiled. "Me, too. I do not want these Comanche to get past us. But I am also wondering what I am doin' here fighting alongside all these Anglos."

"Don't talk like that, Manuel."

"Why not?"

"We ain't Mexicans or Anglos; we're Texans."

"*Amigo*, I would like very much to believe that."

"Then believe it."

"Not all Texans think like you do."

"So what do you care about those fools? We're your friends. You don't need anyone else. The Lewis clan is your second family, Manuel—and there ain't a one of us who would not fight for your rights as a Texan."

"Does that mean that if. . . ."

Manuel did not finish, but he did not have to. Mordecai understood at once what Manuel was trying to say. He turned to face Manuel.

"If you married my sister, Manuel," Mordecai told him emphatically, "I would be pleased and happy to be your best man. It is something I know Angeline wants, my mother, too. The truth of it is, Manuel, that we all want it. You would make us very proud."

Manuel was obviously surprised and pleased at this unabashed acceptance of his love for Angeline and of her love for him. The matter of his acceptance was something that had troubled him since the death of Mordecai's father, and he had come to suspect that when the time came for him to make known his feelings for Angeline, he would see evasion and doubt in the eyes of Mordecai and his mother, along with the other members of the Lewis clan. Now he recognized in Mordecai's emphatic words and manner the unqualified acceptance he had hoped for.

"Well, then," Manuel said, grinning in sudden relief at

Mordecai, "what say we make damn sure none of these Comanches get past us."

"Agreed," said Mordecai.

James was moving down the line toward them, apprising his men of what he had recently learned of the approaching Comanche's disposition. When he reached James and Manuel, he paused longer than usual before them.

"Abe says the Comanche aren't in good shape," he told them. "Fact is, from what the Tonkas just told him, the Comanche warriors are scattered all over the column, mixed in with the women and children, doing what they can to keep their horse herds intact. Abe says their mules are tiring, too."

"Sounds more like a mob than a war party," Manuel remarked.

"That's the way Hays sees it," James agreed. "There's only a handful of Comanche on the column's flanks. The Comanche are more concerned with hanging on to their loot than fighting. He figures once we hit that column it will collapse like a rotten egg."

Manuel said, "I think maybe those mules and the horse herds should be easy to stampede."

"That's the way I feel, too," said Mordecai.

"That's the plan," James said, starting up again. "But remember, nothin' is ever as easy as it looks."

"Amen," muttered Manuel, as he watched James continue on down the line.

III

A moment later, General Houston gave the command to mount up and advance. Keeping to a steady walk, they headed toward the Comanche, their two long, parallel lines meant to close about the Comanche column. James was riding out in front of the two lines in the company of General

Houston, Matt Caldwell, and the other captains. Abe and Jack Hays caught up to them a bit later, Abe pulling up alongside James. James greeted the mountain man cheerfully, pleased to have him and his Hawken rifle nearby.

Once the Texans were close enough to pick out individual Comanche warriors, Houston ordered a halt and suggested that the word be passed for each man to see to his weapons. The men did precisely that, then sat their horses patiently and waited for the Comanche to ride closer.

Even from a distance James was impressed at the grotesque appearance of the Comanche warriors. Some trailed long red or yellow ribbons that were braided into their pony's tails; others carried umbrellas, making a weird and ridiculous contrast with their horned headdresses. As the head of the Comanche column neared the Texans, the Comanche warriors, as was their custom, put on a display of horsemanship designed to impress their foes and give heart to their fellow warriors. That they were superb riders had never been questioned by any Texan who had ever met them in battle, and on this day their gyrations on horseback were truly astounding, some of them pounding directly at the advancing Texans, then jumping off on one side of their ponies, only to remount on the other, all the while filling the air with war cries as terrifying as any that could erupt from a human throat. Other Comanches swept closer and still closer to the Texans, then supported by a strap or leather thong, dropped to the far side of their pony. Thus protected from Texan fire, they turned their horses and rode recklessly along the front of the Texan line to spur swiftly away at the last moment, filling the air with their war cries.

James had faced more than his share of Comanche on the plains and had always admired their horsemanship, but never as much as on this day. Seldom a solid line, the Comanche warriors shifted into swirling, dissolving groups of horsemen galloping closer and closer to the Texans, then abruptly wheeling their mounts to dart out of range before sweeping back once again at the Texans, apparently in a final, resolute charge, only to veer sharply away at the last possible moment.

Watching them was dizzying; it was impossible to keep track of any single warrior, and James sensed that the men behind him were slowly being mesmerized by this magical, shifting line.

What were they really up to? James suddenly wondered. The time was past when this dazzling horsemanship would turn into deadly assault. Why were the Comanches holding off? And even as he asked the question, he knew the answer.

"Matt," he called out suddenly to Caldwell, "they're trying to delay the battle—they need time to get their herds past us."

"Yeah," said Matt suddenly, nodding his head grimly. "You're right, James. That's it for sure."

Matt turned to the general, and James heard him tell the man that now was the time to attack. James saw the general frown and shake his head dubiously. He shouted something back to Matt, and James could barely hear the words, but his intent was clear. He wanted to wait. He wasn't at all sure that now was the time to charge.

Abe pulled closer beside James. "Looks like the general's gettin' cold feet, James."

"A hell of a time for that," James said. "If that herd of horses and mules gets past us, we won't be able to stampede it, and the Comanches will feel free to come at us in force."

"You don't have to convince me, hoss."

Even as they spoke, a tall Kiowa warrior in a feather headdress rode out in advance of his whirling Comanche brothers. Brandishing his lance, his head chopping the air as he hurled his insults, he rode still closer to the Texan lines, a man determined to show the watching Comanche how powerful his medicine was. The feathered warrior was obviously convinced it was equal to any *tejano* bullet.

Ben McCulloch rode up beside James.

"Dammit," he said to James. "What're we waitin' for? We need action. I got men back there loadin' their britches."

Visibly frustrated, Matt Caldwell turned his mount to face Abe.

"Abe!" he said, "Pick off that fool with your Hawken."

Abe swiftly lifted his plains rifle to his cheek, settled the stock snugly into his shoulder, then caressed the trigger, his finger barely moving. The report was sharp, flat—the sound of it cutting through the strident yipping of the watching Comanche. The Kiowa froze in the midst of his challenge, his lance still held high over his head. Then the lance dropped from his grasp, and the Kiowa toppled crookedly from his pony, his feathered bonnet smashing awkwardly into the ground.

A moan swept through the Comanche's ranks.

"Now, General!" Caldwell snapped. "Charge 'em!"

Huston's high, quavering voice broke through the waiting silence and gave the order to charge. At once, the Texans emptied their rifles at the Comanche, then spurred their mounts straight at the advancing column, shrieking like the very Indians they were facing. They came at the Comanche hard and fast, discharging their Colts at the dismayed Indians. With little difficulty, the Texans broke through the Comanche's flanks and plunged headlong into the main body.

Ahead of him, James saw the backs of a thousand horses, and yelling like a banshee, he headed for the vast remuda, whipping past mounted women and old men, aware of a growing body of Texans behind him. When he reached the horses, he began firing directly over their heads. The frantic animals turned and bolted away from the onrushing Texans, carrying with them the Comanche in their midst. Beyond the horses, James saw the mules floundering in a marshy patch, sinking helplessly under the awesome loads they were carrying. Into the mules slammed the maddened horse herd. All about him, James caught sight of the desperate Comanche caught up in the crush of the maddened, plunging herd.

Unable to maneuver, the Indians were helpless before the combined firepower of the charging Texans. Ahead of him, James caught sight of a Comanche warrior desperately pulling his mount around to face the Texans. James fired point blank at the Indian. A portion of his face fell away to be replaced by a yawning red emptiness. As the Comanche tumbled from his pony, James swept past him and overtook a younger warrior. As this warrior turned to loose an arrow at James, a shot from behind James spun the Indian out of his saddle. James turned to see Manuel, his revolver smoking, charging past him on the heels of another Comanche.

He had time only for a short wave at James.

James turned back to the stampeding herd ahead of him and was in time to see another Comanche, his pony caught in the boggy ground, leap from his horse, retaining his lance. James veered toward him, aiming his gun as he rode. He squeezed his Colt's trigger, saw the Indian go down, then turned his mount and kept on.

IV

Mordecai could hardly believe how quickly the Indian force had collapsed. One moment he was in the midst of the churning mass of Comanche warriors, firing right and left at the howling horde, the next he was galloping after panicked, disarmed braves who seemed intent only on fleeing the enraged Texans. He and other Texans chased the Comanche into the creek bottom, and soon it became for him and the other Texans a deadly hunt.

Mordecai found himself executing foes, not killing them, his revolver blasting almost continuously. He kept on into the creek bottom and found himself alone. All about him came the reports of pistols executing hapless Comanche. Disheartened by the slaughter, he dismounted and pulled his horse into high grass. Crouching in the tall grass, he proceeded to reload his two weapons. These new Colts James had brought from Linnville, the models Captain Sam Walker had helped Colt design, were heavier and more powerful than the earlier models Mordecai had used before. To have these weapons was almost equal to carrying a cannon in each hand. The damage they did to a Comanche was a sight that sobered Mordecai more than it pleased him.

From all around him the sound of battle continued: screams, shrill yells of triumph, gunshots, the quick tattoo of hoofs. As he reloaded his two Walker Colts, beads of perspiration poured down his face and stung his eyes. His eagerness to reload caused his sweaty hands to shake slightly, and suddenly he lost the tin filled with his percussion caps and saw it drop out of sight into the deep grass. At once, he dropped to his hands and knees, groping frantically for it. Twice he thought he had it, but each time he reached for it, his fingers closed about tufts of grass or a rotted twig. He tried not to panic, but could not conceal from himself how desperately he needed these percussion caps.

Aware that he was sinking into panic, he sat back suddenly, removing his hat to brush his matted hair off his forehead. He forced himself to take a deep breath to calm himself. At almost the same moment, out of the tall grass beside him hurtled a Comanche brave. Mordecai was not completely surprised; he had been alerted a second before by the crackling of dried grass. Nevertheless, the suddenness of the Comanche's charge was enough to slam him flat on his back.

He felt fingers on this throat, closing inexorably around his windpipe like steel cable. He thrashed desperately, his eyes burning into those of his attacker. He saw the savage's face twisting in rage and saw also that a portion of it had been blown away so that he was missing one eye and a chunk of hair on his left side, including his ear. A great dark scab of blood reached down clear to his shoulder. Seeing this, Mordecai redoubled his efforts to free himself, determined not to be killed by an Indian no better than a dead man. His fingers clawed at the savage's fingers, prying them loose one by one.

And then he was free. He rolled away, snatched up one of the big Colts he had dropped in the grass and began hammering in a demented fury at the savage, catching him first in the rib cage, the side of his neck, and then at the arms the savage flung up to protect himself, smashing almost completely through one of them, and finishing up with blows to the head that crushed the savage's skull. When Mordecai had finished pummelling the lifeless Comanche, he sat back on his haunches, sweat pouring off him, his heart pounding, panting like a man who had run a mile in the heat of the day.

That was when, back on his haunches, still feeling the dead Indian's vise-like grip on his neck, he caught sight of the small blue tin of percussion caps resting upside down in a clump of grass.

V

As James, in company with Manuel and six other members of the Bastrop militia, continued their remorseless pursuit of the Comanche, he witnessed scenes as barbaric as any he had seen before. Either in acts of defiance or in a desperate ruse to delay pursuit, the Comanche began killing the prisoners they had captured. White men and captured negro slaves were found staked out on the ground, impaled with lances, tongues ripped out, scalps hanging loose. One woman, whom one militiaman identified as the granddaughter of Daniel Boone who'd been taken outside Linnville, was tied to a tree, her naked torso filled with arrows.

They buried her and kept on. Then, an hour or so before sundown, James and Manuel, riding at the head of their weary body, topped a rise and saw ahead of them a young boy tied to a tree, his body—like the woman they had just buried—filled with arrows. James spurred quickly down the slope and flung himself from his horse, desperate to find out if the boy had any spark of life left. But even as he approached the tree, he could see that without a doubt the boy was dead. He was a fair-haired lad, not more than twelve or thirteen years of age; his glazed eyes were open, his mouth hanging slack. Flies buzzed around his head. James slapped at the flies, then realized the futility of it and stepped back, choking back a curse of rage and futility.

Manuel dismounted behind him and proceeded to untie the boy. Like they had the woman, they would bury him without a marker. No one would ever know who he was, and those who had borne and loved him would never know where he lay. An anonymous grave was all his luckless fate could grant him.

A half hour later, close on to dusk, having run down three weaponless Comanche braves fleeing on foot, they saw ahead of them still another woman tied to a tree. This one was not completely naked, and as James galloped up, he was startled to realize that he recognized her. It was the widow of Major Watts of Linnville, the pretty blond woman he had seen working at her desk in the customs office. She was alive, sobbing with relief at the sight of James and the other men. What had saved her was her formidable whalebone corset, the same item of clothing that had prevented her rape and mutilation. It had blunted the arrows that had been sent at her, and as James cut her down, he could see that though she was bruised fearfully from the force of the Comanche arrows, her skin had not been broken. Except for a painful sunburn on her exposed limbs, she was unharmed.

As Manuel untied the woman, James took off his dusty coat and draped it over her full figure. She was barely able to form the words to thank him, and as the leather thongs holding her to the tree parted, she gasped out her relief and fell into James's arms. He swept her up, carried her to a shade tree, and let her down gently, standing protectively over her while Manuel brought a blanket to cover her limbs.

"We'll go no farther today," James told Manuel.

Manuel nodded, then turned to the rest of the men. "You can go on boys. Keep after the bastards, but we're stayin' here."

One of the men swept into the lead of the remaining horsemen, casually saluted James and Manuel and rode on, the militiamen following.

VI

After the battle at Plum Creek, the Texans discovered they had suffered less than five serious casualties, while Buffalo Hump had lost at least eighty of his most battle-hardened warriors. In addition, the Comanche had given up all the loot they had gathered.

The Texans divided the spoils. No effort was made to return the goods to their original owners. Members of the militia took sacks of silver and bolts of cloth back to their wives. Some men recovered cases of liquor and kegs of brandy, as well as stores of tobacco. Also divided equally among the victors were the surviving horses and mules, as much as treasure to the Texans as to the Comanche. The Tonkawa, who had run on foot thirty miles to reach Plum

Creek, now appeared on splendid horses, their share of the spoils of battle. It was a reward they undoubtedly appreciated far more than the expansive citation General Huston wrote out to reward them for their services.

With the day ended, the loot divided, the men of the Texan Army on the site of the battlefield drifted off to their homes. Only the fourteen Tonka braves remained behind to hold a victory celebration. While the moon rose over Plum Creek, they danced about their roaring fire, boasting to each other, calling out defiant challenges to the spirits of the Comanche dead.

They concluded their celebration by roasting and devouring the arms and thighs of several butchered Comanches.

PART III

COMANCHERIA

☆ **Chapter** ☆

11

President Mirabeau Buonaparte Lamar was not satisfied. Neither was his Secretary of War. If Plum Creek was a great victory, it was not enough. Both men felt that the Honey Eaters should be made to realize that they were not safe no matter how far into Comancheria they fled. To make this point, President Lamar announced that he was sending a punitive expedition after the Comanche under the leadership of Colonel John H. Moore. Soon after, the call went out for volunteers.

II

During the long ride to the Lewis compound, Manuel's thoughts had dwelt almost entirely on Angeline. He was more than eager to see her again, but apprehensive as well, for by joining this expedition, he would for the first time be leaving behind someone he now realized he loved more than life itself—a woman he had always loved, in truth, from the moment he first caught sight of her in Marie Lewis's kitchen. Since then he had thought of Angeline as his woman—and for almost as long, he had known that she returned his feelings.

A week after Plum Creek, Manuel had settled the matter.

Encouraged by Mordecai's words before the battle at Plum Creek, he had ridden up and formally proposed to Angeline. She had accepted with a shy smile and then had let him take her in his arms. He had held her tightly, aware of her hammering heart beating in concert with his own. At that moment, glancing beyond Angeline, Manuel had seen a proud and happy Mordecai standing in the open doorway with his mother, tears of joy coursing down Marie's careworn cheeks.

Now, as Manuel rode into the yard of what had come to be called the Lewis Fort, he saw two saddled horses waiting at the hitch rack, bedrolls and gear tied snugly on the cantles. Marie and Angeline were standing in the dog trot, watching him ride in. Manuel pulled up in front of the hitch rack and touched his hat brim in salute to Marie and Angeline. As he dismounted, Mordecai and James stepped out past the two women.

"Howdy, Manuel," Mordecai said. "You must've rode through the night."

Manuel nodded. "I guess I'll just have to sleep in the saddle. Where's Jonathan."

"He'll be along," said James.

Manuel turned his gaze toward Angeline. As her eyes caught his, it was as if he had been struck by a gentle hammer, like he was some fool kid suffering from puppy love. He almost blushed. Angeline did blush, and that made her warm, shy smile even more lovely. Dropping his reins over the hitch rail, he stepped up onto the low porch and headed for her.

Sensing the two would appreciate some privacy, James and Mordecai left the porch to see to their horses. Marie vanished back into the house. Manuel escorted Angeline away from the door farther down the dog trot, then he smiled down at her.

"Do be careful, Manuel," Angeline murmured, a palpable fear showing in her eyes and in the lines of her face.

"I will," he assured her. "Don't you worry none."

"I do wish President Lamar hadn't proposed this expedition," she told him. "Wasn't it enough what you men did at Plum Creek?"

"Maybe so, Angelina," he told her. "But I see what Lamar wants."

"What, Manuel? What on earth does he want? There hasn't been an attack on a single settlement since that battle. The Comanche are gone. They have learned their lesson."

He smiled at her and, reaching out, held her close for a moment, understanding her concern and feeling warmed by it. But she just did not know the Comanche, or she would not have said that. He pushed her gently from him and gazed down fondly into her face. He felt a need now to make her understand why the Rangers had to make this expedition.

"Angelina," he told her, "the Comanche will never learn their lesson. They might hold off for a while, change tactics, but they will always consider the *tejanos* their enemies. As long as they breathe, they will be a threat to us."

"Then, my God, Manuel, what's to be done?"

"Drive them back from this borderland. Make it too painful for them to remain so close to us. Punish them. Burn their lodges, their winter stores, drive off their ponies. It is what brought those chiefs in before. That's all the Comanche will ever understand. We must make it so unsafe for them to remain close to us that they will pull back—at least as far as the Red River."

Angeline, gazing up into his face, took a deep sigh and seemed to accept that reasoning. "I suppose you're right, Manuel," she said with some reluctance. "But just do be careful. I implore you."

"I will be very careful," he replied softly, kissing her

lightly on her forehead, then touching his lips to hers for a delicious moment that he found all too brief. "Now I have someone to return to—she who will bear my children."

Angeline stepped closer and hugged him, turning her head so that it rested on his chest. "Our children," she corrected him.

"Yes," he said, "our children."

Then he stepped back.

"I must go."

She nodded, but neither one of them moved.

"You'll be all right here?" he asked. "You aren't worried?"

"Andrew's coming from Austin. He'll be with us. Frank and Sly are nearby. We'll be fine."

"This is some fort," he said, glancing up appreciatively at its reinforced roof.

"Yes."

He stepped quickly forward and held Angeline once again. There was so much he wanted to say, but as always so few words with which to express them. Besides, sometimes words made a liar of a man, expressing so much less than he meant.

"Reckon I'll be going now," he told her.

"Yes, you better," Angeline said, attempting a smile. "James and Mordecai are waiting."

He glanced over at them. They had already mounted up, and Marie's strained face was lifted to Mordecai's as she bid him good-bye. Manuel could see how different this parting was for her. He glimpsed Jonathan on the horizon, riding to meet them.

He looked back at Angeline. "We'll make this a quick expedition, I'm thinking," he assured her, sounding far more confident than he felt. "Like that business at Plum Creek. So don't you worry none."

Angeline nodded, and he saw then that she was fighting

back tears and no longer trusted herself to speak; he realized he would be doing them both a favor to move out now. He turned quickly, pulling his hat down more snugly, and strode swiftly to his waiting horse.

As he caught up his reins and stepped into his saddle, Marie, shading her eyes to look up at the three of them, stepped back from the horses and told Manuel to take good care of himself. As James and Mordecai yanked their horses about and started from the yard, Manuel thanked Marie and dared only one more glance at Angeline before wheeling his mount and following after James and Mordecai.

III

Seven miles farther up the Colorado, outside Lem Skittles cabin, the four riders met the main body under Colonel Moore. Skittles was a newcomer to the Colorado settlements. His brother, also a newcomer, was joining Moore's expedition, while Skittles stayed behind to protect his wife and the two young ones. Not a man in the expedition thought this a bad idea. All told, the expedition numbered ninety-six buckskinned riders, most of them Rangers, and eleven Lipan Apache scouts, with all provisions packed on a string of twenty-one mules.

For the next few weeks, they rode west up the Colorado, actively seeking out Comanche. They saw not a single tell-tale flock of buzzards to indicate an Indian Village. But what they did see was a land that no one man among them would ever forget, a splendid open country that until now had been virtually unknown to any Texan. They crossed mile after mile of lush, gently rolling land just waiting for the plow. By late October they had penetrated farther west than any known Anglo-Texan had gone before. They crossed the

Concho and the Red Fork of the Colorado and were almost halfway to Santa Fe when the weather turned chill.

They were still going, crossing a high semi–arid plateau when the Lipan Apaches smelled out a large encampment of Pehnahterkuh Comanche ahead of them in the bend of a shallow stream that cut through a wide canyon. Moore rode with the Lipan chief to scout the encampment; they counted sixty lodges and estimated a population of perhaps one hundred warriors. Returning to his men, Moore decided it was time for a war council. He sent the Lipan chief and the rest of his scouts back to keep tabs on the Comanche village and then gathered the Rangers around him.

Standing there, surrounded by ranks of hard-bitten Texans, the colonel made a striking figure. At least six-feet-two-inches tall, some whispered that he reminded them of Old Hickory, his tall figure was so rangy and lacking in tallow. In his early fifties, he had a thick mane of white hair and a bushy white mustache. His sharp, unwavering eyes were a flinty gray. A few of the men now crouched about him remembered him at San Jacinto, wielding only a flashing saber as he charged into the solid ranks of Santa Anna's soldiers. A quiet, taciturn man for the most part, the colonel was an officer who led by example rather than exhortation.

Moore started off by telling the men what he had learned of the Comanche's disposition, including the number of lodges, and the fact that the Comanche had apparently set out no pickets.

"What do we do, Colonel?" one of the men asked.

"Now, that's a silly question, ain't it? We've come a long way for this. We attack."

James spoke up then. "That's what I was hoping."

"What's our plan?" someone else asked.

Moore had a stick in his hand. He went down on one knee

and sketched out the canyon and the stream running through it, then the spot where the Indian pony herd was grazing.

"We'll stampede them ponies first thing," he said. "James, you take a few and tend to that." He pointed with his stick. "Drive them ponies right back through here and out onto the prairie. You'll join up with me and my men coming in about here. We'll catch the bastards in between. In West Point, they call it a pincers."

James nodded, then turned to wink at Mordecai and Jonathan.

"And do it right, James. All I want to see is ponies stampeding and Comanche on foot."

"That's what you'll see, Colonel," James replied.

"Owens," Moore said to the lieutenant, "take Manuel and about thirty men across the river. Here." He pointed to the bend in the river he had sketched on the ground, "and wait there for the Comanche to cross. They'll be comin' right at you."

"You sure they'll cross there, Colonel?" the lieutenant asked.

The lieutenant was a young man with jet black hair and dark bushy brows. He had seen action before. A Comanche arrow had left a puckered scar in his right cheek, and the arrowhead had severed a nerve, causing that side of his face to droop permanently.

The colonel replied patiently, "It's the way they'll come, Owens. From the look of that canyon, it's the only way they can go. The other way, they'll be trying to climb a sheer cliff."

The lieutenant nodded quickly, satisfied. "Then we'll be waiting' for 'em."

"Just keep your powder dry, lieutenant."

"You can count on it, Colonel."

Colonel Moore's flinty gaze swept the men circling him.

"I'll be leading the rest of you irregulars in a mounted charge into the village. We'll move as soon as James stampedes them ponies. Our orders are clear, men. This is a punitive expedition. We are to hunt out and kill Comanche." He paused a moment to let that sink in. "And we take no prisoners."

The men exchanged glances. They had figured this was coming, but had kept themselves from thinking what it really meant. But they could hide the reality from themselves no longer and were now face to face with the truth of what they were about. Some were obviously uncomfortable with the order, but many more were grimly pleased at the prospect. They had seen enough burnt-out cabins, mutilated men, and raped women staked to the ground with Comanche lances to hate these savage heathens to the very depths of their souls. Nevertheless, every man there was sobered by Colonel Moore's stark words.

"What time do we attack?" the lieutenant asked.

"First light. That'll give us plenty of time to get set. We'll be tethering our pack animals back here, and we'll need a few men to stay with them. We'll wait until midnight before moving in."

Owens nodded, satisfied. Moore stood up and flung away the stick he had been using. James looked at Mordecai and Jonathan, indicating with a motion of his head that it was time they saw to their mounts.

As they moved off, Jonathan said to James, "Did you hear what Moore said? We ain't takin' no prisoners."

"I heard."

"What about the women and children?"

"Maybe you didn't hear *all* he said, Jonathan. This here's a punitive expedition."

"Sweet Jesus," said Mordecai.

"Amen to that," said James.

IV

From the first James was astonished at how easy it went. With the Lipan Apaches scouting ahead for him, he led his mounted Rangers through the pre-dawn darkness, descended through the timber into the canyon behind the pony herd, and pulled his men up behind it without arousing a single Comanche. Not a dog in the entire Indian village had barked. It seemed incredible to James that these Comanche, so fierce and implacable on the warpath, so satanically cruel to their enemies, could now sleep so soundly in their lodges without a single picket standing guard on the encampment. Apparently these murderous warriors and their families slept without a care in the world.

Turning it over in his mind, James pieced together an understanding of why this might be so. The reputation of the Comanche was so fierce and terrible that no other tribe dwelling on their borders dared enter their domain. It must always have been so from the earliest days of their conquest of this region when, as Abe had pointed out to James, they had driven the Apache from the plains. These Honey-Eaters simply could not conceive of any tribe or group of men daring to journey into their land and to make war on them.

Well, James noted grimly as he sat his horse, President Lamar was determined to show them different.

The sun broke over the hills beyond the canyon. James waited in the thin timber for the sun's rays to fully bathe the canyon, then glanced back at Mordecai and Jonathan and the rest of his men. They appeared ready—more than ready, in fact. He looked back at the bunched ponies, themselves coming alert to the new day. He pulled out his Colt and fired into the air over their heads. At once the ponies lifted their heads almost as one animal, then swung about and bolted away from the sound of the gunshot. Spurring after the herd,

James and the rest of his men continued to fire over the backs of the plunging horses, increasing their panic.

Keeping close alongside the stream, the maddened ponies plunged on. James and his Rangers—letting out high-pitched war cries as shrill as any Comanche's—remained hard on their heels. As they neared the encampment, it became no longer necessary to send more rounds into the air; the ponies, with nostrils flaring and eyes bulging with terror, charged into the Indian camp, a swarming, destructive river of horseflesh intent only on escaping the screaming madmen on their flanks.

Out of the early morning gloom, James saw a branch coming at him. He ducked low fast enough to save his head if not his hat, which went snapping off his head. Its leather strap slapped painfully against his Adam's apple, but he ignored it as he swept on. Ahead of him came the cries of the aroused Comanche as they bolted from their lodges. Beyond the encampment, James glimpsed the dark surge of approaching horsemen as the colonel and his men galloped in from the other end of the canyon to close the pincers.

Shots rang out from the Comanche lodges as James and his men rode in among them. James saw one naked brave plant his lance in the ground, intent on disemboweling his horse. James cut to one side just in time, flung his gun hand out, and sent a bullet into the warrior's naked chest. Straightening in the saddle, he felt a Comanche's powerful hand closing about his thigh as the savage tried to pull James from the saddle. James brought down the barrel of his Colt as hard as he could, catching the Comanche squarely on his forearm. The savage's grip fell away, the sickening sound of his shattered bone lost in the wild confusion of gunshots, shouts, and screams that came at him now from all sides.

V

Mordecai followed close behind James, Jonathan at his side, as they charged through and around the lodges, shooting down surprised and panicked Comanche on every side. He tried not to notice the sex or age of the Indians as he brought them down on all sides of him with a deadly accuracy, resolutely reminding himself that if this were a Texan settlement, the Comanche would have done the same.

The surprise of the attack was so complete that the Indians could do nothing but fly before their attackers. Weaponless and stark naked, the braves and their women and children plunged through the early morning light, heading directly for the bend in the river where Colonel Moore had stationed his sharpshooters. As Mordecai pounded after them, he had the sickening thought that he was driving bleating sheep to the brink of a precipice.

A Comanche fleeing just ahead of Mordecai spun suddenly about and, with an astonishing, lightning-quick motion, leapt astride Mordecai's mount, his bare thighs slapping down hard on the horse's rump. Flinging his arms about Mordecai, the Indian flung himself backward, taking Mordecai with him. Mordecai felt his pistol fly from his hand a moment before he and the Indian struck the ground. Mordecai struck out wildly at the Comanche and managed to roll free of him. Still on his hands and knees, shaking his head to clear the buzzing in it, he saw a second Comanche running at him with lowered lance.

Out of nowhere it seemed, Jonathan galloped, running down the Indian.

Desperation and a vivid sense of his own danger cleared Mordecai's head immediately, and he turned in time to meet the charge of the Comanche who had pulled him off his horse. The Indian was naked, his only weapon a war club.

Mordecai ducked back as the Comanche swung the club, which caught Mordecai's left shoulder a glancing blow that sent a numbing shock clear down his arm. But by that time, Mordecai's bowie was in his right hand. Lunging close enough to the Indian to smell his fetid breath, he plunged the long blade deep into the savage's bowels.

A black, noisome flow of blood and entrails spilled out over his fist. He stepped back and let the Indian fall. All around him now, Rangers were charging past. He heard someone shout his name. He turned and glanced up to see Jonathan galloping back toward him, pulling Mordecai's mount after him. Still holding the blade, Mordecai tried to mount up, but found he couldn't with a bloody knife in one hand. He lurched back from the high-strung horse, bent and wiped the blade on the damp grass, and slid it back into its sheath.

"Is that your Colt!" Jonathan cried, pointing to Mordecai's handgun resting at the base of a cottonwood. He was keeping a tight rein on his horse as he circled Mordecai.

Mordecai retrieved the weapon, holstered it, and this time mounted up without difficulty. His shoulder was beginning to ache like a sore tooth, but it was nothing he couldn't handle. The important thing was he still had his scalp, thanks to Jonathan.

VI

Crouching in the reeds across the stream from the Comanche village, Manuel watched fascinated as the fleeing Comanche boiled out of their lodges and headed for the water. With the Rangers riding herd on them, they were plunging into the water like startled antelopes, just as Colonel Moore had said they would. Manuel checked his rifle's load, then lifted his rifle and held his breath as the Indians, many of them screaming in panic, scrambled through the shallow water toward him. Some, finding themselves in spots that were over their heads, began to swim frantically, while those behind them threatened to overtake and pull them under in their wild haste to escape the Rangers's terrible fire. All around him, Manuel heard the click of rifles being readied as the waiting men listened for the lieutenant's order to fire.

It came suddenly, loud and clear.

"They're close enough, men!" he shouted. "Open up on 'em!"

To get a better shot Manuel stood up, picked out a Comanche struggling in the water, and squeezed the trigger. He saw a splash of red as the Indian's head disappeared beneath the water. He loaded swiftly, automatically, and fired at another Indian, this one close enough to hurl his tomahawk at one of the riflemen in the rushes. Manuel's bullet tore the brave's face away, just as another ball punched into his belly. The Indian spun about in the shallow water and a moment later was floating downstream, only the top of his head showing. Wading out farther into the stream, Manuel joined others picking off Indian after Indian. Soon they found themselves pouring an indiscriminate fusilade into a floundering mass of screaming Indians—men, women, and children. Even as he loaded and fired, loaded and fired, Manuel was aware of Moore's force standing on the far shore, dismounted now, striding into the water, firing upon those Indians who had turned about in midstream and were attempting to make it back.

Abruptly, out of the swirling water in front of him, a woman erupted, knife drawn, fierce black eyes blazing with hatred. She flung herself at Manuel, her shrill cry of defiance cutting through the rattle of rifle fire all around them. Manuel stepped back and raised his rifle, but looking into the woman's eyes found he could not pull the trigger. And then she was on him, bowling him back into the shallow water. He slammed down into the shallow water on his back, the Comanche woman crouched over him, her knife poised high above her head as she prepared to plunge it into his heart.

In that single instant, Manuel recalled his good-bye to Angeline and his promise that he would be careful. He wondered almost calmly how she would react to the knowledge that he had allowed a crazed Comanche woman to kill him. He flung himself to one side, splashed up onto his feet, drew the Colt in his belt, and cut the Comanche woman down, his first shot striking her in the left breast, his second in the neck. She dropped her knife, turned about as if to flee back across the stream, then crashed face-down in the water; a second later she was drifting downstream with all the other dead Comanche.

The killing continued, but Manuel stepped back out of the shallow water and did no more of it that day. There were enough riflemen to kill twice the number of Comanche, and their number was diminishing rapidly.

His rifle was not needed.

VII

It had been a Roman orgy of killing—a complete and casual slaughter of the Comanche. The firing ceased only when the last Comanche was dead or had crawled away. The Rangers made no effort to go after the few women and children who had managed to flee the canyon alive, content to know that they were bereft of all supplies, fleeing on foot across the trackless prairie. When they stumbled at last into the encampments of other bands, they would have a dismal tale to tell—one calculated to sober any Comanche foolish enough to consider retaliation. In all, fifty Comanches had been killed in the camp, more than eighty in the river. Only one Texan had been fatally wounded; as luck would have it, he was Skittles's brother, the newest settler to the Colorado river valley.

Driving the more than five hundred captured ponies ahead of them, the Texans started back down the Colorado. They had been gone almost two months, and it was now close to November. They were weary men who had ridden far into a hostile land and completed the bloody business assigned to them.

It was time to go home.

VIII

Riding point on the pony herd one hot dusty afternoon, Manuel's thoughts turned as usual to the fair Angeline. As he spurred his horse quickly to head off a feisty colt, he asked himself if he and Angeline had waited long enough. Christmas would be coming soon. Was it not time now for them to be wed? Why not a Christmas wedding?

His heart leapt at the prospect. A marriage during the Christmas festivities would be a most favorable time to unite his people with those of the Lewis clan. Were they not his other family, as Michael had always insisted? Indeed, was this marriage not what Angeline's father had always wanted?

Grinning, Manuel could hardly wait for the campfire that night. He could already imagine the pleased grin on Mordecai's face at the news of what Manuel had decided this day.

☆ **Chapter** ☆

12

Three weeks after Manuel rode off with James and Mordecai, Angeline was standing in the bright morning sun feeding the chickens when she saw smoke on the horizon. She knew immediately what it meant. A ranch was going up in flames. Judging from the distance and direction, Angeline had no doubt it was the ranch belonging to the Baileys, newcomers to the valley. She dropped the pan of corn and ran back toward the ranchhouse, calling out to her mother.

As Marie appeared in the doorway in answer to Angeline's call, a hard-riding young man appeared in the distance, heading for the ranch. They hurried to the gate to wait for him to reach them. When the rider reached them, he reined in his trembling horse, but remained in the saddle.

"It's a murder raid," he told them excitedly. "Kiowa and Comanche!"

"How many?" Marie asked, her face pale with apprehension.

The rider told her it was about ten or fifteen, but said he couldn't be sure. He emphasized that his father was certain it was a mix of Comanche and Kiowa, which meant a murder party, and that they had already run off his stock and burned out the Baileys. He had requested water for himself and his horse, and as soon as this was provided, he rode off to warn others.

Not long after, the rest of the Lewis clan—Frank and Hope, Andrew and Petra, Sly Shipman and Annie, along with their offspring—arrived to take advantage of the Lewis Fort. The older children were grave and serious, the little ones excited, not really able to comprehend the gravity of their situation. They were herded into the main bedroom and made as comfortable as possible by Petra, Hope and Annie. Meanwhile, the men busied themselves loading rifles and placed on the kitchen table for ready access the powder, caps, and balls the women would be needing when it came to reloading. Angeline and Marie made many trips out to the well to fill the wooden buckets, placing the two on each side of the windows and one in each corner.

The sod roof would help, but fire was always a possibility. If their attackers were persistent enough and willing to take casualties, they could succeed in setting the roof and building ablaze. Their fire arrows, once buried in the front door, would most probably set fire to it. The Lewis Fort was strong, but it was not impregnable.

With all their firearms loaded, Andrew took up his rifle and strode out onto the dog trot to keep watch, while Marie and Petra set about preparing a noon meal for the family. Angeline, weary from hauling all those buckets of water, joined Andrew on the dog trot. Shading her eyes, she scanned the horizon. The smoke from the Bailey place had drifted away, which meant their cabin and probably the barn were now but smoldering ruins. She knew the Baileys and was deeply affected by their tragedy, knowing how hard they had worked to build their ranch and how much love they had put into its creation. Her silent prayer now was that the Baileys and their two young ones had managed to flee in time.

Standing there beside the grim, watchful Andrew, looking

out over the calm beauty of the sun-bathed landscape, she found it difficult to believe that at that very moment the grasslands around them were most likely crawling with savages whose only delight was in murder and plunder, who found a perverse, devilish delight in the sight of burning homes and in the systematic mutilation of living victims.

Marie called to her for help with the table setting. Angeline hurried back inside.

By midafternoon, the children were ready to burst through the walls, and since there had been no further alarms, it was decided that if they were particularly careful, they could be allowed out into the back yard for a brief while under a constant guard. Released into the sunlight, the children gloried in their release from what had been for them an intolerable confinement. Frank's two older sons, Edward and David, acting as unofficial moniters, helped keep order.

Andrew was out at the well in the front yard, drinking from the dipper, when he glanced up and saw five or six Indians ride into view across the river. They were treating a small bunch of cattle like a buffalo stand, circling them and cutting them down with their lances or arrows. Their yips of delight carried clearly across the river.

"Into the house!" Frank called out.

Sly and Frank, along with the women, erupted from the house and herded the children back inside. Annie's three-year-old protested and tried to twist away from her mother's grasp, but a few swats on her bottom took the fight out of her. In a moment they were all inside, heading once more for the bedroom. Andrew was about to bolt the door shut when a distraught Hope rushed into the kitchen.

"Frank!" she cried. "Billy's not here!"

"My God, where is he?"

"Eddie said he went to hunt frogs! To frighten the girls with!"

Angeline, standing by the door, realized exactly where Billy was. She flung open the door and dashed out through it.

"Angeline!" Frank called from the dog trot. "Come back here!"

"I know where he goes," Angeline called back without slowing. "It's his favorite spot."

Unwilling to allow Angeline to take this risk alone, Frank took after her, amazed at the speed with which the young woman flew over the ground. In a moment she was out of sight behind the steep embankment bordering the river. When he reached the bank himself, he saw Angeline pulling Billy swiftly out of the shallow pool where he had been searching for frogs. The ten-year-old was obviously startled by Angeline's urgency and protested her rough handling of him.

"Get up here, Billy!" Frank told him. "Now!"

At the sound of his father's voice, the fight left the boy, and he broke from Angeline and started to run up the embankment toward him.

At that moment Angeline screamed out a warning.

Turning, Frank saw two mounted Indians erupt at full gallop from out of a nearby draw. He swung up his rifle and fired at the lead Indian, who promptly peeled back off his pony. When the other Indian saw Frank draw his pistol, he cut sharply and galloped down the bank toward the river, swept up the screaming, battling Angeline onto his pony and rode off, his sharp yipping cry of triumph sending a shock of horror through Frank. He lifted his pistol but dared not fire for fear of hitting Angeline. The Indian vanished back into the draw.

Filled with a bitter, inchoate rage, Frank swept Billy up and carrying him under one arm like a loaf of bread, hurried back to the house.

II

That night, the war party, made up of nine Comanche and four Kiowa, left the Colorado behind and set off due north, driving before them a small herd of Kentucky-bred stallions. Angeline, her wrists bound with rawhide, sat in front of the warrior who had captured her, her raw thighs straddling a saddle blanket that smelled of sweat and piss.

As the Indian raiders pounded on over the prairie, Angeline glanced back the way they had come, praying to see riders in pursuit. But all she saw was the nearly full moon, climbing still higher into the sky, sending a bright, shimmering wash over the undulating grassland that extended clear to the horizon—a vast sea of grass that left no trace of their passage as it closed behind them.

Angeline's heart sank. It was no use. She was beyond help. Her worst nightmare had come true. She was the captive of savage horse Indians. Since the time she had first heard stories of Indians carrying off women captives—and especially since that day in San Antonio when she had done her best to comfort Matilda Lockhart—this had been for her a fate more terrible than death.

And now that fate was hers.

III

The warrior who had taken Angeline was a Kiowa, she realized. He and the other Kiowa warriors appeared taller, not as squat as the Comanche, and less bow-legged when they walked. Nor did they speak the same language as the Comanche, communicating in swift, impossible to follow sign language. Not until noon of the next day did they halt, and when they did it was to divide the horses. The Comanche rode off with twelve, leaving eight for the Kiowa, after which the Kiowa continued on a northern course.

The only nourishment Angeline had received during this time was a chunk of dried buffalo meat and water. She had been cuffed unmercifully when she spat out a portion of the buffalo meat, but had taken the punishment stoically, refusing to cry out or respond in any way.

Already, on the war party's first halt, her captor had made foul use of her, his stinking, sweaty body slapping furiously down upon hers, his lust like that of a stallion taking a mare. The agony of the warrior's first brutal entry caused her to bite through her lower lip, but she refused to cry out or respond in any fashion. Apparently in an attempt to arouse some response from her, the warrior invited his three companions to participate in her violation.

When at last the loathesome rutting was done, she was allowed to sleep. She rolled over onto the hard ground, drew her knees up to her chin and closed her eyes, telling herself that none of this mattered any longer. Her life was over. She had no intention of returning or allowing herself to be returned to her people to suffer the scalding indignity of becoming a pitiable spectacle, to be gaped at as had poor Matilda Lockhart. All she could hope for now to end this squalid outrage was a quick death. And she would do all in her power to achieve that end. After that grim vow, her tremendous exhaustion smote her like a fist, and she sank into a dreadful, nightmare-haunted sleep.

For two more days the Kiowa rode north until they crossed a river more broad than any other they had come upon, causing Angeline to wonder if this was the Red River she had heard older men talking about. If it was, she was now deep in Indian country, so deep she might as well consider herself on another planet. When at last they arrived at the Kiowa's village, the warriors made a great show of their entry, putting on their war paint before they entered the village, then displaying grisly trophies as they drove the stallions into the village ahead of them, while the children and old women and a few of the younger braves followed in their wake, the younger women shouting out to the warriors and gesturing obscenely at Angeline.

During this long, appalling journey, what Angeline had been trying to prepare herself for were the women of the tribe, since Matilda Lockhart had given Angeline a vivid picture of their satanic nature, the old crones especially. She had hoped that perhaps the Kiowa women would not be as ferocious as the Comanche women, but now as she rode through them, she realized that her hope was at best a forlorn one.

Before her captor could bring his pony to a halt, hooked fingers grabbed her thighs, black nails scratching deeply. Someone snatched at and ripped her trailing dress. She yanked it out of the hands of one old crone, who promptly spat in her face. The warrior booted the pony out of the crush, then pulled up in front of an ugly old Kiowa chief standing in front of his lodge, his arms folded. Slipping off the pony, the Kiowa warrior lifted Angeline off the horse and flung her to the ground in front of the old chief. Angeline struck hard, but managed to keep herself from sprawling full length on the ground. Striding closer to the chief, her captor swept his arm at the two stallions he had brought back, indicating that in addition to Angeline, the chief was to consider those two horses as his also.

The chief grunted his pleasure, stepped back into his lodge and came out with a young woman who must have been his daughter. Two younger daughters came out with her, along with a woman old enough to be the chief's wife, and were careful to remain in the background, their black eyes glinting with curiosity. The chief's oldest daughter kept her gaze down as the chief spoke to her with some finality, obviously informing her that she had just been purchased. She was to marry this mighty warrior who had brought him such fine presents. The young woman dutifully bowed her head in submission to both men. Satisfied, the warrior spun on his heels and strode off proudly leading his pony, followed by a troop of youngsters and a host of grinning, toothless old women.

On the ground Angeline had kept her face averted, paying little heed to this business, as if it were all happening to someone else. Suddenly she felt powerful fingers digging into her arms and was pulled roughly up onto her feet to find herself staring into the cold eyes of the chief's wife. She heard the chief grunt at his wife, and with a careless shrug, he turned and stepped back into his lodge.

This seemed to galvanize the woman. With a squeal of delight, she flung Angeline at her two daughters. Eyes gleaming with anticipation, they grabbed her hair and dragged her after them so forcefully that Angeline stumbled and fell to the ground. Before she could get up, a heavy stick pounded down onto her back so hard for a moment she could not breathe. Another blow caught her on the back of her neck; she was hauled upright in time to catch a foot in her stomach. Gagging, she sprawled forward onto her hands and knees. From all around her a shrieking hilarity erupted as the chief's two daughters were joined by other women, one of them a hairless, toothless old hag. Her eyes wild, she began jabbing at Angeline with a pointed stick, digging cruelly into her face and neck, cackling shrilly with each poke.

Angeline realized that this old woman could easily blind her—and there was no hope that anyone would come forward to intervene. Instantly Angeline shook off her numbing apathy. Death she wanted; but not mutilation. She recalled what she had learned from Matilda Lockhart. Matilda insisted that had she fought back tooth and nail from the very beginning, she would not have been so brutalized; but once she had allowed herself to become a victim, the plaything of the tribe's women, she found there was nothing she could do to change her status. The pecking order had been established once and for all.

She sucked in her breath, forced herself to breathe at a more regular pace, and kept her head averted so that the old woman's stick could not strike her any more in the face. Then she straightened up quickly, snatched the stick out of the old crone's hand and with a calculated, diabolical fury poked the old woman in the face with it.

The crone shrieked in pain and fled. Angeline pursued her relentlessly and succeeded in digging the point of the stick deep into one of her eyes. The eye exploded from its socket, blood pouring out from behind it, carrying the crimson eyeball down onto her cheek where it hung grotesquely, like some loathesome insect. The old woman's screams were piercing. She danced around in a fury of pain and fright, clutching at the bleeding hole in her face, screaming at the sight of her own blood. So wildly did she dance about that the other women became caught up in her gyrations and began laughing at her.

But Angeline was not out of it yet. One of the chief's daughters spun her around and slapped her in the face. Angeline did not hesitate. She punched the woman in the stomach. As she doubled over, Angeline brought her knee up into her face. The Indian's nose exploded, and as she sagged to the ground, her sister screamed out in fury and flung herself at Angeline from the side. Angeline was pushed violently to one side, but managed to remain on her feet. Spinning about, she lashed out, punching the woman so hard in the chest that it drove her back. Then, with hooked fingers she clawed at the woman's face, doing her best to scratch out her eyes.

The Indian woman put her head down and charged Angeline, catching her in the stomach, bowling her over backward to the ground. Instantly the two were rolling over and over in the dust, biting and kicking with the fury of two wildcats while all around them a circle of gleeful Indians howled, their cries beating dimly upon Angeline's consciousness. By this time she could hardly feel a thing; her fury seemed to have rendered her insensible to pain. And as she punched and scratched and kicked, she felt a strength that was almost superhuman.

Astride the chief's daughter, completely dominant now, she was striking at the woman's face when she felt a man's strong arm hook about her neck and pull her roughly back and off the woman. The pain shocked her back to reality, and she scrambled hastily to her feet to find herself staring into the old chief's impassive face. Seeing his face this close, she was horrified. More than ugly, it was a mask of scarred brutality. One eyelid had been slashed and had healed imperfectly. A puckered scar went from the corner of his mouth clear back to his right ear, the flesh beneath it white and lifeless. To her astonishment his obsidian eyes regarded her with something akin to approval. She felt her flesh crawl.

Abruptly, he nodded with a kind of imperious acceptance—and flung her toward his lodge. As she caught herself in front of it, he gave her a command, pointing to the lodge entrance, indicating she should go in. As she stepped through the hole into it, she glanced back to see the chief roundly chastizing his two daughters. She felt a gray despair. She had established her pecking order, but all it had gained for her was this monster's couch.

But it was not to his couch the chief took her that night. Evidently unwilling to offend his wife, the chief prodded

Angeline out of his lodge and led her to a grassy sward in among a clump of beech trees. The moon was high, the night cool. The chief pushed her roughly to the ground, then ripped off her tattered dress. Angeline wore no corset, but she had two petticoats, and these the chief disposed off with growing impatience. When she was naked at last before him, the chief straddled her, his coal-black eyes shining in anticipation. She tried to keep her face averted so she could not have to look up into his frightening face, but his big hand forced her to look up at him.

Even in the dim moonlight his ugliness was awesome, sending a chill down her spine. And he was ridden with lice. A thin parade of gleaming lice, standing out sharply in the moonlight, marched across his forehead. His breechclout stank fearfully of dried urine and caked feces; it was clear the old chief was so unmindful of personal cleanliness that he made no effort to wipe himself after squatting in the woods.

Angeline inched back on the blanket.

What passed for a smile rearranged the chief's face. Reaching down, he tossed aside his breechclout. Angeline felt his knee thrusting between her thighs. She glanced down in horror and saw his medicine bag dangling from his loins like a third testicle. She closed her eyes and looked away, reminding herself that she had already been violated, that none of this mattered any longer. She told herself to do what she had done with the others, to pretend that it was not happening to her, but to someone else.

She closed her eyes and waited, but the moment the chief thrust into her, his weight pressing heavily down onto her, she found she could no longer escape the horror of it. Unable to restrain herself, furious at these awful invasions, she pulled free and scooted back, fighting with a silent, but unyielding tenacity. The chief kept his temper, grunting in admiration at times. But when her raking fingers almost reached his eyes, he sat back calmly and struck her powerfully with his clenched fist. Her head snapped around, and for a moment she lost consciousness.

With a deep, satisfied grunt he thrust into her and fell forward upon her again, rutting happily, one of his sweaty shoulders pushing heedlessly against the side of her face. She lay back, only dimly aware of the blood flowing from her split lip. When at last the spent chief pulled himself off her, she lay there inert, resigned. As far as she was concerned, her life was over. This man could do anything he wanted with her. It had no meaning to her. All she felt was the pain of it. And that, she realized dully, would pass.

The chief gazed impassively down at her, his reptilian eyes blinking. Though he made no outward sign of displeasure, she could sense that he was not entirely pleased with her. He pushed back off her and pulled on his breechclout. Standing up, he gave what sounded like an order. She did not know what he wanted. Impatient, he bent low and cuffed her on the side of her head, as if she were a troublesome puppy, then pointed to the lodge. Angeline got to her feet and allowed the chief to lead her back to the lodge.

Dully, she wondered when this nightmare would end.

☆ Chapter ☆

13

Manuel, riding with Jonathan, Mordecai, and James, felt a sudden, premonitory dread as he topped the gentle rise and caught sight of the Bailey place—or what was left of it. A moment later, the three riders pulled up beside the ruined homestead to look it over. All that was left of the cabin was its blackened flooring and its fieldstone fireplace. The barn did have one scorched wall standing, but it was leaning precariously, and it looked as if the next strong wind would topple it. A few abandoned chickens were clucking disconsolately as they scratched and pecked at the ground in front of their coop. It looked as if the three Rhode Island Reds were now the homestead's sole occupants.

"Jesus," said Mordecai.

"Comanche?" Jonathan wondered aloud.

"What else," said James grimly. "Maybe an overturned lamp could account for the house, but the barn, too?"

"And there's no sign of the Baileys," Mordecai said.

"Let's go," said Manual, spurring ahead of the others.

When the three caught up with Manuel, all four riders lifted their horses to a lope as they continued downstream toward the Lewis compound. Neither man spoke or revealed the concern he felt. But that was not necessary.

II

Frank was standing in front of the Lewis Fort when Manuel, James, and Mordecai rode through the gate. By this time Annie and Sly had told the three men the grim particulars of Angeline's abduction. As Manual dismounted in front of the hitch rail, Hope stepped out through the door to stand by her husband, her face drawn, a weary droop to her shoulders. Manuel thought he understood. Annie had made it clear to them that Hope had been having a difficult time with Marie.

Manuel took a deep breath and nodded to Frank and Hope as he followed James and Mordecai into the house. He remained in the kitchen while Mordecai and James went on into the bedroom where, Annie told them, Marie had secreted herself. Manuel stood uncertainly in the middle of the kitchen, not sure himself what he would say to Marie when the time came. Ever since he had learned what had happened to Angeline, he had been in a kind of sick daze with a queer, constricting emptiness in the pit of his stomach. Now, standing in the same kitchen where he had come upon Angeline so many times in the past, he could almost hear her voice again. A scalding lump formed in his throat. He pulled out a chair and slumped down at the kitchen table.

He heard Hope come back in, but did not look up. She went past him to the stove and poured him a cup of coffee, then placed it wordlessly down in front of him. He looked up at her and nodded his thanks, but made no attempt to drink the coffee. He didn't trust himself to eat or drink anything.

James reentered the kitchen, and a moment later Mordecai followed in after him. Manuel glanced up at Mordecai. The young man's eyes were bleak, and he was unable to look either man in the eye. Manuel understood. It was bad enough what had happened to Angeline, but it had left a terrible mark on Mordecai's mother as well.

"Can I see her . . . ?" Manuel asked.

"Go ahead," said James. "But go easy. She's not good, Manuel."

Manuel left the kitchen and walked down the dim hallway to the big bedroom. He paused at the door and knocked. There was no response, but from the other side of the door came a curious, metronomic tapping.

He knocked again, then pushed the door open all the way and stepped into the bedroom. The curtains were drawn and in the dimness, Manuel could see Marie rocking steadily in a rocking chair beside her bed. She was wearing a black dress and had wrapped a knitted shawl about her shoulders, despite the stifling heat in the small bedroom. The steady tapping sound Manuel had heard came from her rocking chair as one of the rockers struck a warped board in the floor behind her. A kerosene lamp on the dresser threw a dim, yellowish light over Marie's hunched figure.

"Marie . . . ?" Manuel called.

She did not respond and kept on rocking, her eyes staring straight ahead into the room's farthest corner. Manuel closed the door and walked over to her.

"Mrs. Lewis . . . !" he said.

She lifted her face to look at him, her dark luminous eyes regarding him blankly. Manuel put his arm around her shoulders and was startled at how frail they felt. Her rocking slowed. She continued to look at him without uttering a word. Peering into her eyes, Manuel realized how close she was to a complete and utter despair.

"It's Manuel, Marie. I've come back . . ."

She did not respond.

"Marie, I'm going after Angeline."

A spark of hope gleamed momentarily in her eyes. She

reached out and touched his luxuriant beard, then his brow, wonderingly.

"Manuel?" she asked, her voice barely audible. "Is it you?"

"Yes, Marie."

Her eyes fed on him, devoured him, her face alight now with a sudden, extravagant hope. Then she looked past him at the door.

"Angeline? She's here?"

Manuel's heart sank. "No, Marie . . . she's not with me. But I promise you, I'll go after her."

The glow in Marie's face went out as quickly as a snuffed candle, she seemed to shrink into herself and pulled her shawl more tightly about her shoulders and leaned back in the rocker. Looking away from him, she resumed her agitated rocking, the metronomic beat once more filling the room as she drifted back into the dark world she had been occupying when Manuel entered the room.

Backing away softly, Manuel opened the door and stepped into the hall. As he headed back to the kitchen, he could hear once again the steady tapping of Marie's rocker.

III

Abe arrived two days later, near four in the afternoon. James had ridden down to San Antonio to find Abe and had brought him back along with three wiry, heavily laden mules. Abe and James stomped wearily into Marie Lewis's house and slumped down at the kitchen table, prepared to explain their plan to Mordecai and Manuel. Andrew was back in Austin, and Frank and Sly were off helping a neighbor rebuild a barn the Comanche had burnt down.

Hope provided coffee and doughnuts for them while Petra kept an eye on Marie.

The bearded mountain man finished his second cup of coffee, then leaned back in his chair wearily. "You want to start this?" he asked James.

"Go ahead, Abe," James said.

"That shield James brung me," Abe began, "the one belongin' to that Indian Frank killed, was a Kiowa shield. No question. And that makes things a mite easier."

"How so?" Manuel asked.

"The Comanche're spread all over hell and gone. We could spend years searchin' for the right band. But the Kiowa hunting grounds are just north of the Canadian, and close by to the east of 'em is their traditional enemies—Osage and Wichita. We can mebbe get one of them tribes to help us locate the Kiowa band that took Angeline."

"Why would they help us?" Mordecai asked.

"You seen them mules out there? Theys laden with goodies, hoss. Glass beads, mirrors, vermilion, ammunition, ribbons, cloth, blankets, knives and big black hats for the women. Not to mention the rifles. They's old flintlocks, but they'll be found welcome, I'm thinkin'. With all these fine goods to bargain with, we'll find out what we want to know, for sure. I'm willin' to bet on it."

"Then what," said Manuel.

"We go in get her."

"That won't be easy."

"What difference does that make?"

"None."

Abe leaned back and scratched his beard. "That's what I was thinkin'." Then he looked around the table. "Now, who's goin' with me an' James?"

"I am," said Manuel.

"And me," said Mordecai.

"No," said Abe. "No, you ain't, hoss."

"Why in hell not?"

"You ain't thinkin' clear, hoss. Yer forgettin' yer Ma in there. She's already lost your old man to the Comanche. And now these red devils've taken away your sister. You thinkin' of makin' it three? What'll become of her if you don't come back?"

"Well, I'm pretty damn sure I will be comin' back—and I'll be coming back with Angeline!"

"I already said you ain't thinkin' clear," Abe told him softly. "Likely as not there won't be none of us come back from this."

"He's right, Mordecai," said James, his face grim. "Abe and I, we worked this out ridin' up here. I say it's settled. You ain't going."

Hope spoke up then. "Mordecai," she said, hurrying to his side. "Petra and me, we need your help with Marie. She's just not eating. You saw her. She just sits in that darkened room and rocks and rocks. She'll be gone before you get back. You've got to stay here and snap her out of it."

"Can't you—?"

Hope shook her head firmly. "It ain't me she needs now, Mordecai. It's you!"

Mordecai swallowed, tears suddenly swimming in his eyes. "You mean she's that bad?"

"She hasn't eaten more'n a few scraps since Angeline got carried off."

Mordecai looked past Hope at the dim hallway leading to his mother's room. "All right," he said softly. "I'll stay."

Hope hugged him impulsively.

"I've prepared Marie's favorite potato soup," she said. "Please, take it in to her."

"Now?"

"Yes. Please."

Mordecai palmed the moisture out of his eyes. "Sure," he

said, getting to his feet. "And I won't leave that room until she's finished every bit."

About three quarters of an hour later, a weary but very much relieved Mordecai returned to the kitchen with an empty bowl in his hand, a delighted Petra on his heels. Mordecai smiled at Hope and asked her if there was any more of that potato soup left in the pot.

The next morning, with Mordecai and Hope watching from the doorway, Abe led James and Manuel out through the gate. Leading their heavily-laden mules, the three riders were soon out of sight. They were heading due north, hoping to cross the Red River in a week, and planning to keep on from there until they reached the Indian Territory one, maybe two weeks, later.

☆ Chapter ☆
14

Angeline was immediately made the Kiowa chief's principal wife. But as Angeline sensed, this was not because he preferred her to his other wife, but because he was unwilling to let it be known that he did not find her pleasing to him. He would lose too much face if she did not prove to be as worthy as the two stallions the warrior had brought him in return for his daughter's hand. The chief's wife and his two daughters were sent to a smaller, adjoining lodge.

Despite the difficulty of the Kiowa tongue, Angeline found herself picking up snatches of their language and soon learned that the chief was called Iron Face and his wife Willow Woman. And whenever Iron Face addressed Angeline, he called her New First Wife. Meanwhile, the chief did all he could to please Angeline in an effort to make her a more responsive wife. He presented her with a wolf fur blanket for her cot and gave her a mirror and a comb. But Angeline did not, could not, respond in kind. She found nothing but a crawling horror in the old chief's caresses, and after a few weeks had passed, Iron Face still found little pleasure in his new wife.

Angeline made no effort to listen to or communicate with him. Worse, she made only the smallest effort to learn the Kiowa tongue or to converse either with Willow Woman or his daughters. This made for trouble. His household had two heads, but only one functioned. His new wife did not cook. She could not light a fire nor keep one going. Her attempts at scraping hides or sewing beadwork were futile. She could only perform the duties of a slave: hauling water, gathering firewood, and sweeping the lodge's floor.

Not once did he hear her laugh, and he felt her revulsion whenever her eyes rested on his face. Unlike his own people, who saw in his battle scarred face evidence that he was a great warrior, he could tell that when she looked upon him, she found only ugliness. Indeed, she could barely stand to be near him, so that when he joined her in the night, it was as if he were lying on a slab of stone. She was, for him at least, a dead person, cold and unresponsive.

Some nights, desperate to arouse her, he beat her. But even then she did not react. She lay on the cot under him, taking the blows without uttering a sound, her head drawn in for protection while he continued to strike her. Sensing a contest of wills, Iron Face at such times redoubled his efforts in a grim, determined attempt to draw a response of some kind from her. Panting with exertion, he would flail at her until he succeeded in wrenching from her a single cry of pain.

But Iron Face soon realized that such miserable victories were pointless. He restored Willow Woman to her original place in his lodge and gave Angeline to her and her daughters to be their slave. Perhaps his women might be able to teach her to be useful. But as for him, he was done with her. If the time ever came when, penitent and ashamed of her foolish behavior, she asked to be restored to her former place in his lodge, he promised himself he would only scowl and turn from her.

Angeline was the only white woman Iron Face had ever possessed, and he had no desire to repeat his mistake.

II

Free at last of the chief's caresses, Angeline thanked God for her deliverance. No longer referred to as New First Wife, she found herself called instead She Who Hates The Kiowa. Before long it was simply Hates Kiowa, and though her life became infinitely more difficult, it was far easier to endure. Now that the chief had rejected her openly, Willow Woman and her daughters treated her with a cruel and active contempt. Even so, she remained ready at any moment to turn on them as she had on her first day. Indeed, the memory of her destructive fury on that instance seemed to be what was keeping them at a wary distance. Furthermore, the pathetic sight of the one-eyed crone was a constant reminder to everyone what a truly savage response could be invoked by crossing this bitter, silent white woman. That much, at least, she had established.

She soon slashed off her long hair, since it had long since lost its sheen and become only a straggly, vermin-infested nuisance. Fit now only to lug buckets of water from the stream, the only one in Iron Face's family left to carry the bundles of firewood to the lodges, her work was constant and unremitting. She spent entire days hip-deep in the water, pounding clean Iron Face's buckskins. She spent hours in the hot sun bent over the staked-out hides, scraping them clean with bone knives, the blood from her worn fingers mixing in with the scrapings. She labored as she had never labored before in her life, and if it seemed to any of Iron Face's women that she moved or worked too slowly, they would take delight in shrieking at her and threatening her with willow switches.

One morning, Angeline was hauling two buckets of water up a steep embankment when her feet slipped on the slick mud. She slammed forward, her face striking the side of the embankment, the buckets slipping from her grasp. Pushing herself off the ground, she turned to see them rolling back down the bank. Scrambling hastily after the buckets, she managed to retrieve one of them, but the other jumped lightly into the water, landed upright, and started downstream.

She flung the bucket she had retrieved back up onto the embankment and plunged into the stream and swam after the bucket. But she was not a good enough swimmer and almost drowned before her feet found the bottom and she was able to struggle back to the river bank. The women lining the stream laughed heartily at her dilemma, not one of them making the slightest effort to help her. Glaring up at them, Angeline realized that they would have let her drown, idiot grins on their faces as she went under.

She stood up on the embankment, her buckskin dress heavy, her hair plastered miserably to her face and neck, and looked down the stream in time to see a boy swim out and grab the bucket. Angeline felt enormous relief as she climbed the embankment to fetch it from him. As she hurried along the bank, her moccasins squirted water comically with each step. By this time all the women of the band had lined up to watch her, grinning and laughing wildly, slapping their thighs at Hates Kiowa's sorry appearance.

Suddenly, the old crone she had nearly blinded, Walking Shadow Woman, her white hair flying, her face twisted into a malevolent mask, broke through the ranks of watching women and fell upon Angeline, fresh willow switches whistling as they cut into Angeline's back and neck. The unexpected force of the old woman's attack drove Angeline to the ground. Rolling over onto her back, her arm held up to protect her face, Angeline peered through narrowed eyes at the old woman's panting, convoluted face as she whaled away at her. Suddenly an icy, bone-deep rage galvanized her. For a moment, pitying the old crone she had injured so fearfully, she had held back. But no longer.

She jumped to her feet and bore relentlessly through the storm of slashing willows, reached out and grabbed both of the old woman's wrists and twisted. The willow switches fell from the old crone's grasp. Angeline snatched them up and attacked the old woman, lashing her around the face and shoulders until, shrieking in pain and outrage, the old woman stumbled and fell back to the ground. Angeline continued her punishment without let-up. Only when her arms were too heavy from the exertion to continue did she step back from the pitiful, whimpering old crone sprawled on the ground before her.

Then she turned to face the other Comanche women, expecting the worst. They had been closing in around her, howling out gleefully as she punished Walking Shadow Woman. But now they moved quickly back, their eyes averted. Angeline glanced back down at the old crone. Her face and arms a mass of welts, the old woman raised her bloodied arms piteously to ward off any more blows.

Angeline straightened and took a deep, satisfied breath. Once more she had asserted herself; her place in the pecking order had been reestablished. She would be held in contempt, perhaps, and be hated cordially by every Kiowa woman, but she was still deemed too dangerous to attack openly. How long Angeline could count on this, she did not know. But for now, at least, she was safe.

She flung down the willow switches, retrieved her second bucket, and went back to her labors.

III

During the hottest hours of the day, the women of the band took refuge in a wicky, a cool shelter made of leafy boughs laid across a crude pole frame elevated on four posts. Twice Angeline tried to enter it in order to obtain some relief from the blistering sun. But each time, her appearance raised a howl of protest, and the women inside pushed her back out into the sun. The second time it happened, Angeline realized that there would never be room for her within that leafy shelter.

But she did not break. She grew thinner, all softness burned out of her under the relentless schedule of the work the chief's wife laid out for her. As the days and weeks passed, Angeline grew steadily stronger. Her light skin was soon burnished a deep brown, and she found herself able to do twice the work she had managed at first.

The chore easiest to endure was berry picking. Willow Woman was always astonished at the heavy buckets of fragrant wild berries she brought in at nightfall. Losing herself in this pleasant task, she was almost content as she moved for hours by herself along the river's sandy banks. There, under the cool shade of the cottonwoods, she picked wild plums, chokecherries, pecans, and walnuts. Often she was so intent on her swift-fingered task, a mule deer or an antelope stepping out of the willows to drink would catch her unaware.

It was during such solitary hours that she first began to consider seriously the possibility of escape.

IV

Early in the time of the Yellow Leaf Moon, a recently departed war party, their faces still black with war paint, returned to the village in great haste, forgoing any triumphant entry or ceremony. A hurried council was called as excitement and visible fear spread among the women, who gathered their children, ponies, mules, and their dogs close about them.

When the council broke up, the order came to move out. Though Angeline hardly spoke to any Kiowa, except to acknowledge commands or return insults, she had by this time been able to pick up much of their language. What she heard now was that the Kiowa feared an attack by a large Osage war party. Two days after they had set out for an attack on the Wichita, they had stumbled on a large, attacking Osage war party. A brief skirmish had followed, during which two Osage warriors had been struck down. Even so, the Kiowa had been forced to flee from the large number of Osage warriors.

With remarkable speed, the women broke camp. When Angeline started to help, she was rudely ordered to keep out of the way. But she watched closely as the women worked, amazed at their proficiency. With incredible speed, the lodges came down, and in less than half an hour after the command to break camp had been given, the entire village was on the move. Dogs and ponies and mules were all pressed into service, pulling travois of all sizes, each one of them piled high with household goods, tools, and provisions. Some of the larger, pony-driven travois carried children and old women.

Throughout the day, the long line of fleeing men, women, and children kept going, while mounted warriors raced out ahead of the column, alongside it, or followed behind, their black-painted faces grim. Walking close beside Willow Woman and her two daughters, Angeline realized that now, during the confusion of this flight, might be her only chance to escape. All it would take would be for her to let herself fall back. She was of no account to any of them, and her loss would not even be noticed.

On the second day of their flight, as the sun climbed into the sky, she began to trip occasionally, immediately getting to her feet and hurrying to catch up with Willow Woman and her daughters. But they did not seem to care if she kept up or not and paid very little attention when she fell back. Every now and then they would glimpse her behind them, trudging wearily alongside another family. They apparently gave it no thought when Angeline's stumbling inability to keep up caused her to be swallowed up at last in the curtain of dust raised by the hurrying column.

When the Kiowas came to a wide, meandering stream, an oasis of cottonwoods and bushes, they halted to make camp and fill their water bags. Angeline remained at the rear of the column, waiting to see if Willow Woman made any outcry concerning her absence. There was none. She waited a decent interval and watching for her chance, ducked into a thicket and ran swiftly back upstream, keeping to the cottonwoods and willows, moving with the speed of any other wild thing of the wood.

When she had gone at least a mile, she held up for a moment to catch her breath—and at that moment heard the pounding of unshod hooves. Deep in heavy brush, she peered up at the high ground following the river and saw the grim, painted Osage warriors surging past her in pursuit of the Kiowa column. Judging from their speed, Angeline was certain they would overtake the Kiowa village within the hour.

It was curious and totally unexpected, but watching the Osage war party disappear upstream, Angeline felt an odd sinking in the pit of her stomach. Though she had come to know few of her Kiowa captors, despite their casual cruelty, she had come to enjoy a certain freedom and had been able to observe how close the Kiowa families were. Brothers, sisters, cousins, aunts, and uncles were always fussing over each other. Acts of kindness and affection abounded between them. And it was clear that these savages—for all their brutality—could love each other deeply. Not once had she seen any of them raise their hands to noisy or disobedient children.

In addition, the village had been her home, her source of food and sustenance. She had been provided with a warm shelter for protection against the cold nights that were going chillier with each passing day. Though she had made no attempt to befriend any of the women, some of them had nevertheless smiled shyly at her in passing, some even giving her small gifts. Willow Woman's sister gave her a bone-handled knife so Angeline could slice the meat she was stringing up for drying. Another woman had passed her a comb fashioned out of greasewood. And one very old granny, whose lodge Angeline had passed every day on her way to the river, had noticed early on how worn and nearly useless Angeline's moccasins had become. Despite her failing vision and fingers crooked with arthritis, she had labored over a new pair of doeskin moccasins for Angeline and had pressed them on her without ceremony only a few days before.

These acts of kindness could not make up for the loneliness and despair she felt at her abduction. Nevertheless, they were enough to trouble her as she contemplated the fate of Iron Face's people when that fierce whirlwind of Osage warriors fell upon them.

She set out once more, brushing past brambles and splashing through shallows with a steady pace until nightfall. Even then she continued on, but at a less frantic pace. Well past midnight, she crawled into a thorny patch of brush close beside the river and allowed total exhaustion to claim her.

The next day, watching the path of the sun, she continued on up the stream. When she became certain which way south—and Texas—lay, she left the protection of the water and struck out across the prairie. She had planned her escape meticulously and then waited for her chance. Now that she had taken it, she was well prepared. She carried a large supply of jerky and one large water bag. Under her dress she had hung bags containing berries and in one of them she had secreted a fishhook and a line, something one of the Mexican slaves had given her for cleaning and mending his tattered shirt. She also had six sulfur matches in a tin case. Stolen only a few days ago from Willow Woman, these matches along with her bone-handled knife, were her most valuable items. She needed both to survive.

Two days later, as she headed toward a line of cottonwoods on the horizon, she crested a slight knoll and saw before her, less than a mile in the distance, a long line of carts moving toward the southwest. She dropped to the ground, then pulled herself through the tall grass until she could peer down at the odd-looking wagons and their ungainly wooden wheels, and knew at once that they were Comancheros.

In Angeline's eyes, the only thing worse than Comanche or Kiowa were the Comancheros—New Mexican traders who profited from the horse Indians' burning and looting of Texan and other settlements, giving them in exchange for their plunder the guns, ammunition and other goods the Indians needed to survive. It was while approaching such traders that her father had met his death. And if these Comancheros discovered her, she realized, they would promptly sell her back to Iron Face or some other chief, perhaps a Comanche this time.

She knelt down until the Comancheros vanished into the vastness of the grassy plain, then continued on toward the line of cottonwoods where she knew she would find a stream. Close to nightfall she reached the trees and slumped down onto a small grassy clearing beside a spring-fed brook that emptied into the shallow river that fed the cottonwoods. Though she had rationed her berries and jerky, after three days her provisions were low. Now, watching the dark shapes flitting in the shallows just under the bank, she saw that she had an excellent chance to vary her diet.

Taking out her fishhook and tackle, she caught a grasshopper for bait, cut a birch pole for a rod, and in no time at all hooked a shiner. Using only one of her precious matches, she built a fire. While it burned down to a glowing bed of coals, she dressed the fish with her bone-handle knife, then placed greenpine boughs over the coals, and atop those she placed the fish.

The aroma of the cooking fish was so delicious, it was an effort for her to wait until the fish was done properly. When it was, she ate proudly and with gusto. Alone in this vast steppeland, she was surviving. If she could make it south to Texas before winter, she would be safe at last.

Of course, she had no intention of returning to her people along the Colorado River. She knew what shame she would bring upon them if she showed up in their midst after having been used as she had. How could Manuel possibly accept her now? She had so often dreamed of coming to him as a virgin on her wedding night. Manuel would have to find someone else, and she would try never to think of him again. She would perhaps find a house where she could do the labor for which the Kiowa had prepared her so well, then she would bide her time and work her way east until she had left Texas and her people behind.

They would think her dead—and in truth, after what she had been forced to become, she was dead.

She threw a few sticks more on the fire and inched closer to its warmth and prepared to go to sleep.

A whip cracked in the distance.

She jumped up, her heart pounding. Her hand reached for her knife. The bullwhip's crack had sounded like a gunshot. She thought immediately of the Comancheros she had seen earlier. Could they be camped in these cottonwoods after all? She had seen them heading off to the southwest.

She kicked dirt onto her fire. The whip's sharp crack came again. She stole through the trees toward the sound until she saw the glow of a campfire through the cottonwoods. Moving closer, she peered at the two men lounging about the fire. The crack of the bullwhip came again, and she saw the one who was wielding it. He did not look like a Mexican, and appeared to be mending the whip's handle. After a moment the man with the whip—the taller of the two—shrugged, coiled the whip, and dropped it into the back of his wagon. It was a small, covered wagon with four wheels. No. These were not Comancheros. They were Texans, perhaps. But who were they? Did she dare show herself to them?

She dismissed the thought immediately. These two were men alone on the trail, away from civilizations restrictions; she knew enough now to know they would take her as quickly and as brutally as the Indians had. She was now quite well aware of the hungers of such men.

Carefully, she stole back to her spot along the stream. She noticed she could smell the smoke from her fire long before she reached it. She doused the fire with water from the river, then huddled close against a large cottonwood, aware that she would have to stay hidden until those men left these cotton-woods.

She was almost asleep when she heard a light footfall beside her. She glanced up to see a tall, shadowy figure looking down at her. It was one of the two men she had seen beside the wagon, the one who had been wielding the whip.

"Well, now," the man said softly. "Rest easy, *senorita*. I did not mean to frighten you. It was the smell of your fire and the aroma of fresh-cooked fish that drew me on through the trees."

If he had come through the trees alone and had not told his

companion what he was about, she still had a chance for her freedom. With her knife clutched firmly in her hand, she flung herself up off the ground at him, driving him back with the suddenness of her attack.

She slashed at him, slicing through the sleeve of his coat. Chuckling, he ducked away before she could stab again, then grabbed her right wrist with both hands and twisted. With a sharp cry Angeline dropped the knife. She began to kick furiously at him, more out of despair than of any hope she could free herself. The man stopped chuckling and flung her to the ground.

"Enough, woman!" he told her. "I do not intend to hurt you."

"You are a Comanchero?"

He smiled. "I am from New Mexico, but I am not a Comanchero."

"Then leave me alone."

"Leave you out here? In the middle of this empty land?"

"Yes!"

"I see you do not trust me."

"Why should I?"

"Because you must."

"Why must I?"

He smiled. "Because I intend to take you with me to New Mexico and there ransom you. You are a Texan, are you not? I am sure your people will pay dearly for your return."

"I am not a Texan. I have no people."

"I do not believe that. The Comanche have taken at least thirty women captives in the past two years. I have made a fine living ransoming them. It is what I do."

"You are a pig!"

"A very useful pig, you will find."

"You traffic in human misery."

"Yes. And as I said, it is very profitable."

"I do not wish to be ransomed."

"That is not for you to say, *senorita*. Your people will want you back. They always do—at least, they do at first." He stepped back to look her over. "And you are not in such bad condition, truly. I don't see any signs of mutilation. You must have played your hand wisely."

"I will give you only trouble. And if you touch me, I will report this when you ransom me."

"I will not risk any ransom for such foolishness, believe me. You will be perfectly safe with me. You have my word."

Reluctantly, warily, like a wild animal being offered crumbs from an open palm, she got to her feet, then reached down for her knife. She had no choice but to go with him, she realized, and perhaps it was for the best. Once she reached New Mexico, she would make good her escape from this pig. She would be free then to disappear as she had planned—and this man would be out his ransom.

"Come," he said.

Without a word Angeline followed him..

☆ Chapter ☆

15

For three hours, Manuel, James, and Abe cooled their heels while the Osage band finished celebrating what appeared to be the return of a victorious war party. They had been accepted into the camp with typical Osage hospitality, then shown to an Osage lodge, a circular habitation fashioned of upright poles arched over on top. The poles were interlaced horizontally with slender branches, the roofing covered with mats or skins—a more solid shelter than the portable lodges favored by the nomadic plains Indians. On his way into the village, Manuel had ridden past fields of corn, beans, and squash, and the three of them had already had their fill of corn mush or whatever the hell it was the Osage women had brought them.

"How long they goin to keep us here?" James asked Abe irritably. "We're wasting time."

"Well now, hoss, I wouldn't say that."

"Why not?" asked Manuel.

"I ain't all that familiar with the Osage palaver, but if I'm not mistaken, they're celebratin' a victory over a Kiowa band. If they brung back any prisoners, we jest might learn somethin' about Angeline."

That quieted the two men, and a moment later, the camp chief Standing Wolf entered the lodge, wrapped in a brilliant red and black Navaho blanket. Manuel watched two other chiefs follow in after him. All three chiefs looked properly fierce. The Osage shaved their skulls, leaving only a long scalp lock that extended down the back of their neck, their shiny skulls standing out prominently. It gave them a suitably savage aspect and probably did a lot to cut down the lice population, Manuel figured as he watched the chiefs squat down on the other side of the hearth facing them.

"I'll be usin' sign language with these here chiefs," Abe told his two companions out of the corner of his mouth. "I'll talk out loud, same time I'm makin' the sign so you can foller what I'm sayin'."

"Go to it, Abe," said James.

Before any palaver began, however, a rather elaborate ceremonial pipe, festooned with feathers and ribbons, was brought out and lit. The Osage chief handed it to the chief next to him, who took a few puffs and handed it to the chief beside him. The pipe was passed on to the three men and after they were finished with it and a solid cloud of tobacco smoke hung in the air over their heads, the chief placed the pipe down beside him, its pleasant, incense-like smoke coiling up through the lodge. This very important ceremony seen to, the chief nodded curtly to Abe, indicating he should begin.

Moving his hands with amazing fluidity and dexterity, the mountain man began what sounded like an oration, telling the chief in fulsome terms how impressed he was with the Osage band's extensive fields and the fine ponies he had seen in their pastures. This chief was obviously one who knew how to bring prosperity to his people. The chief listened impassively, only the pleased glint in his eyes revealing his appreciation of Abe's oration.

Abe's hands moved quickly now as he included the chief's warriors in his oration, congratulating them for their recent victory over the hated Kiowa, the same tribe which warred with the *tejanos*, insinuating not so slyly that any enemy of the Osage was an enemy of the Texans.

This Standing Wolf agreed to with a deep grunt of approval.

Manuel leaned back slightly, feeling a bit more easy.

Without further preamble, Abe launched into an account of the Kiowa-Comanche war party's abduction of the young Texan woman, sister to the man who sat on his left. His account of the abduction finished, he asked bluntly for the chief's help in locating Angeline.

Standing Wolf straightened his shoulders slightly and leaned back, his obsidian eyes regarding Abe with what Manuel thought was something close to amusement. Then his hands began to move. What he had to say was soon said, and then he leaned back.

Abe turned to James and Manuel. "The old fox wants to know what we've got for him in those mules."

"So tell him," James said. "That's what we came here for."

"Not so fast, hoss," Abe said. "We want to know if they can help us first."

"Then find out."

Abe looked back at Standing Wolf and asked him what news he might have for them. Had they heard anything about any women captives in the Kiowa bands.

The chief answered swiftly. The Kiowa had many captives. From Mexico and from other tribes. Even the Osage have lost women to these raiders. Abe translated for the two men.

"We know that, dammit," said James. "Ask him about *tejano* captives."

Abe's hands moved swiftly as he inquired about captive women taken from Texas.

The chief again straightened, seemed to take a deep breath to keep his patience; then his hands moved quickly, slashing the air at the conclusion, as if he were saying this was the end of it.

"The old fox knows somethin', that's for sure," Abe told his two companions. "But right now he's peeing in his buckskins he's so eager to see what goodies we got for him. We better take him outside and begin distributin' our goods."

"So let's do it then," said Manuel.

Abe looked back at the chief and with two quick sweeps of one hand indicated he was ready and willing to proceed to the distribution of his gifts. With a quick grunt of approval, the chief picked up his pipe and cleaned out the bowl with a long, feathered stick—a sign that the audience was over.

Abe held his two companions back as the three chiefs preceded them out of the lodge. The mules were tethered to a pole just outside the entrance. Around the mules a closely packed crowd of bronzed Indians were waiting eagerly. Even if they were not to be the recipients of the *tejano*'s bounty, they would get a precarious delight in seeing what presents were given to their chiefs.

"How the hell're we going to work this, Abe?" James asked.

"First we take good care of Standing Wolf. Then the other chiefs. But we hold back the real goodies, the big kettles and pots, and the guns. We don't let them goods go until we get something we can chew on. Now give me a hand, you two."

With great deliberateness and elaborate courtesy, Abe and Manuel, under Abe's careful direction, gave out first hats, then umbrellas to the chiefs. The eyes of the onlookers widened in wonder at such gifts. The chiefs could not resist putting on their fine hats immediately, opening their umbrellas and strutting about in front of their admiring tribesmen, who filled the air with hushed cries of wonder and envy. Manuel had all he could do to keep from laughing at the sight of the chiefs screwing their big hats down over their upright, quill-like ridges of hair until only their shining bald pates were visible.

Next, summoning the chief's women, Abe had the men hand out to them ribbons—yellow, pink, and rose—then bolts of cloth. Tins of tea and coffee followed, then sacks of salt, flour, sugar. After that came a few cooking utensils: long-handled spoons, baking pans, and earthenware bowls, reducing the first mule's burden to a mere fraction of its former bulk.

This done, Abe halted the distribution, folded his arms, and waited.

Standing Wolf immediately demanded to see more, indicating this with a quick jab at the other two mules. Abe stood his ground, repeating with equally fierce jabs his desire to gain information on any woman captives held by the Kiowa. The chief stared for a long moment at Abe, and watching all this, Manuel realized that the chief would have no difficulty in cutting this session short and taking by force every item Abe was now denying him.

But the chief's sense of fair play and the universal rules of hospitality prevented any such action. With a shrug, he gave an order to a brave in the crowd. The brave vanished and a moment later returned with what was obviously a Kiowa warrior. He was missing both ears and there was little left of his nose. The blood was still shiny on his neck and chin. Despite his appalling condition, he still appeared openly defiant, determined to give his captors no satisfaction.

An Osage woman ran toward the mutilated warrior and with a quick flash of her skinning knife, removed a chunk of his cheek, then darted off. Her action was greeted with a great shriek of approval, the women's cries sounding the loudest, Manuel noted. The Kiowa warrior straightened his shoulders and uttered not a sound. He was going to die, he realized, and all he could do about it was make certain that he died as a Kiowa warrior should, his medicine intact.

The chief said something to the brave who had brought the Kiowa. The brave grabbed the Kiowa by his hair and unceremoniously dragged him off. His eyes glinting with some merriment, Standing Wolf turned to Abe and made a few quick signs.

Abe translated: "Standing Wolf says he is sure that soon this Kiowa will tell us all about the women captives he has heard about—and some he has not heard about. The old fox has a sense of humor. Guess it's time to open the rest of them presents. Just hold back on that third mule."

Pipes and tobacco came next for the chiefs, along with beads and tiny bells to be sewn into the seams of their finest regalia. Vermilion followed next, and the women of the chiefs were not left out as Manuel presented to each of them an iron kettle. Immensely pleased with these gifts, the chief turned to another warrior and gave him an order.

When this one returned, it was alone. He spoke quickly to Standing Wolf, who turned to Abe and made a few quick signs.

"This is more like it," Abe told Manuel and James. "He says the Kiowa war party they just decimated had a young white woman captive. For a while she was the wife of the chief, fellow named Iron Face."

"Where is she now?" Manuel demanded.

Abe asked Standing Wolf. The chief shrugged and looked at the third mule.

"Well, hoss," Abe said to James, "I guess this is it. We're goin' to have to shoot our full wad this time. But I don't see we got any choice."

The last mule contained bullet pouches, powder horns, and even worms for cleaning out rifle barrels, which the chiefs accepted with grave pleasure. Then came the rifles. Abe had taken the precaution of polishing each weapon so that the ironwork and barrels shone like new. Despite the chief's attempts to remain impassive, their eyes opened wide as Abe himself presented these fine old Kentucky rifles to them. He kept only two of the rifles back, and then placed on the ground in front of them one of their three remaining boxes of ammunition.

That did it. The Osage chiefs were well pleased, and Standing Wolf immediately spoke to two waiting braves. They vanished to return a moment later with a captured Kiowa woman. She was reasonably young, and it was clear she had been taken alive only because of her youth and beauty. This did not mean, however, that she was being treated gently. Manuel and James had to jump back quickly when the captured woman was flung to the ground in front of them.

An Osage woman, obviously fluent in the Kiowa tongue spoke to the captive. There was no mistaking the sharpness of her tone. The woman, her head bowed piteously, answered in a low, frightened tone. The Osage woman told Standing Wolf what she had said.

The chief turned to Abe, his hands moving swiftly.

"We got news, hoss," Abe said to James as he translated, "but it ain't all good."

At the conclusion of his message, the chief folded his arms. Abe turned to James and Manuel.

"It's good news and its bad news," he told them. "Angeline was with that Kiowa band, all right, but she escaped. The band was high-tailin' it from the Osage war party, and she took the opportunity to make herself scarce."

"My God," said James. "You mean she's out there somewhere alone?"

"Look at it this way, hoss," said Abe. "It's a good thing she wasn't on hand when these Osage caught up to this Kiowa band. That there woman we just saw is the only one survived. The Osage have no love for the Kiowa."

"What do we do now?" Manuel asked, his voice tight.

"What do you think, hoss? We go after her."

"But we don't know where she is," James said.

"If I know Angelina," Manuel said, "she's on her way back to Texas."

"But that would take her through Comanche country," James reminded him.

"Abe," said Manuel. "What do we do now?"

"That's for you two gents to tell me. "

"I say we find out for sure where that Kiowa village was attacked, then go after her," said Manuel. "She couldn't be far."

"Not if she's on foot," agreed James, brightening.

"That's right," said Abe. "Course you can't be sure o' that."

"It don't make no difference," said James. "Manuel's right. We go now. We still got at least five hours of daylight."

"Soon's I settle up with this chief, hoss," Abe told him. "Maybe he can spare us a couple of horses—in trade for the mules. We might be needing them."

"Why?" Manuel asked.

"Angeline may not be on foot—and she may not be headin' back to Texas."

This possibility had not occurred to Manuel until that moment. His heart turned leaden. Abe was right. Earlier, he had spoken without thinking. Everyone knew how women carried off by the Comanche or Kiowa were treated upon their return. How could Angeline know that she would be welcomed back by her own people? Or by him?

He took a deep breath and sought desperately for some consolation in what he had learned so far. Angeline had been the wife of a Kiowa chief. She was no longer a virgin, no longer the sweet, innocent, tender shoot of a girl he had bid good-bye to when he rode off. But as Abe had just pointed out, it could have been worse. Angeline could be dead now, struck down by that Osage war party when it stormed the fleeing Kiowas. He felt a sudden surge of admiration for the woman he loved so much. She had acted bravely, had refused to accept her fate, had taken the only chance offered her and escaped from her captors.

Manuel crossed himself quickly. *Please, Madre de Dios, do not let me lose her!* he prayed silently.

II

The two men she had seen about the fire were Esteban and Santos. From the first, Angeline realized she could not trust them. For one thing, they were not heading west toward New Mexico as Esteban had told her. They were heading northeast, too contemptuous of her intelligence to consider the possibility that she might be able to tell the difference. Esteban's partner was Santos, a small, filthy, unshaven man with a whining voice and a sidelong glance that never looked directly at her but whose eyes were filled with furtive desire. Whenever he passed closed by, he made her skin crawl. He drank tequila constantly from a jug he kept beside him on the wagon seat.

Esteban was taller than Santos and more trim—a dark mestizo with a thin mustache and bright, shifty eyes. He laughed a lot, but at matters and circumstances that only he and Santos seemed to understand or appreciate. He kept his coat and trousers cleaner than his partner's, and his clothing was of a more expensive cut. He made an effort to keep his face clean-shaven and his hair combed back. He wore a black, wide-brimmed hat and dark trousers and kept his boots polished with a tin of lampblack he kept in his saddlebag. The wagon was drawn by a span of mules and contained not only piles of furs, but a host of provisions, potatoes, pinto beans, rice, sourdough starter, salt, tea, a can of sugar, and plenty of coffee. She was soon cooking their meals, since she could not eat what Santos prepared for them.

Esteban rode alongside the wagon or just ahead of it astride his big roan, while his partner crouched like a fat spider on the wagon seat, driving the patient, floppy-eared mules. Inside the jouncing, bone-jarring wagon, Angeline made herself as comfortable as she could. Before the second day was out, she discovered the wagonbed's false bottom, and with the edge of her knife, she managed to pry up a board and glimpse the rifles, at least twenty, that were stored under it. Not only rifles, but pistols and boxes of ammunition and gunpowder. These men were gunrunners, she realized, and that explained why Esteban had lied to her, why he was not heading for New Mexico as he had told her.

She said nothing of her discovery and secured for herself two flintlock pistols. Her father had made it a point to teach both her and Mordecai how to load both rifles and pistols, so that in case of attack she could work beside her mother, loading the guns and handing them to him. It had never come to that, as it turned out. What had happened instead had been far worse, but at least now she could put what she had been taught to good use. She loaded the two pistols, then tied both ends of a rawhide strip to the stocks and draped the rawhide around her neck and down through her burgeoning cleft, allowing the pistols to hang down her front inside her buckskin shirt. It was dangerous to carry loaded pistols in this fashion, she realized, but not as dangerous as it would be without them, for she had no illusions about these two men or their mission out here on this plain. She waited grimly for them to make their move, determined to make them pay dearly for any attempt they might make to take her.

III

Three days after Angeline joined the two men, what she had been expecting took place. They had halted beside a stream, preparing to camp for the night beside it in the high grass. The stream was flowing at a fairly brisk pace even this late in the season, and Angeline suggested that the two men bathe upstream, while she remained close beside the bank to keep an eye on the wagon.

There was enough light left in the sky for Angeline to catch a glimpse of the two men coming toward her along the bank. Santos was in the lead, grinning. Esteban, his tall figure almost dwarfing the other, was right on his heels. Both men were naked. Angeline swam to the bank as casually as possible. As she stood boldly and walked up the embankment toward her clothes, she could see the men crouching in the grass, leering at her. She dropped beside her folded garments, and reaching under them, pulled out two pistols. The two men had stood back up and were striding toward her, brushing aside the heavy grass as they approached. Holding the two pistols at arms length, she stood up and caught both men in their sights.

They halted, amazed.

"Go back and put your clothes on," Angeline told them.

"Look who's talkin'," said Esteban.

"Just do like I say."

"You shoot us, and you'll die out here. You need us."

"I don't need you. I don't need anyone. Not now. I'm as good as dead as far as my people are concerned. It don't matter to me how or where I die. But maybe it does for you."

"Hey, now, Angelina," Esteban said, "No sense in you talking like that. You got a long life ahead of you."

"It ain't a life I want. Not with you two takin' turns. I been through that already."

"But Angelina, we wasn't goin' to hurt you."

"Don't call me Angelina."

"That's your name, ain't it?"

They were inching toward her. She knew why. They had no confidence in her ability to load the guns correctly and were willing to gamble that even if she did know how to load them, she would not be up to firing them accurately.

But that, too, was something her father had taught her.

"*Por favor*," pleaded Santos, still inching closer. "Be reasonable, *senorita*. We are but men, healthy men. We need the caresses of a woman."

Esteban was more cautious than Santos. Perhaps he remembered that moment when Angeline had leapt from the grass at his feet and tried to stab him. He reached out to hold Santos back, but the little man was too greedy and too hungry. He brushed Esteban's arm aside and rushed Angeline, positive she would not shoot him.

"I warn you!" Angeline cried, taking a hasty step back, both pistols still aimed at the two men.

But Santos's blood was up, his eyes alight. He was thinking now of only one thing, and behind him Esteban's eyes were also gleaming. As Santos neared her, she realized she had no choice but to shoot.

She fired pointed blank at him. The pistol kicked in her hand, but not as much as she had thought it would. The round caught Santos high on his left shoulder. It was only a flesh wound, but its impact was enough to stop him in his tracks. Close to panic, he sagged down onto one knee, his hand clapped over his wound, blood oozing through his fingers.

Angeline swung her other revolver up, this time aiming at Esteban. The man paled and backed away hastily, holding up both hands. "Hey, don' shoot, *senorita*! *Por favor*! We are only joking!"

"No," Angeline replied, advancing on him boldly. "No

you ain't. You told me you would not let such foolishness interfere with your chances of ransoming me. But you have no such intention. You and this pig here want only to share me as would any Kiowa or Comanche.''

"That is not fair, Angelina!"

"Don't call me that!" Angeline cried, jabbing the muzzle of the pistol at him. "My name is Angeline!"

"Of course!"

"Help me!" pleaded Santos, looking up at them both. He appeared to be crying. "I am wounded bad. My blood, it covers me!"

"Take care of this stuck pig," Angeline told Esteban. "Then stay clear of me."

"But that will not be easy, Angeline. We are a party. We must work together!"

"Work together? With you?"

"Yes."

She smiled coldly. "Are you making me a partner?"

He shrugged, as if he were accepting the inevitable.

"Tell me what you are up to, Esteban. What are you doing out here in this Indian country with a wagon full of rifles?"

"It is simple." He shrugged. "I sell them to the Indians."

"To the Comanche?"

"No. Not to the Comanche. They will not trade with Esteban. Once I sell to the Comanche. The guns, they were not very good. So now they will not trade with me. But," he went on, shrugging, "there are other Indians."

"Kiowa?"

"No. They do not like Esteban, either."

"Then which Indians?"

"The Osage."

She thought that over for a moment. She had not heard of the Osage attacking Texan settlements. They were savages, but perhaps they would not treat her as would the Comanche or the Kiowa. Besides, was it not their war party that had attacked the Kiowa village? Any enemy of the Kiowa was an ally of hers, she told herself.

"All right," she said. "We will go to the Osage tribe. How far is it?"

"Two, maybe three days from here," Esteban told her, shrugging his shoulders, his dark eyes crawling over her body, a tiny smile of anticipation lighting his dark features.

Angeline snatched up her buckskin shirt and covered her nakedness.

"Leave me alone now," she told him, "and take that one with you."

"You have wounded me, *senorita*!" Santos cried. "Have you no pity?"

"Get him out of here, Esteban," Angeline said.

Esteban pulled the whining Santos to his feet. Crestfallen and thoroughly cowed, Santos turned with Esteban and the two plunged back through the grass. Twice they looked nervously back over their shoulder at her, like wary apes. As soon as they were gone, Angeline sank to the ground and took a huge, gulping breath of relief. But she had no illusions about her situation. She had only one loaded pistol left, and it was unlikely she would be allowed to reload the other.

But she still had her knife.

IV

For two full days, Esteban and Santos had been forced to keep the wagon within a swampy thicket alongside a narrow stream while an enormous herd of buffalo rumbled across the plain from north to south. The herd turned the patch of willow and cottonwood into an island of green surrounded by a nearly solid black sea of horns, humps, and clotted tails. Moving calmly along the fringes of this vast buffalo herd were smaller herds of deer, wild cattle, wild horses, antelope, even wolves. A truly peaceable kingdom, Angeline told herself in wonder.

Santos had stopped whining and blubbering about his shoulder wound, and now the two men were passing the time as they had from the first day the herd had surrounded them—they were drinking the rum they had been keeping aside for their trading session with the Osage and were now as drunk as Indians. And just as dangerous.

Keeping away from them as best she could, she realized that it would not be long before they made another attempt to take her. As she had feared, Esteban had nailed down the board she had pried up to get at the pistols, making it impossible for her to reload the one she had emptied at Santos. So far, her constant vigilance had saved her; but she knew it would only be a matter of time before the two men succeeded in satisfying their lusts, especially now that Santos seemed to be no longer hindered by his shoulder wound.

With this miserable prospect before her, she set about taking advantage of their inebriation to saddle up Esteban's roan and lead him off into the thicket. Tethering him to a sapling, she returned to the wagon to load up Esteban's two saddle bags with what provisions she could take without their knowledge. As she moved among them, she was kept busy evading their drunken embraces. Once she had loaded the two saddle bags, she took them to the roan, taking Esteban's saddle roll as well. Then she returned to the wagon, keeping herself visible but well out of reach of their clumsy embraces.

The buffalo herd had been steadily thinning out since midafternoon. When night fell, she planned to steal away from the wagon, mount Esteban's roan, and ride to the farthest part of this patch of timber and move out as soon as the herd allowed her to do so. She was almost certain she would be able to leave it by morning at the latest, well

before Esteban and Santos recovered their senses and realize
she was gone. If Esteban could be believed, they were only
few days from the Osage. She would try her luck with them
It was a frightening prospect, but she preferred it to staying
with these two pigs.

V

She left the wagon earlier than she had planned, while i
was still light. Despite their piggish drunkenness, Santos an
then Esteban went for her in a series of stumbling lurches
forcing her to realize that the two men were too far gone to b
intimidated by any threats she might make. She would have
to injure them fearfully, and she preferred not to have to d
this, not if she could ride off without hurting them.

She had almost reached the roan when she heard then
calling her name, shouting it out drunkenly and whistling
shrilly. A moment later came gunshots. Wincing at the sound
she stepped into the roan's saddle and rode through th
shallows toward firmer ground. Dimly she heard the rumbl
of the few buffalo still remaining on the plain as the gunsho
sent them into a mild stampede.

She kept on through the tall grass, and the roan was almos
out of the shallows when she heard the high, yelping cries o
a Kiowa war party. Her scalp prickled at the sound. Fightin
her panic, she slipped off the roan's back and pulled it deepe
into the tall grass; then after a quick, desperate struggle, sh
succeeded in pulling the horse off its feet. She crouched dow
behind it, holding her left hand close to the roan's snout t
prevent it from whinnying if a Kiowa rode close.

Three mounted Kiowa warriors in full war regalia gallope
up the river past her, *ki-yi*-ing like fiends newly sprung fron
hell. They did not see her as they galloped past. Sh
shuddered, terrified. It was a nightmare for her to see thes

Kiowa again. They reminded her of her capture and humili-ation. Had she come this far, only to be pulled back into their hellish bands? She vowed to herself that she would die before she would allow it.

Soon the gathering darkness resounded with the pounding of unshod hooves as the Kiowas spread out to look for still more victims on both sides of the stream. One mounted warrior charged across the river vanishing into a clump of birch not fifty feet away, the sound of his horse crashing through the brush fading rapidly.

Meanwhile the sky in the direction of Esteban's wagon went bright as the wagon went up in flames. She recalled Esteban telling her how both the Comanche and Kiowa were unhappy with the rifles he had sold them and wondered with a shudder what kind of fool courage had prompted him to continue to run guns through their land. Shrieking, terrified cries followed, and she realized at once that they were coming from the throats of Esteban and Santos. She felt no affection for either man; nevertheless, she winced at the sound. Such a death she would not wish on her worst enemy.

VI

The screaming, howling, and hoarse pleadings continued unabated as the Kiowa braves warmed to their task. The sobbing cries and whoops of pain they drew from Esteban and Santos rose to an awful crescendo. Meanwhile, Kiowa warriors rode back and forth through the breaks, searching for more victims. Had the attack come earlier, while it was still daylight, the Kiowa would have had no difficulty finding her tracks and following them into the grass. They came close, but not close enough. Twice she had to clamp her hand over the roan's snout to prevent it from whinnying.

It was close to dawn when Angeline heard someone

crashing through the brush downstream. She lifted her head to peer in that direction. The first light was pretty dim, but it was bright enough for her to see Esteban staggering toward her through the water. He was hatless and his face was a bloody mess. It looked as if the man had been mutilated almost beyond recognition, then left for dead. Angeline was debating whether or not to go to his assistance when the sudden drumbeat of hooves warned her.

She ducked low. Down the middle of the shallow stream rode a Kiowa, his pony kicking up a spray of water. The Indian had spotted Esteban and was heading straight toward him. Hearing him coming, Esteban flung himself around and began to head for the brush on the far bank. The Kiowa lowered his lance, and as Esteban scrambled up the bank, the Kiowa's lance caught him in the small of his back. Still urging his pony on at full speed, the Kiowa lifted Esteban's limp body from the lance and slammed him down over his pony's neck. Uttering a high, piercing cry of triumph, the Kiowa swung his pony out of the stream and galloped off.

It was full daylight when the Kiowa let loose a series of high-pitched yells. A moment later came the swiftly receding thunder of their ponies as they rode off to the south, the same direction the herd had taken. For a long while after the pound of their hooves had faded into the early morning stillness, Angeline did not move, not daring to believe that she had escaped.

Slowly, cautiously she stood up, then pulled the horse upright and rode back down the stream heading toward the wagon. A moment later she nudged the roan out of the thicket behind the wagon and dismounted. Only black tattered remnants of the canvas remained and the wagon had been looted thoroughly. The false bottom had been ripped out and not a weapon or provision remained. As she walked around to the front of the wagon, she saw Santos's quiet, staked-out body. She saw it, but she did not allow herself to look directly at it.

Esteban was hanging from a wagon wheel, the only one not burned through. She was about to turn away, when she saw his head move and realized in horror that he was still alive. Careful not to sever anything vital, the Kiowas had sliced and peeled and cut with the prowess of surgeons trained in hell. The gunrunner's eyelids had been torn off. Skin hung from his naked torso in long, raw strips. The Kiowa had made certain that he must eventually die from his wounds, but that his death would come slowly, primarily of exposure—a truly terrible death.

He looked unblinkingly up at Angeline, his mouth hanging open. He had no tongue left, only a stump so that when he moved his mouth to speak, nothing came out but a terrible, whistling groan. Then he caught sight of the pistol in her hand, and from the look in his eyes, she saw at once what he wanted her to do.

Angeline did not think she could do such a thing. On the other hand, she knew she could not leave him like this. His horribly mutilated body, his pleading eyes would haunt her through all her remaining days. She took a deep breath, cocked the pistol, then aimed it at a spot just above his ear, turned her head and squeezed the trigger. She felt the faint spray of his blood on her wrist and quickly yanked her hand away. She thought she was going to be sick. With frantic speed she wiped her wrist on her skirt and sprang back a few steps from the wagon, not allowing herself to look directly at the ruin she had made of Esteban's head.

Then she flung the pistol away, hurried to the roan and mounted up. In a moment she had crossed the river and was threading through the timber. All she could hope now was that she was not heading from the frying pan into the fire.

☆ Chapter ☆
16

Riding east toward a low line of wooded hills, Angeline caught sight of a dark green smudge of cottonwoods to the south. She immediately turned the roan toward it. The trees indicated a stream. The sun had been pounding down on her mercilessly throughout the day, and she was close to exhaustion, not having slept a wink for nearly twenty-four hours. The roan, too, was having difficulty. She had filled Esteban's canteen when she saddled the roan, but she and the horse had long since drained it, and she could tell that the horse was close to foundering. Her hope now was that she could reach the stream in time.

She had gone a considerable distance toward the line of timber and was close enough to make out individual trees, when she saw four Kiowa or Comanche warriors heading toward her from the west. Her first hope was that they had not seen her and were intent on some other destination. But when she urged the roan to a lope, she was dismayed to see the four Indians lift their ponies to a belly-down gallop, intent on catching her before she reached the line of trees.

II

Watching astride their mounts from a hill above the stream, Manuel shaded his eyes in order to see the lone rider more clearly. He knew it was a woman, but that was all he could tell. Abe had his telescope out and was tracking her also.

"Looks like an Indian squaw, all right," Abe said. "But somethin' don't look right about her."

"Let me have that telescope, Abe," Manuel said. He had a queer, nervous feeling in the pit of his stomach.

Abe handed it to him. Manuel had a maddeningly difficult time catching the horse and rider in the lens. At last he succeeded. Horse and rider loomed suddenly closer. The woman's hair was short, her face almost black. He could barely see her face because she kept her head turned as she looked back at the four Comanche chasing her.

The he caught something. His eye still glued to the eyepiece, he cried, "Abe, she's riding a saddle horse, a roan. It's not a pony."

"Let me see that," said James, taking the telescope.

James studied the rider for a full thirty seconds. "You're right," he said. "That's a saddle horse, all right. And she's got a full Mexican saddle. She's a Mexican."

"So she's Mexican," said Abe. "And she's in trouble. I say we ride on down there and even up the odds some."

"We do that, Abe, we're liable to waste ourselves," James reminded him. "Don't forget. It's Angeline we're after."

"Well, you can stay up here if you want, hoss," Abe drawled, taking back the telescope and dropping it into his saddle bag, "but I'm ridin' down there."

"I'll go with you, Abe," said Manuel.

"All right," said James. "We'll all go."

The three riders urged their horses off the hill and headed down the slope at a hard gallop. There was a river in front of them, and they would have to cross it before they could cut through the timber. As Manuel spurred into the river after Abe, he knew that James and Abe were certain this was only a hapless Mexican woman fleeing from the Comanche, but it could just as easily be a white woman. It could be Angeline!

III

She was so close she could almost smell the trees and the stream that fed them. And so could the roan, she knew. But it was still too far for both of them. She felt the horse's gait shift. It uttered a kind of strangled gasp and then collapsed under her. The horse's forward plunge was so violent, she was flung headlong over the horse's neck, her left shoulder striking the ground first. She kept tumbling and came to rest finally on her back, the storm of Comanche riders bearing down on her, their yells piercing the air.

She brought the knife out of her skirt and jumped to her feet. A Comanche warrior, a wide grin on his round, ugly face, leapt to the ground and hit it running, his coup stick in hand. It was clear they did not mean to kill her, just torment her, then take her. And once they discovered she was a white woman, they would take turns. It would be the whole, miserable nightmare all over again.

She crouched, hiding the knife. The Comanche brave could not have been much more than sixteen or seventeen, his eyes malignant black coals in a round, almost pudgy face. He smiled as he looked her over, sizing her up, she had no doubt, for future play. Then he rushed at her, his coup stick extended playfully. She waited just long enough, then snatched at it. The Comanche was too quick for her and pulled the stick back, laughing. But he was now close enough for her to attack. She ran suddenly at him, holding her knife high.

Startled, the Indian ducked aside, but Angeline brought the knife down swiftly. She felt the blade sinking into the brave's left shoulder and saw the sudden grimace on the Indian's face. She was past him then, and as he whirled angrily to punish her, the knife went flying.

The three other Comanche riders were circling the two of them, shouting taunts at the brave Angeline had stabbed. It was clear they felt she had bested him, having drawn first blood. What made it all the worse for the brave was the fact that she was a woman. As the circling riders howled derisively at him, rubbing in his disgrace, his face darkened in fury. No longer laughing, he rushed at her. Angeline tried to duck away, but he caught her by the arm and yanked her close enough to catch her on the side of the head with a hard, bludgeoning fist that sent her spinning to the ground.

Grunts of approval came from the watching Comanche. The side of her head numb, Angeline stared up at the brave and considered rushing him, forcing him to kill her. But he turned to the others and said something to them. It sounded like an invitation. The riders laughed and seemed about to dismount. Angeline knew what was coming next.

She scrambled to her feet, snatched up the fallen knife and hurled herself at the Comanche. The mounted warriors warned him in plenty of time. He spun about and deftly grabbed Angeline's right wrist and twisted. Angeline cried out in spite of herself and let go of the knife. The Comanche spun her to the ground a second time. The back of her head hit hard. Her senses reeling, she saw the Comanche drop his breechclout and start toward her.

Suddenly, from the direction of the trees, came the shuddering pound of shod hooves. The mounted Comanche yelled a warning to the young brave as three riders stormed out of a hollow toward them. Angeline sat up to see three white men, Texans! The rider in front was vaguely familiar, a big man with a huge beard. His rifle barked, and one of the Comanche peeled from his horse. Then from the fists of the other two riders came the rapid bark of gunfire. The Comanche on the ground hastily pulled up his breechclout and darted for his horse; before he reached it, a bullet caught him in the back of his head, exploding it.

The two remaining Comanche, screaming out their battle cry, charged full tilt at the onrushing Texans. The big, bearded rider in the lead met the foremost Comanche head on. Using his rifle as a club, he knocked the Comanche from his horse, then jumped free of his mount to finish him off with a huge knife. The other two riders swept head-on at the remaining Comanche, their guns blazing, their combined gunfire sweeping the Comanche off his horse.

They were close enough now for Angeline to see their faces clearly. At once she recognized the other two riders. One was James, the other Manuel!

IV

Manuel leaped from his horse and grabbed Angeline. Hugging her to him, he couldn't believe his luck. He felt Angeline sobbing, her whole body shaking. He felt like crying himself as he clung to her, holding her as tightly as he could.

At last she pushed away, wiping the tears from her face.

"You must not!" she cried. "You must not!"

"But why? We found you!"

"I'm unclean. Don't you understand?"

James strode up to her and without preamble took her in his arms and pulled her close. "Don't talk nonsense, Angeline," he told her, unashamed tears in his eyes. "You're comin' home with us to where you belong. None of what happened was your fault."

"But . . . don't you understand. I'm different now. I'm not the same girl I was."

"You mean you growed up fast. No one's goin' to blame you for that."

"No, that's not what I mean. I'm . . . different. I can never be the same. I'm a different person. I've . . . killed a man."

"Hush, Angelina," Manuel said softly. "The only important thing is that you are safe."

"But . . . don't you see? I can't marry you, Manuel. Not now!"

He grinned at her. "No, you can't. Not now. I've already decided that. You can ask James. We'll be waitin' until Christmas!"

A dripping scalp in his belt, Abe strode over.

"Mebbe you can tell us, Angeline," he drawled. "Any more Comanche near here?"

"I . . . don't know. But last night there were Kiowa."

"Then I say it's best we get the hell out of here and head for home. I'll saddle one o' them Comanche ponies for you."

Home! The sound of that word hit Angeline with such force, she felt dizzy. It was a word she thought she would never use again. Could never use again. But she had been wrong!

She was going home!

V

James entered the bedroom first, Manuel following in after him. Angeline remained in the doorway. She had been advised by Hope not to show herself immediately to her mother, lest the shock of her sudden appearance be too much for the grieving woman. Angeline had been home for nearly two hours. She had promptly bathed and was now dressed in a light blue, freshly-ironed dress that had always been her favorite; her short hair was combed out and neatly trimmed by Petra. She was so squeaky-clean she fairly shone.

James approached Marie carefully. Leaning over, he took her gently by the left shoulder. She stopped rocking and looked up at him, her face gaunt now, her eyes staring up at him out of dark hollows. James swallowed nervously.

"Marie, we're back."

Marie looked blankly up at him, then away, her eyes once again staring into the room's farthest corner. Manuel stepped over to the window and took it upon himself to pull aside the curtains to dispel the room's suffocating gloom.

"We went after Angeline, Marie," James prodded gently. "Do you remember? Do you remember?"

Marie's eyes brightened slightly. "Angeline?" she said.

"And we brought her back."

Marie frowned in sudden concentration, but said nothing. It was clear she had drifted so far from them all that she was almost too far for them to reach. It was as if her spirit had retreated to another land entirely. In the doorway behind them, Angeline wept softly.

Manuel went down on one knee in front of Marie and took her hand in his. "Marie," he told her softly, "I said I was going after Angeline. Do you remember?"

Marie seemed to quicken. Her eyes brightened. "Manuel?" she asked, reaching over to touch his beard, just as she had done before. "Is that you? Have you brought back my little girl?"

"Yes, Marie," he told her gently, carefully. "I have."

His words seemed to shake Marie. Her face went pale. Tears sprang from her eyes as she looked toward the door. "Angeline?" she said.

"Mama!" Angeline cried, bursting through the doorway. She threw herself down before Marie and flung her arms around her shrunken waist. Tears bathed her cheeks as she looked up into Marie's ravaged face. At that moment all she wanted was to comfort her mother—even if it took the rest of her life.

Marie was crying, too, her gaunt face twisting as anguish she had bottled up for so long burst from her, wracking her frail body. The two women embraced each other and hung on, their sobs shaking them both. And then, as the two men watched in pure wonderment, the sobbing subsided and there came from Marie a torrent of questions and cries of joy as, for the first time in months, Marie began to communicate with another human being.

Both men backed hastily out of the room and gently closed the door. As Manuel walked down the hallway beside James, he realized with a deep sense of joy that never again would he hear that steady, metronomic tapping from Marie's rocker. Her little girl was home again.

VI

Angeline's fears that she would suffer from the stigma of her abduction were not ill-founded. Indeed, as she took up residence once more in the Lewis Fort with her recovering mother and devoted brother, curious neighbors who had seldom had the time to visit before began dropping by unannounced; it soon became apparent that Angeline was the real focus of these visits. The women and their men peered at her sidelong, their glittering eyes watching for some sign, it appeared, of her shameful involvement with a Kiowa chief. As the months passed and it became apparent that Angeline was without child, the interest in her subsided somewhat, but did not abate. She could not attend any public function, dance, or festivity without being aware of the curious eyes that followed her everywhere or the sudden silence that greeted her entry into a crowded room or onto a dance floor.

It was the solidity and strength of the Lewis clan that kept this mean interest at bay and made it, however unpleasant for Angeline, at least bearable. No family who knew the Lewis men had any wish to arouse their displeasure. They were a clan everyone respected, true sons of Texas who had long since proven their worth to their fellow settlers in this flaming borderland. For Angeline, they proved a massive bullwark, a source of comfort and warmth that culminated in the Christmas wedding that Manuel had so eagerly sought and which, brought a pure, cleansing joy to Marie and the rest of the Lewis clan.

The snow that followed, along with the complete absence of Indian predations throughout that winter, seemed the final, beatific benediction on their union.

VII

The following spring, reports drifted back to Andrew in Austin that the southern Comanche had had enough. The loss of their major chiefs in the Council House Massacre, followed by a series of devastating routs—of which Colonel Moore's punitive expedition had evidently been the final straw—had prompted the Pehnahterkuh to desert the hills and canyons they had roamed for so many generations and withdraw north of the Red River.

But Lamar's draconian method of dealing with the Comanche had drained the infant republic's meager treasury and only served to strengthen Sam Houston's hand. With the horse Indians apparently no longer a threat to the western border settlements, with new settlers pouring into the lands abandoned by the Comanche, the Indian threat was deemed solved, and Houston was returned to the presidency, primarily on the strength of the vote of those eastern Texans who had had no real experience dealing with the horse Indians.

Upon taking office, Houston abandoned Austin and moved the republic's capital back to his namesake city near the gulf, promptly announcing a policy of accommodation with the horse Indians. He disbanded the Ranger companies and sent emissaries to the Comanche and Kiowa bands; he appointed Indian commissioners to proceed with his pacification program and proposed the opening of trading posts in the region to supply the Indians's needs so that they would no longer feel the need to raid Texas for those goods and products on which they had come to depend.

That Andrew did not approve of these policies went without saying. No one along the border saw anything but disaster in such policies.

VIII

The Lewis clan were gathered in the kitchen of the Lewis Fort. Abe was on hand as well. The occasion was Andrew's retirement from politics. With Lamar no longer in office and with Houston pursuing policies that could only bring disaster to the borderland, he had washed his hands of politics and was now back with Petra, determined to improve his holdings.

Frank had just suggested that possibly there might be some merit in Houston's pacification policy. At least, he maintained mildly, the policy should be given a chance.

"A chance?" blurted Mordecai. "For what? A chance to see our cabins go up in flames once more, you mean."

James muttered his agreement.

"You've hit the nail on the head, Mordecai," admitted Andrew. "This policy will give the Comanche a chance to lick their wounds and make preparation for their next assault.''

Sly spoke up then. ''What we should do then, is make good our own defenses. Build more block houses, arm every able-bodied man.''

''The Rangers have been disbanded,'' Frank reminded them.

''And without them, our backsides are pretty near bare,'' Andrew remarked bitterly.

''Mebbe not,'' said Abe, clearing his throat and taking his pipe from his mouth. ''There ain't no law says a man has to park his rifle in the closet. He can meet with his neighbors and drill if he wants to, and nothin's to prevent him from joinin' up with his fellows and patrolling if he's a mind to do so.''

''You mean like the minutemen?'' Mordecai asked, his voice eager.

''That's just what I mean, hoss,'' replied Abe.

Marie brought the mountain man another cup of coffee and then pushed the platter of doughnuts closer to him. It was obvious she approved of this grizzled trapper and Indian fighter.

Manuel chuckled, winked at Marie, then reached out for one of the doughnuts.

''Abe is right, Andrew,'' Manuel said. ''We do not need the law to show us how to protect our people. It's up to us now. Has this not always been so? Never have I counted on these fat-bellied politicians to do for me what I can do better for myself. Our home is nearly finished, and it will be as strong as this fine Lewis Fort.''

''And there will be others built like it along the Colorado,'' predicted James.

''Amen,'' said Frank. ''I'm putting sod on our roof before this summer is out.''

Petra spoke up then from the stove. "Andrew?"

Andrew turned in his chair and smiled with sudden warmth at her. Laughing, he said, "All right, Petra. All right. I hear you." He looked back at the others. "You heard Petra. Looks like we'll be forting up, too."

"I'll help," said James.

"Me, too," added Sly.

"All of us will," suggested Manuel. "The way you have helped us."

As he spoke, he glanced over at Angeline. She was at the sink, peeling carrots with Hope. At that very moment, she turned to gaze upon him, and once again he felt that powerful rush of affection and love for his woman. Her hair was completely grown out now, and it fell down her back like a single dark sheath of silk. The pure and simple truth of it was that she grew more lovely by the day, a loveliness that awed and humbled him. His throat suddenly constricting with gratitude for her deliverance, he looked back at his companions around the table.

Sly was making the point that Houston would soon enough realize the error of his ways and possibly change his policies.

"Not on your life," said Andrew, shaking his head in frustration. "I know the man. He thinks all Indians are like the Cherokee, peaceable agrarian savages."

James broke in bitterly. "Hell, I heard Houston thinks he's got Indian blood in him. The way I see it, he wants to be their savior. He is blind to their threat and will be until the day he dies."

"Then let it be soon!"

This sharp rejoinder startled every man at the table. It came from Angeline, her angry words cutting through the kitchen with startling clarity. Surprised at her vehemence, the men turned to stare at her. Manuel got to his feet and went quickly to her side. He could see that Angeline had held her tongue for as long as she could, and now must speak her mind.

"I'm sorry," Angeline said, a little flustered as every man's eyes regarded her. "I didn't mean to say that, I suppose. Mr. Houston is probably a good man. But he is mistaken. The Comanche will never give ground to the Texans. It is not trade they want, but vengeance. They seek warfare the way a child seeks a peppermint stick. For the sheer pleasure of it. They cannot be reasoned with. They will have to be wiped out completely. We must do to them what they have done to those tribes that opposed them in the past. The Tonkawa, the Apache. It is the only way."

Everyone there knew from what bitter wellsprings of memory those words flowed, how dearly won was the experience that gave her words such powerful endorsement. Not a man in the room felt qualified to comment further. What Angeline had just said so clearly was true, indisputably true, and its implications could not be ignored. With her words, the discussion had effectively ended. The men, and their women, knew what had to be done, and they would do it.

Manuel put his arm around Angeline's shoulders, and together they left the kitchen and went outside onto the low porch. There he stood silently beside her, gazing out over the land beyond the river and the distant rolling plains beyond, as if, like Angeline, he could see in his mind's eye the plundering hordes of Comanche, faces painted, lances glinting in the sun, moving once more on their land.

Marie followed them out onto the porch and moved close to Manuel. He reached out and pulled her close to him also, thinking of Michael—the man he had loved almost as a father—and of all the other sons of Texas who had given their blood to gain this fair land.

It would not end here. If they were good enough, if they were bold enough, they would survive . . . they would endure.

Fury knew something was wrong long before he saw the wagon train spread out, unmoving, across the plains in front of him.

From miles away, he had noticed the cloud of dust kicked up by the hooves of the mules and oxen pulling the wagons. Then he had seen that tan-colored pall stop and gradually be blown away by the ceaseless prairie wind.

It was the middle of the afternoon, much too early for a wagon train to be stopping for the day. Now, as Fury topped a small, grass-covered ridge and saw the motionless wagons about half a mile away, he wondered just what kind of damn fool was in charge of the train.

Stopping out in the open without even forming into a circle was like issuing an invitation to the Sioux, the Cheyenne, or the Pawnee. War parties roamed these plains all the time, just looking for a situation as tempting as this one.

Fury reined in, leaned forward in his saddle, and thought

about it. Nothing said he had to go help those pilgrims. They might not even want his help.

But from the looks of things, they needed his help, whether they wanted it or not.

He heeled the rangy lineback dun into a trot toward the wagons. As he approached, he saw figures scurrying back and forth around the canvas-topped vehicles. Looked sort of like an anthill after you stomp it.

Fury pulled the dun to a stop about twenty feet from the lead wagon. Near it, a man was stretched out on the ground with so many men and women gathered around him that Fury could only catch a glimpse of him through the crowd. When some of the men turned to look at him, Fury said, "Howdy. Thought it looked like you were having trouble."

"Damn right, mister," one of the pilgrims snapped. "And if you're of a mind to give us more, I'd advise against it."

Fury crossed his hands on the saddlehorn and shifted in the saddle, easing his tired muscles. "I'm not looking to cause trouble for anybody," he said mildly.

He supposed he might appear a little threatening to a bunch of immigrants who until now had never been any farther west than the Mississippi. Several days had passed since his face had known the touch of the razor, and his rough-hewn features could be a little intimidating even without the beard stubble. Besides that, he was well armed with a Colt's Third Motel Dragoon pistol holstered on his right hip, a Bowie knife sheathed on his left, and a Sharps carbine in the saddleboot under his right thigh. And he had the look of a man who knew how to use all three weapons.

A husky, broad-shouldered six-footer, John Fury's height was apparent even on horseback. He wore a broad-brimmed, flat-crowned black hat, a blue work shirt, and fringed buckskin pants that were tucked into high-topped black boots. As he swung down from the saddle, a man's voice, husky with strain, called out, "Who's that? Who are you?"

The crowd parted, and Fury got a better look at the figure on the ground. It was obvious that he was the one who had spoken. There was blood on the man's face, and from the twisted look of him as he lay on the ground, he was busted up badly inside.

Fury let the dun's reins trail on the ground, confident that the horse wouldn't go anywhere. He walked over to the injured man and crouched beside him. "Name's John Fury," he said.

The man's breath hissed between his teeth, whether in pain or surprise Fury couldn't have said. "Fury? I heard of you."

Fury just nodded. Quite a few people reacted that way when they heard his name.

"I'm . . . Leander Crofton. Wagonmaster of . . . this here train."

The man struggled to speak. He appeared to be in his fifties and had a short, grizzled beard and the leathery skin of a man who had spent nearly his whole life outdoors. His pale blue eyes were narrowed in a permanent squint.

"What happened to you?" Fury asked.

"It was a terrible accident—" began one of the men standing nearby, but he fell silent when Fury cast a hard glance at him. Fury had asked Crofton, and that was who he looked toward for the answer.

Crofton smiled a little, even though it cost him an effort. "Pulled a damn fool stunt," he said. "Horse nearly stepped on a rattler, and I let it rear up and get away from me. Never figured the critter'd spook so easy." The wagonmaster paused to draw a breath. The air rattled in his throat and chest. "Tossed me off and stomped all over me. Not the first time I been stepped on by a horse, but then a couple of the oxen pullin' the lead wagon got me, too, 'fore the driver could get 'em stopped."

"God forgive me, I . . . I am so sorry." The words came in a tortured voice from a small man with dark curly hair and a beard. He was looking down at Crofton with lines of misery etched onto his face.

"Wasn't your fault, Leo," Crofton said. "Just . . . bad luck."

Fury had seen men before who had been trampled by horses. Crofton was in a bad way, and Fury could tell by the look in the man's eyes that Crofton was well aware of it. The wagonmaster's chances were pretty slim.

"Mind if I look you over?" Fury asked. Maybe he could do something to make Crofton's passing a little easier, anyway.

One of the other men spoke before Crofton had a chance to answer. "Are you a doctor, sir?" he asked.

Fury glanced up at him, saw a slender, middle-aged man with iron-gray hair. "No, but I've patched up quite a few hurt men in my time."

"Well, I am a doctor," the gray-haired man said. "And I'd appreciate it if you wouldn't try to move or examine Mr.

Crofton. I've already done that, and I've given him some laudanum to ease the pain.''

Fury nodded. He had been about to suggest a shot of whiskey, but the laudanum would probably work better.

Crofton's voice was already slower and more drowsy from the drug as he said, ''Fury . . .''

''Right here.''

''I got to be sure about something . . . You said your name was . . . John Fury.''

''That's right.''

''The same John Fury who . . . rode with Fremont and Kit Carson?''

''I know them,'' Fury said simply.

''And had a run-in with Cougar Johnson in Santa Fe?''

''Yes.''

''Traded slugs with Hemp Collier in San Antone last year?''

''He started the fight, didn't give me much choice but to finish it.''

''Thought so.'' Crofton's hand lifted and clutched weakly at Fury's sleeve. ''You got to . . . make me a promise.''

Fury didn't like the sound of that. Promises made to dying men usually led to a hell of a lot of trouble.

Crofton went on, ''You got to give me . . . your word . . . that you'll take these folks through . . . to where they're goin'.''

''I'm no wagonmaster,'' Fury said.

''You know the frontier,'' Crofton insisted. Anger gave him strength, made him rally enough to lift his head from the ground and glare at Fury. ''You can get 'em through. I know you can.''

''Don't excite him,'' warned the gray-haired doctor.

''Why the hell not?'' Fury snapped, glancing up at the physician. He noticed now that the man had his arm around the shoulders of a pretty red-headed girl in her teens, probably his daughter. He went on, ''What harm's it going to do?''

The girl exclaimed. ''Oh! How can you be so . . . so callous?''

Crofton said, ''Fury's just bein' practical, Carrie. He knows we got to . . . got to hash this out now. Only chance we'll get.'' He looked at Fury again. ''I can't make you promise, but it . . . it'd sure set my mind at ease while I'm passin' over if I knew you'd take care of these folks.''

Fury sighed. It was rare for him to promise anything to anybody. Giving your word was a quick way of getting in over your head in somebody else's problems. But Crofton was dying, and even though they had never crossed paths before, Fury recognized in the old man a fellow Westerner.

''All right,'' he said.

A little shudder ran through Crofton's battered body, and he rested his head back against the grassy ground. ''Thanks,'' he said, the word gusting out of him along with a ragged breath.

''Where are you headed?'' Fury figured the immigrants could tell him, but he wanted to hear the destination from Crofton.

''Colorado Territory . . . Folks figure to start 'em a

town . . . somewhere on the South Platte. Won't be hard for you to find . . . a good place.''

No, it wouldn't, Fury thought. No wagon train journey could be called easy, but at least this one wouldn't have to deal with crossing mountains, just prairie.

Prairie filled with savages and outlaws, that is.

A grim smile plucked at Fury's mouth as that thought crossed his mind. ''Anything else you need to tell me?'' he asked Crofton.

The wagonmaster shook his head and let his eyelids slide closed. ''Nope. Figger I'll rest a spell now. We can talk again later.''

''Sure,'' Fury said softly, knowing that in all likelihood, Leander Crofton would never wake up from this rest.

Less than a minute later, Crofton coughed suddenly, a wracking sound. His head twisted to the side, and blood welled for a few seconds from the corner of his mouth. Fury heard some of the women in the crowd cry out and turn away, and he suspected some of the men did, too.

''Well, that's all,'' he said, straightening easily from his kneeling position beside Crofton's body. He looked at the doctor. The red-headed teenager had her face pressed to the front of her father's shirt and her shoulders were shaking with sobs. She wasn't the only one crying, and even the ones who were dry-eyed still looked plenty grim.

''We'll have a funeral service as soon as a grave is dug,'' said the doctor. ''Then I suppose we'll be moving on. You should know, Mr. . . . Fury, was it? You should know that none of us will hold you to that promise you made to Mr. Crofton.''

Fury shrugged. ''Didn't ask you if you intended to or not. I'm the one who made the promise. Reckon I'll keep it.''

He saw surprise on some of the faces watching him. All of these travelers had probably figured him for some sort of drifter. Well, that was fair enough. Drifting was what he did best.

But that didn't mean he was a man who ignored promises. He had given his word, and there was no way he could back out now.

He met the startled stare of the doctor and went on, ''Who's the captain here? You?''

''No, I . . . You see, we hadn't gotten around to electing a captain yet. We only left Independence a couple of weeks ago, and we were all happy with the leadership of Mr. Crofton. We didn't see the need to select a captain.''

Crofton should have insisted on it, Fury thought with a grimace. You never could tell when trouble would pop up, Crofton's body lying on the ground was grisly proof of that.

Fury looked around at the crowd. From the number of people standing there, he figured most of the wagons in the train were at least represented in this gathering. Lifting his voice, he said, ''You all heard what Crofton asked me to do. I gave him my word I'd take over this wagon train and get it on through to Colorado Territory. Anybody got any objection to that?''

His gaze moved over the faces of the men and women who were standing and looking silently back at him. The silence was awkward and heavy. No one was objecting, but Fury could tell they weren't too happy with this unexpected turn of events.

Well, he thought, when he had rolled out of his soogans that morning, he hadn't expected to be in charge of a wagon train full of strangers before the day was over.

The gray-haired doctor was the first one to find his voice. "We can't speak for everyone on the train, Mr. Fury," he said. "But I don't know you, sir, and I have some reservations about turning over the welfare of my daughter and myself to a total stranger."

Several others in the crowd nodded in agreement with the sentiment expressed by the physician.

"Crofton knew me."

"He knew you have a reputation as some sort of gunman!"

Fury took a deep breath and wished to hell he had come along after Crofton was already dead. Then he wouldn't be saddled with a pledge to take care of these people.

"I'm not wanted by the law," he said. "That's more than a lot of men out here on the frontier can say, especially those who have been here for as long as I have. Like I said, I'm not looking to cause trouble. I was riding along and minding my own business when I came across you people. There's too many of you for me to fight. You want to start out toward Colorado on your own, I can't stop you. But you're going to have to learn a hell of a lot in a hurry."

"What do you mean by that?"

Fury smiled grimly. "For one thing, if you stop spread out like this, you're making a target of yourselves for every Indian in these parts who wants a few fresh scalps for his lodge." He looked pointedly at the long red hair of the doctor's daughter. Carrie—that was what Crofton had called her, Fury remembered.

Her father paled a little, and another man said, "I didn't think there was any Indians this far east." Other murmurs of concern came from the crowd.

Fury knew he had gotten through to them. But before any of them had a chance to say that he should honor his promise to Crofton and take over, the sound of hoofbeats made him turn quickly.

A man was riding hard toward the wagon train from the west, leaning over the neck of his horse and urging it on to greater speed. The brim of his hat was blown back by the wind of his passage, and Fury saw anxious, dark brown features underneath it. The newcomer galloped up to the crowd gathered next to the lead wagon, hauled his lathered mount to a halt, and dropped lithely from the saddle. His eyes went wide with shock when he saw Crofton's body on the ground, and then his gaze flicked to Fury.

"You son of a bitch!" he howled.

And his hand darted toward the gun holstered on his hip.